CIRCLE OF FIRE

OTHER BOOKS BY AL LACY

Angel of Mercy series:
A Promise for Breanna (Book One)
Faithful Heart (Book Two)
Captive Set Free (Book Three)

Journeys of the Stranger series:
Legacy (Book One)
Silent Abduction (Book Two)
Blizzard (Book Three)
Tears of the Sun (Book Four)

Battles of Destiny (Civil War series):
Beloved Enemy (Battle of First Bull Run)
A Heart Divided (Battle of Mobile Bay)
A Promise Unbroken (Battle of Rich Mountain)
Shadowed Memories (Battle of Shiloh)
Joy from Ashes (Battle of Fredericksburg)
Season of Valor (Battle of Gettysburg)

CIRCLE OF FIRE

AL LACY

M U L T N O M A H   B O O K S

Louisburg Library

Bringing People and Information Together

CIRCLE OF FIRE
© 1996 by Lew A. Lacy

published by Multnomah Books
a part of the Questar publishing family

Edited by Rodney L. Morris
Cover design by David Uttley
Cover illustration by Sergio Martínez

International Standard Book Number: 1-59052-787-9

Printed in the United States of America.

For information:
Questar Publishers, Inc.
Post Office Box 1720
Sisters, Oregon 97759

Library of Congress Cataloging-in-Publication Data
Lacy, Al.
   Circle of fire / by Al Lacy.
      p.   cm. -- (Journeys of the stranger ; bk. 5)
   ISBN 1-59052-787-9
   I. Title. II. Series: Lacy, Al. Journeys of the stranger ; bk. 5.
   PS3562.A256C57   1996
   813'.54--dc20   96-19764
                                                        CIP

05 06 07 08 — 10 9 8 7 6 5 4 3 2

For Don Jacobson,
my publisher, my friend, and my brother in Christ.

We share a love and an admiration
for a big black horse
whose hoofbeats are heard thundering out of
the *Circle of Fire.*

I love you, Don.

PHILIPPIANS 1:3

CHAPTER

ONE

They came out of the night. Eight of them. Indistinct shapes wearing hooded masks beneath their hats, leaning in their saddles against the slanting rain.

With their hats pulled low and slickers wrapped tight, seven of them formed a semicircle in front of the small ranch house. The eighth rider halted his mount under a tall cottonwood tree twenty yards away. Lightning slashed the sky and thunder rumbled as the rider under the cottonwood slung a rope over a limb. At the end of the rope was a hangman's noose.

"All right, Jake!" the rider said.

The man called Jake nudged his horse closer to the house and shouted above the sound of wind and rain, "Sullivan!"

Inside, Ted Sullivan was sitting in an overstuffed chair, reading a book by lantern light. When the booming voice sliced through the walls from outside, Sullivan laid the book down and made his way to one of the front windows and pulled back the curtain. The lanterns burning behind him made the outside a black void.

"Ted, did you say something to me?" the rancher's wife called from a rear bedroom.

Ted was trying to see through the rain-spattered window

when lightning flashed, illuminating the yard. His heart skipped a beat when he saw the hooded riders.

Myrna Sullivan entered the room carrying a hairbrush. She was clad in an ankle-length woolen robe and slippers. Her long dark hair hung loosely about her shoulders.

"Ted, what is it?" she asked.

Ted was about to answer when the same harsh voice came from outside. "Sullivan! Come out here!"

Myrna hurried to the window. "O Ted, is it—?"

"It's them, honey. I only got a glimpse of them when the lightning flashed, but I think I saw seven. They're wearing hoods as before."

"What are we going to do?"

Ted glanced toward his Winchester .44, which stood in a nearby corner.

"No!" Myrna said. "You can't shoot it out with them! They'll kill you!"

Ted wiped a shaky hand over his face. "You're right. I'll have to go out there and talk to them."

"Oh, no, you mustn't! If you step out that door, there's no telling what they'll do to you!"

"Sullivan!" Jake hollered again. "We're runnin' out of patience!"

"Ted, please. Don't go out there!"

"I don't have any choice. If I don't go to them, they'll break the door down and come in here."

Ted Sullivan brushed past his terrified wife and picked up the Winchester. He jacked a cartridge into the chamber, handed it to her, and said, "Bolt the door behind me. Don't open it for anyone but me. If they try to force their way in, shoot through the door!"

Before she could say another word, Ted was outside, closing the door behind him. With trembling hands she slid the bolt, then rushed to the window, biting her lower lip and fighting tears. Lightning slashed the sky. By its eerie light, Myrna saw the rider at the cottonwood tree and the noose swaying in the wind. Her heart froze. Her hands went clammy against the cold metal of the rifle.

Ted moved to the edge of the porch. Water was dripping off the roof and the rain sprayed his face. He saw the swaying noose and the eighth rider as the lightning flashed. He steeled himself and forced steadiness into his voice. "All right, I'm here. Now what?"

"You've ignored the two notes we stuck on your door, and you've ignored our little visit of a week ago. Looks like there's only one way we're gonna get rid of you!"

Ted glanced toward the wind-whipped noose, then back at the hooded rider. "We and the other small ranchers are on our land legally, and you know it! You can't keep harassing us and get away with it! The sheriffs of both counties are going to nail your hides for this!"

"I wouldn't count on that, mister. They'll have to catch us first, and that ain't gonna be easy."

"They will, in time. Keep this up and you'll be sorry."

"Idle threats don't scare us, *nester!*"

"I'm not a nester, and neither are the others!" Sullivan said. "Just because we don't run herds in the thousands like Beaumont and the other big guys doesn't make us nesters. We need time to build our herds."

"Well, you ain't gonna get time."

"There's plenty of land for everybody! Why do you cattle kings have to be so greedy?"

"We gave you plenty of time to pack up and get out, Sullivan. You seem to be the leader of the nesters. Until you leave, the rest of 'em ain't goin'...so it looks like we gotta take stronger measures."

"And murder is your answer?"

"Oh, murder is such an ugly word. Let's just call it necessary elimination. We figure if we hang *you*, that'll be enough to scare the rest of the dirty nesters out before the same thing happens to them!"

Jake slid from his saddle and headed toward Sullivan, and the others—except for the man at the cottonwood—dismounted too. "Enough talk, boys. Let's hang 'im!"

———◆———

TWO

A frenzied wildness surged through Ted Sullivan as the seven riders sloshed through the mud toward him. Jake reached him first, and Ted swung a fist at his jaw. It connected, staggering the man backward. Then the rest of them were on him.

Ted was a strong man, but no match for that many. He dumped two of them in the mud, but the others soon had him locked in their grasp. He struggled as they dragged him toward the cottonwood tree where their leader still sat astride his horse.

Dear Lord Jesus, don't let them hurt Myrna, Ted prayed. Deliver her from their evil hands!

Inside the house, Myrna Sullivan was praying as well. Though she had hurriedly doused the lanterns, she still could barely see. Terror gripped her as she heard the big-voiced man call for Ted to hang.

She was about to dash to the door and take her chances with the rifle when another flash of lightning let her see Ted's assailants drop him in the mud, laughing. She heard the man who had slung the noose over the limb laugh heartily and say, "Scared you good, didn't we, cowboy?"

Ted scrambled to his feet, mud-splattered and soaking wet,

blinking against the driving rain. The man Ted had punched stood in front of him and said, "I oughtta bust your skull for punchin' me, Sullivan!"

"You expect a man to just lie down and let people like you walk on him?"

"Ain't you one of them Bible-lovin' fanatics? I thought Christians were supposed to turn the other cheek!"

"You have no idea what you're talking about. Just because I'm a Christian doesn't mean I have a yellow streak down the middle of my back like you bullies! I never saw a bully yet who'd fight a real man unless his pals were there to help him if he started getting whipped."

The big man swore and started for Ted.

"Jake!" their leader said from astride his horse. Jake stopped and looked at his boss. "Let it go."

"But you heard what he said!"

"And I said let it go."

Jake turned back to Ted and gusted through his mask, "I'm warnin' you, nester! If you're not packed up and gone in two weeks, you're a dead man! We *will* hang you!"

"And you better take them other squatters with you," another masked man said. "If they stick around, they'll be plenty sorry! You tell 'em we said so."

"Yeah, Sullivan," another one said. "We could've hung you just now...and we still can! You better think it over."

"Get off my property!" Ted said. "You're trespassing!"

The masked leader nudged his horse close to Ted. Rain dripped off the brim of his hat as he looked down and said, "Two weeks, mister. You'd better be gone by June second."

Ted Sullivan only stared at him.

The leader wheeled his horse about and said, "Mount up, boys. We've given our warnin'. It's up to this nester to use his good sense and get out before it's too late."

The men mounted and galloped away, their horses' hooves

kicking up mud. They soon disappeared in the dark.

Ted could hear Myrna's footsteps in the mud behind him. He turned to meet her, and she rushed into his arms and broke into sobs. "O Ted, thank the Lord He kept those vile men from hanging you! Thank You, Jesus! Oh, thank You!"

"Let's go inside, honey," Ted said, guiding her toward the house.

They moved inside, and Ted held her tight in his arms. She was trembling, and she wept uncontrollably with her head pressed against his chest. He talked to her in low, soothing tones, trying to calm her.

After several minutes, Myrna looked up at her husband and said, "Ted, we've got to leave. They mean business. They'll hang you next time."

"We are not going to allow those big ranchers to run us off. This is our land." He paused, brushed tears from her cheeks with a tender hand. "Well, it's ours and the bank's. We've been doing well, honey. With that last sale of fifty head, we were able to pay the bank ahead of time on this quarter's installment. There's a great future for us here. I'm not going to let Baxter Beaumont and the rest of his pals steal our future from us."

"But what can we do? The law hasn't been able to track those men down."

"I'll go see Sheriff Gross in the morning," Ted said. "When he hears that they almost hanged me—and promised to do so if we're still here in two weeks—he'll come up with something. These bullying tactics have got to be stopped."

"You really feel that the Lord would have us stay, with your life being threatened?"

"Yes, I do. Just because we're Christians doesn't mean we're supposed to cower before them and let them steal what's ours and let them destroy our lives. We put honest, hard-earned money down to buy this land, and we're paying the bank loan off by working hard."

Ted released her, moved across the parlor to a small table, and picked up his Bible.

"I was reading in Ecclesiastes just this morning and came upon this verse: 'Behold that which I have seen: it is good and comely for one to eat and to drink, and to enjoy the good of all his labour that he taketh under the sun all the days of his life, which God giveth him: for it is his portion.'

"This ranch and the good life it is giving us is our portion from the Lord, Myrna. It came from His hand, and it's ours to have and to hold. Those big ranchers have no right to drive us from it. I could never look myself in the mirror again if I turned tail and ran."

Myrna wrapped her arms around her husband's waist, hugged him tight, and said, "I love you, Ted. If you say we stay and fight...then we stay and fight. And pray that the Lord will give us victory."

Two days later—on May 21—Sheriff Lloyd Gross and Sheriff Hank Hawkins of Jefferson and Deer Lodge Counties in western Montana Territory emerged from Gross's office and walked together toward the town hall. Several riders were gathering there in the warm morning sunlight.

Jefferson City was the Jefferson County seat, and Deer Lodge City, the Deer Lodge County seat. Deer Lodge City was thirty-five miles due west of Jefferson City across a heavily forested valley, which was part of the rugged Rocky Mountains. The county lines joined halfway between two towering ranges, and some of the large cattle ranches sat in both counties.

"Hank," Lloyd Gross said, "when you hear Ted Sullivan tell about his experience two nights ago, it's gonna make your blood boil."

"Got rough, did they?"

"They swung a noose over a tree limb and dragged him

through the mud as if they were gonna hang him. Poor Myrna was about out of her mind with terror."

"Ted fight them?"

"Punched one of 'em. Big man. The leader stopped him from retaliating. Seems all they wanted to do was throw enough of a scare into the Sullivans to send 'em packin'."

Hawkins nodded. "They know Ted's pretty much the leader of the small guys. Guess they figure if they can scare him off, the rest will follow."

"Ted don't scare easy...and neither does Zach Meadows. If the big guys have it figured out, they'll know that gettin' rid of Sullivan won't completely solve their problem. Meadows would be right there to encourage the rest of 'em to stay put."

"I'm just glad they didn't go ahead and hang Ted. Mean as they are, it seems they're being careful not to actually kill someone."

"That may be next, though. Wouldn't surprise me none."

The lawmen greeted the small ranchers collected at the front door of the town hall and stepped inside. Ted Sullivan was at the podium in discussion with four ranchers, including Zachary Meadows of the *Diamond M Ranch*.

Ted spotted the lawmen and went to greet them. He shook hands with Hawkins, whom he hadn't seen for some time, and said, "Thanks for coming, Sheriff. I appreciate your making the trip over here."

"My pleasure," Hawkins said. "Besides, half of the ranches represented here are in my county. I owe it to them to be here."

Gross eyed the clock on the wall; it was nearly time for the meeting to start. "There are more outside talkin' than have come inside, Ted. You want I should go out and tell 'em to get their carcasses in here?"

Ted glanced at the clock. "Won't be necessary, Sheriff." He called to one of the ranchers who was standing near the door to go outside and tell the rest of them it was time to start.

As men filed in and took their seats, Ted did a quick count.

He knew there were just over a hundred small ranchers in the two counties. For two days word of the meeting had been spread by mouth from one rancher to another. He hoped that all had been informed.

It was two minutes after ten when Ted finished his count. There were seventy-eight ranchers in attendance. Maybe more would show up within a few minutes, he thought, but he decided to go ahead and start the meeting.

Ted raised his hands to gain their attention and said loudly, "All right, gentlemen! Time to get started!"

The rumble of voices quickly tapered to silence. Every eye was on Ted. Sheriffs Gross and Hawkins were seated a few feet to Ted's right, facing the audience. Ted was about to speak when the door opened and five more ranchers appeared.

"Come on in, fellas," he said. "We're just about to start. You all know Sheriffs Lloyd Gross and Hank Hawkins. They are here at my request, and want to hear what we have to say."

One more rancher came through the door and quickly took a seat in the rear.

"Men, all of us have been agitated by this bunch of masked riders. Is there anyone here who has not at least had a note tacked on your door telling you to get out of the valley?"

The ranchers looked around at each other, but not a hand went up.

"All right," Ted said, "then you all know what this meeting is about. According to my count, there are eighty-four of us here. That means eighty-four of us have at least been contacted by that bunch. Now let me ask you this: How many of you have been visited by the masked riders and had at least one conversation with them?"

As hands went up all over the hall, Ted turned and said to the lawmen, "Over half."

Both sheriffs nodded solemnly.

Ted looked back at the crowd and asked, "Have any of you been roughed up?"

One man stood and said, "Ted, they came onto my place

about a week ago. My sixteen-year-old son spoke back to the leader, and one of them kicked him in the stomach. I was about to retaliate, but they put guns on me and said if I did, they'd shoot me down like a dog."

Another stood up. "They come to my place four nights ago. Before they left, they threw rocks through the windows of my house."

Many others described property damage the masked riders had done. There was anger in their voices and fire in their eyes. Some told of property damage done on ranches not represented at the meeting. The voices grew louder as the anger mounted.

Ted raised his hands for silence, waited till he got it, then said, "Take your seats, gentlemen. I believe Sheriffs Gross and Hawkins can see that these riders are a threat to be reckoned with."

"That's right, Ted," called out one. "If they don't get what they want, they're liable to kill someone next!"

"Tell them about your latest experience, Ted," Zachary Meadows said.

"That's actually why I called this meeting, men. I want you all to know what happened at my place two nights ago."

The ranchers listened intently as Ted told in detail what had happened at his ranch. When he finished, one rancher rose to his feet, looked at the lawmen and said, "You sheriffs have got to do something about this! Next time they'll carry out their threat and hang Ted…or someone else in this room!"

"That's right!" shouted another, jumping to his feet. "We came to the rich grass of this mountain cattle country, paid for our land honestly, and have a right to raise and build our small herds as much as the cattle kings have a right to raise and build theirs!"

Others joined in, shouting their agreement.

Ted Sullivan raised his hands for quiet. It took several seconds. When the noise had diminished, he said, "I told you a few minutes ago that Sheriffs Gross and Hawkins have come at my request to hear what you have to say. If you want to express yourself to them, you can do it one man at a time."

A hand went up about halfway back. Ted recognized rancher Bill Hathaway. "Yes, Bill."

"Ted, the sheriffs know what's going on. I think I can sum up what's in the minds of all the men here. We want to know what they're doing about this menace. We all know that in the past three weeks, seven of our kind have been intimidated enough that they pulled up stakes and left the valley. From what I can make out, about twenty small ranches within the two counties are not represented here today. Did they not hear about the meeting, or are they packing up and planning to pull out, too?"

"I'll ask the sheriffs to respond in a moment," Ted said. "But first, let's try to answer your last question."

Ted then asked if the men knew of ranchers who had been told about the meeting, but were absent. It took some ten minutes to ascertain that every small rancher who was not present had been informed of the meeting.

"We can't properly speculate on why the others are not here," Ted said. "However, since in every case you men who informed them are their neighbors, I will ask you to go to them when you head for home. Let them know what went on here today, and see what they have to say. If you find some who are planning to leave, let me know…and let the appropriate sheriff know. The lives of seven families have already been disturbed and their dreams shattered. I don't want this happening to any more of us."

The men nodded their heads, and some called out their agreement.

Ted turned to the lawmen. "Sheriff Gross…Sheriff Hawkins… I think Bill Hathaway put it well. The main thing these men want to know is what you are doing about this, and we'd all like to hear who you think the troublemakers are."

Both lawmen rose to their feet and stepped to the podium. Sheriff Gross said, "Men, I can speak for both of us when I say we have tried to track down these masked riders. We have been to your ranches when we've learned that you had threatening notes, and when you have had personal visits from them. But up to this point, none of you have been able to give us a solid clue that would give us something to go on."

"Right," Hawkins said. "Since they appear only at night, it's hard to even get a good look at their horses. Some of you have given us vague descriptions, and we've kept our eyes open to try to spot the animals, but to no avail. Sheriff Gross and I are of the opinion that they ride different horses around the valley in the daytime than the ones they use to make their night visits."

"So up to now," Gross said, "we have nothing to go on that would tell us who they are, or where they hole up."

A man raised his hand, then stood to his feet. "Isn't there some way to set an ambush for these no-goods?"

The lawmen looked at each other, then Hawkins said, "This is big country, sir. Sheriff Gross and I each have one deputy. We're quite limited as to just how much ground we can cover...and we certainly can't be in more than one place at a time. There are over a hundred small ranches in our two counties. There's no way for us to know where the masked riders will show up next."

"What about if we arm ourselves and try to set a trap for them?" the same man asked.

"I'm all for you," Hawkins said. "The only problem is... where will they strike next? You might get lucky and guess the right spot, but chances of that are pretty slim."

Another man stood up. Gross nodded at him.

"Sheriff, why don't you go to the source? We all know these masked riders have to be from the big ranches. Why not nail them right where they live?"

"Because we have no proof," Gross said. "There hasn't been one bit of evidence that Sheriff Hawkins or I could use to nail them down."

Another stood. "Both of you believe the riders are from the big ranches, don't you?"

The lawmen looked at each other. "Go ahead," Hawkins said.

"We don't mind telling you our thoughts on the subject," Gross said. "We both feel sure that the big guys have formed this gang with some of their ranch hands. And we don't mind telling you that we believe Baxter Beaumont is their leader. Everybody knows he's the Big Bull in these parts."

"There's really no questions in our minds," Hawkins said, "that Beaumont is the one who's contrived this scheme to remove you as competition in the beef market."

The ranchers nodded their agreement, exchanging glances all over the room. Another man asked if the sheriffs had talked to Beaumont and the other big ranchers.

"Yes, we have," Gross said. "We've met 'em on their own ground, looked 'em in the eye, and flat asked 'em if they are in on this. To a man, they looked right back at us and denied any knowledge of it...even the Big Bull. Course, he got pretty mad at bein' suspected."

Subdued laughter swept over the crowd.

"So what next, Sheriff?" asked another.

"We wait till they make a mistake. One of these times they'll blunder and give away their identity. Then we'll nail everybody involved."

Bill Hathaway was on his feet again. "So in the meantime, we just stand against them and don't let them intimidate us, right?"

"That's about it," Hawkins said. "Sheriff Gross and I will continue to do our best to catch them. We want all of you to report any future confrontations with them, and do your best to look for something that will identify them."

Zach Meadows rose to his feet. "Ted, they threatened to hang you if you're still here June second. What about that?"

Before Ted could answer, another rancher said loudly, "Let's set a trap at Ted's place on June second! Catch 'em in the act!"

"They're too smart to make it that exact date, Clarence," Ted said. "They'll give it a few days...make it a surprise visit."

"So what're you gonna do? Let 'em hang you?"

"I don't know exactly what I'll do yet, but I guarantee you, I'll fight them!"

"That's what we'll all have to do," Zach said. "Fight them with everything we've got every step of the way! They're nothing but yellow-bellied bullies. The only way to handle bullies is to fight them!"

Zachary Meadows was not a man to be pushed around. Only recently he had been in a confrontation with one of the big ranchers on Jefferson City's Main Street. Dolph Jungerman was belittling Meadows in front of a crowd of onlookers, calling him a "nester," and telling him he should get out of the valley. When Jungerman couldn't put shame or fear on Meadows, he lost his temper and took a swing at him. Zach ducked the fist and knocked Jungerman out with a right and left combination.

A rancher named Walt Nelson stood up and said, "Ted, I appreciate what you're saying about fighting these men, but...everybody knows you're a pillar over at the church. I thought Christians were supposed to be peaceable folk."

Zach glanced at Ted, then looked at Nelson and said, "Walt, somebody's given you the wrong idea about Christians. In the Bible, God tells His people, *'If it be possible,* as much as lieth in you, live peaceable with all men.' God knows it's not always possible to live peaceably with all men. Just because a man's a Christian doesn't mean he can't stand up and fight for what's right. In fact, he's a shame to the name if he doesn't. If he's a genuine Christian, he will stand up and fight for what's right. Real Christians won't go around looking for a fight, but neither will they duck one!"

Walt Nelson grinned. "I like that. You're different than some Christians I've met."

"Come on over to the church this Sunday," Zach said. "You'll find a whole bunch like me over there, including Ted Sullivan and some of the other men in this room."

Some *amens* sounded through the crowd.

"I'll say one more thing, men," Zach said, "then I'll sit down and listen to whoever else wants to talk. I have a wonderful wife and two precious children. Well, they're hardly children anymore. Steve is sixteen and Sage is nineteen. But it's my duty as husband and father to fight Baxter Beaumont and his pals, if must be, in order to stay on the *Diamond M Ranch*. The *Diamond M* is our home, and I will fight for it tooth and toenail!"

The crowd cheered, and both sheriffs commended Zach for his determination to stay and fight for what was his. Ted Sullivan spoke of his determination to win out in the fight, and every rancher present joined in. They were not going to be intimidated by Beaumont's bunch. They had put down their roots in this rich cattle country, and they were going to stay.

When things quieted down, Sheriff Gross spoke. "Men, let me say this…we could be wrong about the masked gang being ranch hands assembled from some of the big ranches and backed by all of them. It could be just a few of the big kings who are in on it. Or it could be Baxter Beaumont alone who is providin' the masked men."

Bill Hathaway was on his feet again. "Sheriff, I've been thinking."

"Yes, Bill?"

"I don't mean to be out of sorts here, but since Beaumont has denied having any part in this, how can you be sure he is involved? I mean…I know he's crusty, hard-headed, and has a mean streak, but that doesn't necessarily make him guilty. Maybe it's someone else entirely."

The lawmen exchanged glances, then Hawkins said, "Bill, you could be right. At this point there is no proof that Baxter's fingers are in the cookie jar. When these men make their big mistake, we'll know. But I'll say this here and now. If it turns out that the Big Bull isn't in on it, I'll be totally shocked."

A murmur made its way through the crowd.

Ted stepped up beside the lawmen, looked at the crowd, and

said, "Any questions before we close the meeting?"

A young rancher stood up. "Yes, sir, if in resistin' these men we have to kill any of 'em, are we gonna be in trouble?"

"Not in the least," Hawkins said. "If they're on your property and you feel you have to use your gun to defend yourself and your family, it's just too bad for them! The tough thing here is that there are eight of them. Just don't play the fool and get yourself or some member of your family killed unnecessarily."

"Any more questions?" Ted asked.

"We got the main question answered just now, Ted," a middle-aged man called out.

Ted spoke words of encouragement to all. United they would stand against whoever the masked men were, and they would anticipate the day when they tipped their hand, gave away their identity, and every guilty party involved would be brought to justice. With that, Ted dismissed the meeting.

A rancher named Paul Grant came up to Zachary Meadows and said, "Zach, if it turns out the Big Bull *is* the instigator of this, how's it going to affect things between your daughter and Cory Beaumont? I mean, they're pretty serious about each other, aren't they?"

"Well, they're not quite ready to get married yet, but I can see the day coming. It's not too far off. But whatever turns out about Baxter won't affect the love Sage and Cory have for each other. "

"Well, I hope nothing happens to hurt either of them," Grant said. "They're both wonderful kids."

"Can't argue with that. See you at church Sunday?"

"Sure will."

THREE

I t was high noon at the *Box Double B Ranch*. The sun's single blazing eye looked down from a nearly cloudless sky, pressing its growing warmth on the land, an omen of heat to come as summer drew near.

Baxter Beaumont stood on the front porch of his sprawling ranch house and let his dark eyes take in the view. The great valley that reached north and south to points unseen was a long sweep of green grass and dense forests, rolling into a shaded distance against the jagged mountain ranges to the east and west.

He was proud that a great deal of the land that met his gaze belonged to him. The *Box Double B* covered more than ten thousand acres of rich grass, dotted with thousands of head of cattle among green patches of conifer, wild berry bushes, and white-barked aspen.

The big ranch house faced west toward the timbered valley that lay out of sight. Down there were countless canyons amid the forests and massive rock formations. Some six hundred yards due west, the land broke off sharply for a span of better than a mile and fell over a hundred feet of sheer rock. Thirty feet from the bottom of the cliff, sparkling springs cascaded from the fractured rock into a winding stream that flowed to the distant floor of the valley.

Baxter heard the door open behind him, followed by light footsteps. He turned to see his wife of twenty-five years moving toward him with a smile.

"Dinner's ready," Lillian Beaumont said.

Baxter nodded, then looked back at the breathtaking scenery.

Lillian moved up beside him, slid a hand inside her husband's arm, and said softly, "Never gets old, does it?"

"That's for sure. Mother nature did a mighty fine piece of work right here." Lillian looked up at him and smiled. "I know… you'll say it wasn't Mother Nature, it was Father God."

"That's right, Bax. My heavenly Father created all that beautiful scenery." Lillian and her husband had crossed swords on several occasions since she had become a Christian nearly two years ago.

"So dinner is ready?" Baxter said.

"Mm-hmm."

"Where's Cory?"

"I don't know. He must be tied up with something. You go on and eat with Joline, and I'll see if I can find him."

"Vice versa. You go eat with Joline, and yours truly will find Cory."

Lillian watched her husband step off the porch and head for the mess hall, where the ranch hands were eating dinner. She knew he figured to find their eldest son either there or somewhere around the corral. She entered the house, stepped through the spacious vestibule, and moved quickly down a wide hallway into the kitchen.

Joline, who had recently turned seventeen, stood at the stove, stirring the soup pot. "Where's Daddy?" she said over her shoulder.

Lillian never ceased to marvel at how much Joline favored her as much as both Cory and nineteen-year-old Mason favored their father. Though neither son was as large as Baxter, they were both tall and muscular. Joline, however, was nearly the same height as her mother and only a few pounds lighter. They looked so much alike,

Lillian felt as if she were looking at herself whenever she set eyes on the girl.

"Your father is looking for Cory."

"Oh. Should we go ahead and eat?"

"Might as well. The search could take a while. You know your brother. He could be anywhere between here and the back forty."

"Or the front forty."

The soup was poured, and the two women sat down, facing each other. "Well, at least we can pray aloud since Daddy's not at the table," Joline said with a tight grin.

Lillian led in prayer, thanking God for the food and asking that the Lord would work in the hearts of both Baxter and Mason—who was on a ride with friends in the mountains—and bring them to salvation. Joline echoed her mother's *amen* and they began to eat.

When the boss stepped into the mess hall, conversations cut off and every eye looked at him.

"Anybody know where your foreman is?" Baxter said.

"Last time I saw him, he was in the bunkhouse talking to Dave Nix, sir," a cowhand named Darrel Bates said.

Beaumont nodded, turned and left without thanking him. Bates looked at the men who sat across the table, shrugged, and they went back to what they were talking about before the interruption.

In the bunkhouse, Cory Beaumont was sitting on a bunk next to ranch hand Dave Nix. They held an open Bible between them, and Dave was reading Matthew 27 aloud when the outside door swung open and a massive form appeared in the doorway, silhouetted against the brilliant sunlight. Both young men looked up to see Baxter Beaumont.

"What's going on here!"

"I was just talking to Dave about—"

"You get to the mess hall and eat your dinner, Nix!" Baxter said. "There's repair work needed on the corral gate. Didn't Cory give you the message? That's your assignment!"

"Yes, sir." Nix laid the Bible on the cot and stood up. "He told me about it a few minutes ago. I...I figured it was all right to talk to my foreman on my own time, so I decided to skip dinner. I'll be on the gate as soon as dinner time's over."

"How do you expect to put out a half-day's work without eating?"

"Well, sir, I can handle it. Cory's been talking to me about what Jesus Christ did for me on the cross, and I—"

"You head for the mess hall now! Eat your dinner and get on that corral gate!"

David Nix flicked an *I'm sorry* look at Cory and hurried for the door.

When he was gone, Baxter set burning eyes on his son. "I've told you not to go spreading your religion around to the men on this ranch!"

"Pa, I've told you before...what I'm spreading is not religion. I am giving them the gospel of Jesus Christ. There's a big difference between the two. As a Christian it's my duty and my pleasure to bring others to Christ, just as Zach Meadows brought me."

Baxter cursed the name of Zachary Meadows, then hissed, "He's nothin' but a half-witted religious fanatic! And what's worse, he's made you into the same kind of half-wit!"

Cory prayed in his heart for wisdom and held his voice steady. "Pa, it's not what you think. If you'd only let me explain—"

"Shut up! There's nothin' to explain! I'm not blind, and I'm not stupid! It's bad enough my oldest son has become a fanatical fool, but you also had to drag your mother and Joline to that church in Jefferson City. You and the Meadows and that Bible-thumpin' preacher made fools outta them, too! Now the only sensible person in the family besides me is your brother!"

Cory looked at his father with compassion. "Pa, I love you. You're all wrong about the new life Mom and Joline and I have found in the Lord. If you'd only let me show you in God's Word what Jesus did for you at Calvary, you'd understand why we turned to Him."

Baxter's ham-like fist lashed out and caught Cory flush on the jaw, knocking him off his feet. He picked Cory's Bible up off the cot and began ripping out pages, flinging them over his shoulder. They fluttered to the floor.

Cory struggled to his feet. His brain was a bit fuzzy from the effects of the punch. He saw his father ripping the Bible apart while swearing and blaspheming God. When he had torn more than half the pages out, Baxter flung the remains against the nearest wall, then turned and faced Cory. "That's what I think of your holy book! You want to beat me up for it? C'mon, fanatic, fight me! I'm gonna knock this Jesus stuff right outta you!"

Cory's inward pain showed in his eyes. "Pa, I'm not going to fight you."

"This religion of yours has made you a sissy, Cory!"

"You're wrong, Pa."

"Prove it then! I tore up your book of fairy tales. If it means so much to you, you oughtta want to punch me out!"

Cory bent over and picked up the remains of his Bible. "I won't fight you because of who you are. This Book tells me to honor my father, so I will do so by not fighting you."

Baxter kicked the cot and let out a string of profanity.

When he stopped to take a breath, Cory said, "Pa, the Bible says, 'God commendeth his love toward us, in that, while we were yet sinners, Christ died for us.' That's the gospel, Pa. Jesus paid the—"

"Nonsense! It's just a bunch of nonsense!" Baxter wheeled and stormed out the door.

Cory began picking up the torn pages from the floor. He thought of the conflict that had been in his home the last two years, ever since he, his mother, and his sister had found the Lord. More complications had come six months ago when Cory and pretty Sage Meadows developed deep feelings toward each other. When Baxter Beaumont learned of it, he exploded. With heated words he had told Cory he didn't want him getting serious with Sage. Sage had told Cory she would not marry him if she had to live on the Beaumont ranch. She would not live under the control of Cory's domineering father. Somehow her comments had reached Baxter's ears.

Baxter Beaumont did not want to lose Cory as his foreman. He had made it known to both his sons years ago that when they married, he would build houses for them on *Box Double B* land. His plans were that when he passed off the scene, his sons would be joint-owners of the ranch. Sage Meadows posed a threat to that plan.

Cory let his mind go back to the day he went to the *Diamond M Ranch* to discuss the situation with Sage and her parents...

Cory Beaumont could feel the butterflies flitting against the lining of his stomach as he dismounted in front of the ranch house at sunset on a cold, wintry day. Trudging through the snow, he mounted the porch steps and was about to knock when the door came open, revealing Sage's smiling face.

"Hello, man of my dreams," she said.

Cory smiled at her as they stepped through the door together. Sage's parents were there to greet Cory, as was Sage's brother, Steve, who was three years younger than his sister.

Jasper, the family mutt, came bounding in, wagging his tail. He and Cory had become fast friends. The shaggy-haired "duke's mixture" whined and wiggled to show his friend he was glad to see him. Cory patted Jasper's head and ruffled the brown and white fur around his neck.

When the greeting was done, Zach told Steve to take Jasper out on the back porch. The dog would be fed after supper. Jasper gave Cory one more whine of welcome, then followed Steve toward the back of the house.

"I'm glad you could come in time to eat with us, Cory," Wanda said. "Supper's just about ready."

"My pleasure, ma'am. When it comes to whose cooking is best, yours and Mom's run neck and neck."

Wanda smiled and gave him a quick hug. "I'm flattered. Let's head for the kitchen. Sage and I will have the food on the table before you men can get your hands washed."

Moments later, as they sat down to the table, Zach said, "Cory, will you voice our prayer?"

"I'd be honored to, sir," he said.

Later, when the food had been passed and everyone was eating, Zach said, "Sage tells me the two of you have been talking seriously about your future together."

"Yes, sir," Cory said. "We're facing a problem with my pa though. That's why I told her I would like to talk to you and Mrs. Meadows. I need your advice."

"Don't want any advice from me, eh?" Steve said.

The others laughed.

"Maybe on how to be smart and handsome at the same time, Steve, but not on this subject," Cory said.

"More fried chicken, Cory?" asked Wanda as she handed him the platter.

"Don't mind if I do, ma'am." He took the platter and spilled two more pieces on his plate.

"Sage has discussed the problem with us," Zach said. "If you and she were to marry, she feels your marriage would be on shaky ground if you had to live on the *Box Double B*. Let me say right off that we agree with her. She would not be happy living under that kind of pressure."

"I understand that, sir," Cory said. "It's no secret that Pa wants to boss everybody and live everybody's life for them. But there's more to it than that. It's the financial side of it."

"Oh?"

"Pa knows Sage is dead-set against ever living on the *Box Double B*. He has threatened to cut me totally out of my inheritance if I ever leave the ranch to work elsewhere."

"I see," Zach said.

"So my problem is...I don't feel I'd be able to properly provide for Sage simply working as a cowhand on a ranch somewhere at thirty dollars a month."

Sage laid a hand on Cory's arm. "Cory, I appreciate your desire to provide for me, but I don't have to have expensive clothes and a mansion to live in with silk curtains and marble floors. I just want a happy home—no matter how humble—with the Lord in the center of it and a husband who loves me with all his heart."

"Cory," Zach said, "Wanda and Steve and I love you. We admire you as a fine Christian young man. We understand that you are pulled two ways, but if you want our advice—that is what you're here for, isn't it?"

"Yes, sir."

"We know our daughter. Sage would be miserable having to live under your father's thumb. It would put a strain on your marriage that would soon break it apart. It's better not to go into marriage than to go into it knowing it's already on a crumbling foundation."

Somber-faced, Cory nodded. "I understand that, sir. It's not that I want to stay under Pa's power, either. I just want to provide sufficiently for Sage if she accepts my marriage proposal when I feel the time is right."

"I appreciate that," Zach said. "You please me by having that desire. As you know, I'm building a small bunkhouse out by the barn because I anticipate having to start a crew within another few months. I could offer you the first job, then make you foreman when I add more men later. I could even pay you a pretty decent wage. Much more than you would get at the average ranch as a cowhand. But…"

"But it would start a war with my pa," Cory finished for him.

"Precisely. If I hired you away from him so you could marry my daughter, it would put him on the rampage for sure. The kind of trouble it would cause between him and this family would bring us only misery and unhappiness. I can't allow that to happen."

"I understand that, sir. I…I'll just have to ask the Lord to work it all out." Turning to Sage, he said, "I appreciate your sweet attitude. More than I could ever tell you. But I must know that I can support you properly before I put an engagement ring on your finger."

Sage smiled, tears surfacing in her eyes.

"My advice is this," Zach said. "As soon as we're finished eating, let's pray together about the whole situation. And let's covenant to pray about it every day until the Lord brings about the perfect solution. He's God, and He can do it."

Cory picked up the last torn page and pressed it inside the front cover of the Bible. He recalled with pleasure the many times Zach and Wanda Meadows had prayed with Sage and himself, asking the Lord to work out the problem in His way and in His time.

He left the bunkhouse carrying the tattered Bible and headed toward the big ranch house. Cory could not bring himself to discard the sacred pages, though the Bible was beyond repair. He would keep it in a box in his closet.

Cory entered the kitchen and found his mother and sister washing dishes and cleaning up the cupboard.

Lillian set tender eyes on him and said, "We figured your father was having a hard time finding you, so we went ahead and cleaned up. Did he find you?"

"Yes."

"Where is he?"

"I don't know."

Lillian squinted and focused on her oldest son's face. "Is that a bruise on your jaw?"

Cory's hand went to the spot where his father had hit him.

Then Lillian saw the battered Bible. "What happened?" she asked, moving to her son.

"Pa tore my Bible up. He came into the bunkhouse where I was showing Dave Nix about the crucifixion. Pa went into a rage. Sent Dave to the mess hall, and knocked me down and ripped my Bible to shreds."

Lillian put an arm around Cory and said, "I'm so proud of you for talking to Dave about the gospel. You'll have another opportunity, I'm sure."

"I've talked to him a few times already. This was my first chance to get a Bible into his hands. He's very interested. I'm sure we'll talk again soon."

"Wonderful! We need to be praying for him."

"And for Daddy," Joline said.

"Yes. And Mason," Cory said.

"Let's get you something to eat," Lillian said.

"I really don't have time, Mom. I've got to take some of the men to the south forest and cut down a few trees. They should be just about through with dinner, and they'll be expecting me."

"But you've got to be hungry."

"I'll survive," he said, kissing his mother on the cheek.

Cory saw the men filing out of the mess hall as he stepped off the porch. The crew he had assigned to go with him was collecting at the wagons parked beside the barn. As he moved their direction, he saw his father and Dave Nix standing near the door of the mess hall in conversation. Baxter had a stern look on his face and was waving his arms. Cory couldn't make out his words, but he knew what his father was raving about. He would let things cool down a bit, then find a time to talk to Dave again.

Two days passed. Cory was in the workshop next to the toolshed, working on a saddlebag. One of the straps had broken, and he was cutting a new piece of leather at the workbench to replace it. Movement caught his eye through a window. He looked up to see Dave Nix heading his way, carrying a section of harness.

Cory's heart picked up pace. Lord, let me win him now.

Dave wore a wide smile as he stepped into the shop and said, "Howdy, Cory!" He laid the harness section at the other end of the bench.

"Hello, Dave. Harness broken?"

"Yep. Buckle came off. It's been one of my 'things to get done.' When I saw you come in here, carryin' your saddlebags, I figured you had somethin' to fix and might be here a while."

"It'll take me 'bout half an hour."

"Do you have a little longer?"

"Well, since I'm the foreman around here, I pretty well set my own schedule. Why?"

"'Cause as long as we're in here where...where your pa can't see us, I'd like to finish what we started the other day."

"You mean—"

"Yeah. I want to know how to go to heaven."

Cory smiled. "Well, it just so happens I have a Bible here in my saddlebag. I want to let you finish reading about the crucifixion, then we'll go from there." He paused, then said, "I saw Pa talking to you at the door of the mess hall after the incident the other day. Was he trying to talk you out of listening to me?"

"He said I should steer clear of you and your 'Jesus stuff.' But Cory...I see somethin' different about you. You're not like your pa, that's for sure. And you're not like most other people. You seem to have a spring in your step and somethin' to really be happy about."

"It wasn't that way till I came to know the Lord two years ago. You weren't here then, but if you had been, you'd have seen a real change in me. Jesus did it. He washed my sins away, put my name in the Lamb's book of life, made me a child of God, guaranteed me I'd never see hell, and has me a place reserved in heaven. When a person has his eternity settled, he can really enjoy this life to the fullest."

"Sounds great to me! Where do I sign? Just show me the dotted line."

C H A P T E R

A week later, it was nearing ten o'clock at night as the Meadows family gathered at the kitchen table for Bible reading before bedtime, which had been a family custom ever since Zachary and Wanda had married.

Outside, a full moon was clear-edged and pure against the deep blackness of the night, spraying the mountains and valleys of western Montana with a silver sheen.

Sitting at the head of the table, Zachary noted that each family member had his or her Bible before them. He looked at his son and said, "Steve, I believe it's your turn to read tonight."

"Yes, sir."

"And where are we in our reading?" the father asked.

"At Psalm 37."

"An appropriate passage for us at this time, what with the masked riders lurking in this valley," Wanda said.

Sage opened her Bible and read the first few words. "Very appropriate, Mom."

"All right, Steve," Zach said.

Steve cleared his throat and began. "'Fret not thyself because of evildoers, neither be thou envious against the workers of iniquity.

For they shall soon be cut down like the grass, and wither as the green herb.'"

Steve paused and said, "This is good, Pa! 'They soon shall be cut down'—I like that!"

"And the Lord is going to do the cutting," Sage said. *"He* will put a stop to all this harassment."

Zach smiled. "Go ahead, Steve."

"'Trust in the LORD, and do good; so shalt thou dwell in the land, and verily thou shalt be fed.' Yeah! Those dirty skunks aren't gonna drive us out!"

"Why don't you hold your comments till we've read the entire Psalm, son?" Zach said.

"Sorry, Pa. It's just that this fits so well for what we're going through right now."

"You'll find much more that fits as you read on. Go ahead."

"'Delight thyself also in the LORD; and he shall give thee the desires of thine heart. Commit thy way unto the LORD; trust also in him; and he shall bring it—"

Steve's words were interrupted by Jasper, who lay on the floor next to his chair. The dog whined and jumped to his feet, looking toward the front of the house. The whine was repeated.

"What is it, boy?" asked Steve, reaching down to stroke his back. "He's trembling, Pa. Something's wrong."

Jasper's whine turned into a deep growl, and he darted into the parlor, barking.

Steve started to get up, as did his mother and sister.

"Hold it!" Zach said, rising to his feet and shoving his chair back. "You three stay here."

"But, Pa," Steve said. "If it's something bad, I ought to be with you!"

Jasper was barking viciously at the front of the house. As Zach passed through the door, he said, "I want you to stay here with your mother and sister."

When Zach reached the parlor, which was not lighted, he

could barely see the dog at the door, scratching to get out.

"Hush, boy!" he said, drawing up to the large parlor window. He peered through the sheer curtain and saw a band of horsemen outside in the moonlight.

From the corner of his eye, Zach saw his family standing at the kitchen door, looking on. Jasper continued growling, barking, and scratching at the door. "Steve," Zach called, "come get him and take him to the kitchen."

Steve hurried to the parlor, took Jasper by the scruff of the neck, and began forcing him toward the kitchen. The dog stiffened his legs, wanting to stay at the door. He kept barking and looking back while Steve forced him down the hall. Once Jasper was in the kitchen, Steve talked to him, settling him down. He whined in a low tone, but stopped the growling and barking.

Wanda was about to ask Zach if it was the masked riders when a familiar voice bellowed from outside, "Zach Meadows! Come out here!"

Wanda left Sage at the kitchen door and hurried to her husband. "Zach, you're not going out there!"

"I have to."

"No! You know what they almost did to Ted Sullivan! They mean business, darling! They'll hang you!" Wanda clung to both his arms.

Sage was now at her mother's side, eyes wide with fear. "Daddy, don't do it!"

"Sage, you stay here with your mother," Zach said, keeping a calm in his voice. "They're not going to hang me."

"Please, Zach!" Wanda said. "Don't go!"

"Wanda, if I don't go out and talk to them, they'll break the door down and come in here. I can't let them do that. You and Sage go back to the kitchen with Steve. Hurry!"

"Please, Daddy, stay in here!" Sage begged. "They'll kill you!"

"They haven't killed anyone before. I'll be all right. Now you two get on back—"

Suddenly heavy footsteps were heard on the porch, and the man with the loud voice hollered, "Meadows! Open the door!"

"Quick, Wanda!" Zach whispered. "You and Sage get to the kitchen and stay there!"

Zach watched as his wife and daughter dashed to the kitchen, holding hands, then called "Hold on!" through the door.

Jasper had heard the man's voice and was barking and growling loudly. Zach could hear Steve trying to hush him, and he could hear the dog's claws scratching wildly on the floor of the kitchen.

Zach took a deep breath, slid the bolt on the door, and turned the knob. A heavy body rammed the door, slamming it against the wall. Five men plunged into the parlor, holding cocked revolvers on Zach, eyes glaring through the holes of their dark hooded masks.

The big man with the booming voice said, "How come you're still here, Meadows? You've had three weeks to pack up and get out!"

"You have no right to force me and my family to leave this valley! We have as much right to our land as you do yours. We're not trying to drive you off. Why can't you leave us alone?"

"When it comes to rights, pal, you're kind don't have any! You squatters just mess up good cattle land. We don't want you here clutterin' up the valley."

Zach asked the Lord for courage and said, "Well, we're not going! We're staying right here!"

The big man took a step closer. "Well, since you insist on stayin' here, we'll just let you! We'll bury you and your family six feet under one at a time, and you can stay here forever!"

"Murder will bring the law on you!" Zach said.

"The law! Hah! We don't fear those two lame-brained sheriffs. Grab him, boys! I'm tired of jawin' with him."

Jasper came charging down the hall, lunged for the nearest masked man, and sank his teeth into his thigh. The man yelled and brought the barrel of his revolver down savagely on Jasper's head. The dog let out a yelp and fell to the floor, unconscious. Zach started to move toward his fallen pet.

"Stay where you are!" bellowed the big man, waving his gun at him.

The bitten man holstered his gun, picked up the limp dog, and carried him through the door and into the night.

"Hey! Where you going with my dog?" Zach said.

"Shut up!" the big man said. "I want your family in here now!"

"Leave my family out of this! They haven't done anything to you."

"Tell 'em to come out here, or these men will go back and get 'em!"

Reluctantly, Zach called, "Wanda, bring the kids and come out here!"

Wanda appeared with Steve on one side of her and a terrified Sage on the other.

"What are they going to do?" Wanda asked, setting fearful eyes on her husband.

"He don't know yet, lady. I want all four of you to step out here on the porch."

The Meadows family moved out onto the front porch at gunpoint.

They all saw it at the same time. A hangman's noose hung from a low limb on a tall oak tree in the yard. It swayed in the breeze under the full moon. A lone horseman sat astride his mount next to the oak, and another was anchoring the rope to its trunk. Another led a riderless horse directly beneath the noose and stopped.

"No! Please don't hang my husband!"

"It ain't your husband we're gonna hang, lady. It's your son!"

Strong hands grabbed Steve and dragged him off the porch. He struggled to free himself, but to no avail.

"No!" yelled Zach, plunging off the porch.

While the man forced Steve toward the tree, two more leaped

in front of Zach, guns aimed at his chest. "Get back!" one of them said. "You get in the way, and we'll hang your wife and daughter, too!"

Zach's heart pounded like a trip hammer in his chest. Wanda and Sage clung to each other in stark terror, eyes bulging. Both began to weep. Zach rushed to them, wrapped his arms around them, and turned to watch Steve's hands being tied behind his back.

The big man stepped close to Zach and said, "You should've listened to me three weeks ago, Meadows. All of this could've been avoided." He motioned with his head toward the house. "Inside."

Zach was glad to take his wife and daughter in the house. "Come on," he said in a low tone. "Let's go inside."

"They can't hang my boy!" Wanda wailed. "They can't!"

"Please, honey," Zach said softly, "let's go." His heart was heavy and he despised his helplessness to save Steve's life.

Sage was trembling from head to foot. As Zach ushered them toward the porch, she looked back and screamed, "Please! Have mercy!"

The last thing the three of them saw as they moved through the door was Steve being hoisted into the saddle, his hands tied behind his back. His ragged breathing revealed his terror.

When Zach, Wanda, and Sage entered the parlor, they saw that the masked men had placed three straight-backed chairs side-by-side, facing away from the door. They were forced to sit on the chairs, and their hands were quickly tied behind them.

"What are you doing?" Zach demanded.

"Shut up!" the big man said. "We're bein' real nice to you. This way, you can't watch the kid stretch the rope." He looked through the open front door and called, "Be sure to cinch the noose tight! I want his neck to snap quick so he don't suffer too much!"

"You beasts!" Wanda screamed. "You won't get away with this!"

"Shut up, lady! Ain't no stupid sheriff gonna catch us!"

"*God* will!" she said. "You can't get away from Him! O Zach, they're actually going to do it!"

Zach was praying fervently that somehow the Lord would deliver Steve.

"Okay, boys!" called the big man. "Hang 'im!"

Sage wailed at the sound of leather slapping horseflesh. Hooves pounded, quickly fading away. They could hear the rope grating against the tree limb as it swung with the weight in the noose.

Steve's strangulated wheezing and choking seemed to fill the night. Zachary Meadows closed his eyes and clenched his teeth. Wanda and Sage sobbed.

The gang's spokesman stood before Zach and ground out his words. "You can't say I didn't warn you last time we were here, Meadows. You really should've listened. If you don't pack up and move outta these parts, we'll hang another member of your family next time!"

The masked men filed through the door, mounted up, and thundered away into the night. Now the only sound was the grating of the rope on the tree limb outside.

"Wanda...Sage...I'm sorry," Zach said, his voice breaking. "I...I just didn't think they would actually go through with it."

"We should've done what they told us," Wanda said. "We should've packed up and left long ago."

"It's my fault," Zach said. "I should've at least taken you and the kids somewhere else."

"It's *not* your fault, darling. I wanted to stay here as much as you did."

"I'll scoot my chair back-to-back with yours," Zach said. "Let's see if I can untie your wrists."

Pushing the chair about, Zach soon had his back to Wanda's. It took him only a couple of minutes to loosen her knot so she could pull her hands free. Quickly, she untied her husband, then Zach freed Sage.

The three of them stood there a moment, rubbing their arms

and wrists, not wanting to go outside. Their arms felt almost too heavy to move.

Zach worked the numbness from his fingers and said, "You two wait here. I'll go out and…and cut Steve down."

"You can't go out there alone," Wanda said in a choked half-whisper. "I'll go with you. Sage, you stay in here, honey."

"Steve was my brother," Sage replied with a tremor in her voice. "Please let me go with you. I'll see him anyway when Daddy carries him inside the house."

While the women were talking, Zach swung the door open and looked toward the tree. What he saw made his head bob. A sharp intake of breath followed.

Both women looked at him, then hurried to his side and looked at the body hanging at the end of the noose. There was a mixture of relief and sorrow, for it was not Steve's body but Jasper's.

"Where's Steve?" Sage gasped.

"I'll find him," said Zach, bounding off the porch.

The two women were on his heels as Zach rushed about, calling for Steve. Suddenly he spotted a shapeless lump lying near a clump of bushes about forty yards from the oak tree. He ran toward it. Steve was lying on his side with his hands bound and his bandanna tied over his mouth. He had been pummeled into unconsciousness and was just coming to.

"Steve, it's Pa. Can you hear me?"

Steve blinked glassy eyes and rolled his head. "Yeah, Pa. I…I can hear you."

Wanda knelt beside her husband and began stroking her son's bruised face. "It's all right, honey. Those wicked men are gone."

"They…they didn't hurt any of you, did they?" Steve said.

"No, honey," Wanda said. "But I'm afraid they hanged Jasper. He's dead."

"Oh, no!"

"Dirty scum!" Sage said. "I hope God kills them!"

Ordinarily, Zach or Wanda would have scolded their daughter for such an attitude, but they were having the same thoughts themselves.

"Thank You, Lord, for sparing our boy!" Wanda said, tears of gratitude running down her face.

"Yes, Lord, thank You," Zach said, blinking at his own tears.

Steve sat up, rubbing his face. "I…saw them lay Jasper down near the tree. Then they took me off the horse. I had no idea what they were doing."

"There's no way you could have known," Zach said.

"What are we going to do now?" Wanda asked him. "That big-mouthed one said they would hang another member of the family next time."

"We've got to go into town right now and report this to Sheriff Gross. I'm thinking maybe the best thing would be to put you and the kids up in the hotel until those devils are caught. You'd be safe there." His jaw tightened. "I'm not going to let them drive us off our ranch!"

"We're not going to leave you here alone," Wanda said.

"The stock have to be fed and cared for, honey," Zach said. "I've got to stay. Besides that, the first cutting of hay is about ready."

"I'll stay here with you, Pa," Steve said. "You'll need my help putting up the hay."

Sage saw the stubborn look in her mother's eyes, knew what she was about to say, and beat her to it. "Daddy, if you and Steve aren't going to stay in town, Mom and I aren't either. This family has to stick together."

Wanda nodded. "My thoughts exactly."

"What did we just read tonight?" Steve said. "'Fret not thyself because of evildoers for they shall soon be cut down like the grass.' We lost Jasper, but at least the rest of us are unharmed. Let's not fret. Let's trust the Lord to handle those wicked men."

"It's right to trust the Lord, son," Zach said, "but He expects us to use our heads. Let's tell Sheriff Gross about this, then we'll decide our next move."

The family walked toward the house together and came upon the lifeless form of their dog hanging at the end of the rope.

"Steve, run in the house and bring my hunting knife," Zach said.

While they waited for Steve to return, Sage looked up at the dog and wept.

"Bless his heart," she said. "He put his life on the line to protect us."

Wanda's lips were quivering, and Zach thumbed tears.

"He wounded one of them, too," Zach said.

"I hope the dirty scum gets blood poisoning," Sage said.

"The Lord will handle him," Wanda said, "along with the rest of them."

Steve returned, and Zach cut the rope where it was anchored to the tree trunk. The rest of the family eased Jasper's body to the ground. Steve carried Jasper toward the house as the family walked that direction together.

"We'll put him on the back porch and bury him tomorrow," Zach said.

Sheriff Lloyd Gross sat beside his wife, Allison, in their parlor and listened as the Meadows family gave them the details of the incident. When Allison heard about Jasper's death, she wept, telling them how sorry she was.

"The brazenness of that bunch galls me," Gross said. "You know Tim Wylie and his family?" The Meadows nodded. "Tim was here not more than an hour ago. He said just after darkness fell, he and his family heard a series of gunshots coming from somewhere around their barn and corral. When they went to investigate, they found all five of their horses dead. A note left on the latch of the barn door said: 'Better get out while the getting's good. Next time it will be worse!'"

"Are Tim and his family going to leave the valley?" Wanda asked.

"Yes, ma'am. Tim's going to buy two horses to hitch to the family wagon in the morning, and they're pulling up stakes. I tried to talk him into sticking around till we nail those...those scoundrels, but it didn't do any good."

Wanda looked at the floor and shook her head.

Zach rubbed the back of his neck. "Sheriff, how are we going to stop these no-goods?"

"Well, Sheriff Hawkins and I came up with the idea of enlisting men from both towns to form what you might call posses. We realize that you ranchers can't ride in the posses because you need to be with your families at night. It's still a long shot, but we'll have four posses riding every night—two in this county and two in Deer Lodge County. Sheriff Hawkins will lead one posse, and his deputy, Murray Hill, will lead the other. I'll lead one here, and my deputy, Jerry Zeller, will lead the other."

"So you'll ride amongst the small ranches and hope to catch them red-handed, right?" Zach said.

"That's it. That's why I say it's still a long shot. There's a lot of territory to cover."

"Well, I like the idea, Sheriff," Wanda said. "At least it's a move in the right direction."

"That's what I told him," Allison said.

"We're trying to work it so we have different men in each posse every night of the week," Gross said. "That way no man has to ride with us lawmen more than one night a week."

"So how many will ride in each posse, Sheriff?" Steve asked.

"If all goes as planned, there'll be six to eight men, plus the man with the badge."

"Good!" Sage said. "I hope you catch them and make them pay for all the misery they've caused!"

Gross pulled his mouth into a thin line. His eyes showed his determination as he said, "Sage, dear, when we catch those hoodlums, they're going to pay to the fullest extent of the law!"

Zach ran his gaze over the faces of his family, then said, "Sheriff, we're in total agreement. Come what may, we're not going to let them drive us off our ranch."

"Good!" Gross said. "If every family will just stick together in this, we'll win yet!"

Wanda smiled at her husband. "You heard what he said, didn't you, darling?"

Eyebrows raised, Zach said, "Of course I heard what he said. Why?"

"We can't stick together if you make Sage, Steve, and me stay in town at the hotel."

Zach knew he couldn't make his family hole up in a stuffy hotel room indefinitely. "Okay, family," he sighed. "Let's go home and work on how to fortify ourselves for the next nighttime visitors."

FIVE

ame the first week of June. High in the Montana Rockies above the sweeping Deer Lodge Valley, Wilson Kyger and his seven men were getting ready for their night ride as dusk settled over the rugged mountains.

Wilson was the younger brother of Wade Kyger, who had been an outlaw leader for nearly six years, running his gang of robbers and murderers in western Dakota Territory and eastern Montana. Trains, stagecoaches, and banks were ready prey for the Wade Kyger bunch, and they often rode away leaving lifeless bodies behind.

Wilson had ridden with his older brother until a year-and-a-half ago, when he formed his own gang. He and Wade were still on good terms. With Wade's consent, Wilson had taken three men who had been faithful members of Wade's bunch—Bill Arkin, Leo Davey, and Fred Vogel—further west with him.

The Kyger brothers exchanged letters periodically, channeling them through mutual friends. It was done, of course, for a price. Both brothers wanted to know where the other one was at all times.

Jake Ransom, Wilson's right-hand man, had done time in prison on two occasions—for armed robbery and for manslaughter.

The manslaughter charge was for bludgeoning a man to death with his fists in a saloon fight. Jake was the only member of Wilson Kyger's bunch who had not committed cold-blooded murder, though he was not against it. He had said on several occasions that he would like to kill some of the small ranchers to put fear in the hearts of the others and send them packing.

Baxter Beaumont, who had hired the gang to harass the "squatters," was against cold-blooded killing. He was paying them well, but part of the deal between himself and Wilson Kyger was that no one would be murdered.

None of the other big ranchers were in on it. Each of them suspected Beaumont was behind it, but since there was no proof, they did not accuse him. All of them, except for Dolph Jungerman, were satisfied to let the small ranchers move in and build their herds as they, themselves, had once done.

The only other person who knew about Baxter's involvement was Mason Beaumont, Baxter's youngest son. Lillian, Cory, and Joline had asked Baxter about it when the harassment first began, and he denied having any part in it. They had not questioned him again.

Wilson's other three men, Roy Coulter, Clete Sarno, and A. J. Titus, had escaped jail in Wyoming while waiting for a circuit judge to try them for murder committed during several robberies. They had headed into western Montana and had run onto Kyger in Butte.

When they were almost saddled and ready to ride, Jake Ransom said, "Baxter's gonna be happy when he learns we got that Tim Wylie to scoot outta these parts."

"You bet," A. J. Titus said. He was nursing a sore leg from a recent dog bite. "So who we goin' after tonight, boss?" he asked Kyger.

"We'll ride into Deer Lodge County tonight, A. J. Depends on how the time goes. First, we'll pay Walt Nelson a visit. I'll decide what to do when we get there."

"He's a stubborn one," Clete Sarno said. "I think it's time we get tough with him."

"We will. Then we'll look in on his neighbor, Bill Hathaway. I think Hathaway's almost as hardheaded as Sullivan and Meadows. Has the potential of developin' into a leader. We gotta scare the livin' daylights outta him. If there's time, we'll move on down the road from Hathaway's place to the Clarence Upland ranch." He swung into the saddle. "Right now, it's Nelson we're aimin' for. Let's go!"

Darkness had just fallen when Delia Nelson heard a rumble of hoofbeats in the yard and went to the door. It was a warm evening, and the door stood open. The Nelsons had one small child, Walt, Jr., who was four years old. The boy followed his mother to the door. He had not forgotten the thundering hooves when the bad men with the masks had threatened his parents, telling them to move away.

Wide-eyed, Walt Jr. watched the biggest rider dismount and approach the porch. He could hear his mother's labored, shallow breathing.

Delia held onto her son's hand, squeezing it hard as the masked man said, "Where's your husband?"

"He's at the barn, milking," she said with strained voice.

Wheeling, Jake Ransom said, "He's at the barn, boys."

Walt Nelson was sitting on a milking stool, sending streams of milk into a bucket he held between his knees. The barn door was on the other side of the cow, and Nelson's head came up when he heard it swing open. He kept on milking, waiting for someone to appear. When they didn't, he called, "Delia...that you?"

Suddenly he saw a masked Jake Ransom come around the cow. The big man glared down at him through the holes in the hood and said, "I see you're still here, Nelson."

Walt stood up, nearly overturning his milk bucket. "Get off my property! Leave us alone! We came here to build a new life, and you're not going to keep us from it!"

"It's a big world, Nelson. You can be just as happy elsewhere. All we want you to do is get out of this valley."

"Well, we don't always get what we want, do we?"

"You're just askin' for trouble, mister! Maybe we oughta hang you from one of those rafters up there."

Four more masked men filed in. Walt Nelson felt a tinge of fear, but his anger overrode it.

"You go tell Baxter Beaumont I said he's got enough land, and he's got enough cattle!"

"What makes you think we're here by orders of Beaumont?" Ransom said.

"Don't play games with me. You guys keep this up, and Sheriff Hawkins is gonna nail you. And when he does, Beaumont's going down with you." Trembling inside, Nelson slowly sat and started milking again.

Ransom pulled his revolver, cocked the hammer, and placed it at Nelson's temple. "That kind of talk will get you dead, squatter!"

Ransom glanced at the four gang members who stood looking on, then took the muzzle of his gun from Nelson's temple and placed it behind the cow's right ear.

"This your only milk cow?"

"What business is that of yours? Get off my property! You're trespassing."

Delia Nelson stood at the front door of the ranch house, holding her little son's hand. Three of the masked men had remained with her, and one sat his horse a few yards behind the others.

"Mrs. Nelson," Wilson Kyger called from his horse, "you'd better hope your husband listens to my men. If he doesn't promise to take you and the kid outta this valley for good within two weeks, they'll kill him."

Delia looked toward the barn. "Go away and leave us alone!" she said. "Why do you have to—"

The report of the gun being fired inside the barn stole away the rest of Delia's words. Her knees went watery. Walt Jr. began to cry, looking up at his mother, who leaned on the door frame, trying to get her breath.

"Looks like that husband of yours didn't satisfy my boys, Mrs. Nelson," Kyger said. "Life'll probably toughen up, you bein' a widow and all."

"No-o!" she wailed. "You filthy murderers!"

She gathered her sobbing four-year-old into her arms and ran for the barn. Her legs gave way, and she fell. Her son was crying, "Mommy! Mommy!" as she struggled to rise. She saw the five masked men returning from the barn. Gaining her feet, she held the boy close and hurried toward them.

"You filthy murderers! You'll hang for this! I promise, you'll hang!"

They only glanced at her as they continued toward their horses.

"I think maybe we got his attention this time, boss," Jake said as they drew up.

"Good. Leave 'em a little note, and let's move out."

Tears half-blinded Delia as she carried her son through the barn door and, by the light of the lantern overhead, saw her husband lying on the floor. She gasped when she saw him move.

"O Walt!" she cried, kneeling beside him. "You're still alive!"

Walt Nelson moaned and turned his head. There was blood

on his temple, coming from a knot where a gun barrel had connected with his head.

He reached up and touched Delia's face as she leaned over him, sobbing.

It was then that she saw the cow. It lay dead, its head twisted in the stanchion. There was a bullet hole and a trickle of blood behind the animal's right ear. The milk bucket lay on the floor, and milk was spilled in a foamy white pool.

When the Nelsons returned to the house, they found a note on a small table in the parlor. It read: *Next time the dead body won't be the cow's.*

Bill Hathaway, his wife Mandy, and their three daughters were on the front porch of their small ranch house, enjoying the warm summer night. An owl hooted from an unseen limb somewhere nearby, and countless crickets were giving their evening concert.

The Hathaway girls, ranging in age from four to seven, were seated on the top step of the porch, holding their factory-made dolls, which had come by mail-order from back East just before Christmas last year. Each doll had beautiful long hair with a red bow in it and wore a bright-colored dress.

Bill and Mandy sat in the porch swing that hung by chains from hooks attached to an overhead beam. The moon was a thin silver disk in the star-spangled sky. Lanterns burned at the two parlor windows, shedding their yellow light onto the porch.

"Happy, honey?" Bill asked, holding Mandy's hand.

"Superbly," she sighed. "This is such a wonderful place to live. I miss our family in Missouri, but this is home now."

The girls were pretending that their dolls were talking to each other, each using her voice to speak for her doll.

"I wonder if we're ever going to get a little brother?" seven-year-old Tessie's doll said.

"I don't want a baby brother," six-year-old Lydia made her doll say. "Papa would like him better than me."

"Lydia!" Mandy said. "That wouldn't be true!"

"Uh-*huh,*" Elizabeth said. "Tessie said Papa would like a little boy so he could grow up and work on the ranch."

"I'd love to have a son," Bill said, "but I sure wouldn't like him better than I do my girls."

"But girls can't milk cows and pitch hay and all that stuff, Papa," Tessie said.

"Some girls do," Bill said. "But I wouldn't want you girls working in the fields. God didn't make girls for heavy work."

Four-year-old Elizabeth adjusted the doll on her lap and said, "Mama, how much does a baby brother cost?"

Mandy glanced at her husband, who was grinning from ear to ear. "Well, honey, baby brothers cost the same as baby sisters."

"Mama, how come your tummy got big before you bought Elizabeth?" Lydia asked.

Mandy was trying to come up with a reasonable answer when suddenly the thunder of hooves came from somewhere south of the house. She stiffened, gripped Bill's hand tight, and said, "It's them again! Why can't they leave us alone?"

"Mandy, take the girls inside," Bill said, leaving the swing. But before it could be done, the eight riders galloped into the yard.

"Everybody stay put!" the largest of the riders yelled.

Mandy gathered her girls close to her as Bill moved to the edge of the porch.

"You men are trespassing! Get off our property!"

"Why don't you make us, cowboy?" another rider said.

"You were supposed to be gone by now, Hathaway," said the big man, swinging from his saddle. Six others followed suit.

Jake Ransom strode leisurely to Wilson Kyger, who leaned from the saddle and said something only Ransom could hear. The big man nodded and headed toward the porch.

"You land hogs don't own this valley!" Bill said. "Why can't you get that through your skulls?"

"You're flirtin' with death, Hathaway!" Ransom said. "We warned you that night we plugged up your well. Did you think we were kiddin'?"

"I said get off our property! You have no right to be here!"

Ransom moved to the bottom step of the porch. The others pressed in close behind him.

"Looks like we don't have your attention yet, cowboy," Ransom said, letting his gaze run to the three girls who stood next to their mother.

Hathaway saw it and stepped in front of Ransom. "Don't even think about touching them."

Ransom laughed. "And what are you gonna do about it if I do?" His gun was cocked and lined on the rancher's midsection. He took a step in the girls' direction and said, "C'mere!"

Mandy stiffened, clutching her daughters close to her.

One instant Bill Hathaway stood rigid, unmoving. The next instant his fist came down on Ransom's gun hand, knocking the weapon to the porch floor. It clattered and fired, and the bullet chewed into a tree near the end of the porch.

Mandy started to back herself and the girls toward the door, but another masked man leaped onto the porch, pointed a gun at her, and commanded her to stop. The girls were crying.

Ransom cursed and lunged for his gun. Hathaway hit him with a solid blow to the jaw, sending Ransom to his knees. He followed with a punch to the back of the neck. Ransom howled and fell flat.

Roy Coulter and A. J. Titus closed in on Hathaway. Coulter cracked him across the face with his gun barrel, and Hathaway staggered and fell on his back. He started to get up, but froze when Titus pointed his gun between his eyes and said, "Stay right there!"

Mandy's face was a mask of terror as she watched Ransom rise to his feet, wrath blazing in his eyes. He picked up his gun and jammed it into its holster. Then he sent a savage kick into Hathaway's rib cage. Hathaway collapsed, gasping for air.

"Watch him!" Ransom roared to Titus and Coulter.

While the rest of the outlaws looked on, Ransom walked over to Mandy and her daughters.

"Time to shoot three little girls," he said.

Mandy screamed and tried to strike him, but he grabbed her arms and shoved her out of the way. He snatched the dolls from the girls' hands and tossed the dolls into the yard, pulled his gun, and fired six shots, blowing them to pieces.

Tessie, Lydia, and Elizabeth screamed repeatedly, their faces white with horror.

Ransom stood over Bill and said, "I hope you get the message. If you're still here in two weeks, it'll be the *other* three girls scattered all over the yard."

Bill rose to his feet, wiping blood from a deep gash on the bridge of his nose. He was unable to speak. His teeth were clenched, and the muscles in his neck and jaw were bulging.

Jake Ransom laughed and said, "Let's go, boys. I think the thick-headed rancher finally got the message."

The gang mounted up, and just before Wilson Kyger led them away, he shouted, "So long, Hathaway! Only a fool would still be here when we come back in two weeks. You aren't a fool, are you?"

With that, the riders of the night galloped away.

An hour later, Clarence Upland, along with his wife and two children, found themselves tied to trees in the front yard of their ranch house. They wept as the eight riders thundered away, leaving their barn and other outbuildings on fire.

Three days later, Sheriff Lloyd Gross was at his desk, concentrating on some paperwork. The door was open, and the noonday sun was brilliant on the dusty street. The weather had been dry, and residents of Deer Lodge Valley were wishing for rain.

As people passed by on the boardwalk, some of them called to Gross in greeting. Each time, he smiled and greeted them in return.

Suddenly hasty footsteps could be heard on the boardwalk, and the sheriff looked up to see his young deputy, Jerry Zeller, move through the door.

"Sheriff! Three of the small ranchers and their families are at the general store. They're pulling out!"

"Oh, no! Not when we're just getting organized so we can stop that masked bunch! Who are they?"

"Kyle Egan, Ernie Wevik, and Gene Langdon."

"I want to talk to them," Gross said, rising from his desk.

Gross and Zeller stepped out the door together and saw Sheriff Hank Hawkins's deputy, Murray Hill, dismounting at the hitch rail.

"Howdy, gents," Hill said.

"Hello, Murray," Gross said, moving his direction. "What brings you to Jefferson City?"

"I had to deliver some papers to Chuck Caldwell this morning. Sheriff Hawkins said since I would be that close to Jeff City, I should come by and let you know we've got another small rancher pulling out."

Gross glanced up the street and saw the Egan, Wevik, and Langdon wagons parked in front of the general store. The women and children were apparently inside. Kyle, Ernie, and Gene were talking to a group of townspeople.

"Who else is leaving?" Gross asked, looking back at Hill.

"Clarence Upland. Those skunks burned their barn and outbuildings a couple of nights ago. Got a couple more who've been roughed up pretty bad. Same night they burned the Upland's place, they killed Walt Nelson's cow. For a few minutes they had Delia believing they'd shot Walt. Then they rode onto Bill Hathaway's place and scared his little girls half to death. Shot their dolls to smithereens. They told Bill and Mandy if they're still there in two weeks, they'll shoot their girls like they did the dolls."

Lloyd Gross's features darkened. He mumbled something to himself, then asked, "Do you think the Hathaways and Nelsons will pull out?"

"I'm not sure. Sheriff Hawkins talked to them quite a while. They seemed encouraged now that we're riding with our posses every night."

"I sure hope they stay. Jerry and I were just heading up the street to talk to three families pulling out right now."

"Aw, no," Hill said. "I sure hate to see it. Hope you can talk them out of it."

"Gotta try. I guess you probably heard about Tim Wylie leaving."

"Yeah. I sure hope we get a break before any more good people pull out. Well, gentlemen, I've got to head back for Deer Lodge."

Twenty minutes later, the two lawmen returned to the office, dejected. The Egans, Weviks, and Langdons were too frightened to stay.

SIX

The morning sun peeked over the horizon, spreading its light across the prairie, through the streets of Denver, and on to the rugged Rocky Mountains westward. The sunrise brightened the base of that majestic range—which hoisted itself one rocky tier upon another—all the way to the regal peaks that took their jagged bite out of the brightening blue sky. Though it was nearing mid-summer, the highest peaks were still capped with snow.

Denver's streets, deserted through the long night, were now showing activity as another day was born.

At the Bluebird Café on Tremont Street, the aroma of hot coffee, combined with that of potatoes, pancakes, bacon, and eggs, filled the place. Nearly half the tables were occupied when the door swung open, and a tall, dark man entered, removing his black, flat-crowned hat. People whispered to each other, eyeing him with admiration.

He was dressed completely in black, except for his white shirt. He wore a black string tie, and a bone-handled Colt .45 Peace-maker rode his right hip low and tied down in a black holster and gun belt. There were a pair of twin white-ridged scars on his right cheek, highlighting the sharp-angled edges of his rugged but handsome features. His eyes were colored by a gray that seemed to have no bottom.

He smiled at his admirers and made his way amongst the tables toward a vacant one in a back corner. He was easing onto a chair when he saw two middle-aged men leave their table and head his direction. They were smiling warmly as they drew up.

"Mr. Stranger," said one, "I'm Brad Wells, and this is Lou Kirby. We're members over at First Baptist where you preached yesterday. We just wanted to tell you how much we were blessed by your sermons. The clarity of the gospel in your morning message certainly had its effect. What was it…eleven adults and about fifteen teenagers who came for salvation?"

"Something like that," Stranger said.

"And the way you exalted the Lord Jesus Christ in the message last night—powerful!" Lou Kirby said.

The tall man gave them a broad smile. "He *should* be exalted after all He did for us when He went to that cross."

A waitress appeared with coffee cup and steaming coffeepot in her hands. "Did you gentlemen want more coffee at your table?" she asked Wells and Kirby.

"No, thank you, Lila," Wells said. "We're about to leave." The men said parting words to John Stranger and walked away.

"Coffee, Mr. Stranger?"

"Please." Stranger noticed that the waitress's eyes were puffy and red. "Didn't I see you at First Baptist yesterday, young lady?"

"Yes, sir. My husband, Eric, and I are members there. Eric wasn't able to go to church yesterday. He's nursing a broken leg."

"Oh, I'm sorry. How did that happen?"

"On his job. Have you…ah…had a chance to look at the menu?"

"Not really. Give me a couple of minutes, okay?"

"Sure." Lila hustled off to take care of her other customers.

Stranger lifted the cup to his lips and blew on the steaming coffee. At the same time, he saw a man and woman come through the door. Their eyes roamed the room in search of an unoccupied table. The husband spotted John Stranger in the back corner, said something to his wife, and they both headed toward him.

Stranger rose to his feet and said, "Good morning."

"Good morning to you, Mr. Stranger," the man said. "Do you remember us?"

"Sure do. You both received Christ yesterday morning. I...I believe your last name is Chandler."

"That's right, sir," the man said. "Don and Betty Chandler. We've been visiting the church for several weeks, but your sermon finally opened our eyes to how desperately we needed to be saved. We can never thank you enough."

"It really wasn't anything different I said...Pastor Larribee preaches the same gospel I do. It's just that after hearing him preach for several weeks, the Word of God was doing its work in your hearts. Just give the glory to the Lord Jesus. He's the One who saved you."

"Oh, we understand that, Mr. Stranger," Chandler said. "We just want to thank you for making the gospel so plain and clear just when we needed it."

Stranger smiled. "The pleasure is mine. It's a great privilege for a sinner saved by grace to preach the Word of God."

"Is Pastor Larribee going to have you preach again for him anytime soon?" Chandler asked.

"I'm out of town most of the time, but he often has me preach when I'm here."

"Someone told us Sunday night that the young lady we saw on your arm after the service is your fiancée," Betty said.

"Her name is Breanna Baylor, ma'am. And yes, we do plan on marrying one day. Breanna is a certified medical nurse, and like me, does a lot of traveling. Most of her work is as a visiting nurse."

"I see. Well, she certainly is a beautiful young lady."

"Thank you, ma'am."

Lila came over to take Stranger's order.

"I'm afraid I still haven't looked at the menu yet," Stranger said. "How about bringing me a healthy helping of whatever it is that smells so good?"

"I'll do it," Lila said with a smile and hurried toward the kitchen.

The Chandlers excused themselves and headed for a table in the middle of the room.

Moments later the waitress returned, bearing Stranger's breakfast and a fresh pot of coffee.

"I don't mean to stick my nose in where it doesn't belong," Stranger said as she filled his cup, "but I can see that you've been crying. Is there anything I can do to help?"

Tears filled her eyes.

"Your name is Lila, I know. What's your last name?"

"Clark, sir."

"And you said your husband's name is Eric?"

"Yes."

"Does this have anything to do with Eric's broken leg?" he asked.

"Yes." Lila thumbed tears from her cheeks, avoiding his gaze. "Eric and I just moved to Denver a month ago from Illinois."

"And he broke his leg on the job, you said."

"Yes. It was your Miss Breanna who helped Dr. Goodwin put the splint on Eric's leg. She told us about you while they were working on Eric, and that you would be preaching at our church."

"Do you mind telling me what the problem is?"

"There's nothing you can do, Mr. Stranger. It's our problem."

"Try me."

Lila looked around and saw that customers were needing her. "I'll be back in a few minutes," she half whispered.

Stranger looked up to see Denver County Sheriff Curt Langan and his deputy, Steve Ridgway, enter. When they saw him, they smiled and headed for him.

"Oh, no!" Stranger said as they drew up. "They've sent two

lawmen after me! Am I under arrest, Sheriff?"

"Yeah!" Langan said. "We're arresting you for being gone from home so long at a time. We've missed you."

"Whew! I thought maybe you'd mistaken me for some tall, dark, handsome outlaw who looks like me!"

"Tall, dark, and handsome outlaw who looks like you, eh?" Langan said. *"Nobody* looks like you, John. And the only part I see of you from that description is that you're tall and dark."

The three men laughed together, then the sheriff asked, "Mind if we join you, John?"

Stranger gestured toward three empty chairs and said, "Shoot yourself. I mean *suit* yourself."

Sheriff and deputy laughed again as they sat down.

Lila Clark came, poured coffee for the lawmen, and took their orders. Before she left the table, Stranger said, "Lila, I want to talk to you before I go."

She managed a smile. "All right, Mr. Stranger."

Langan's gaze touched the waitress's face and held fast until she walked away. Looking at Stranger, he said, "I'd say she's been crying, John."

"Girl's got troubles," Stranger said. "I'm trying to pry them out of her so I can see if there's something I can do to help. You know her?"

"Only vaguely. She's been here a matter of only four or five weeks."

"Her husband's got a broken leg. She said he broke it on his job. I think maybe it's a financial problem."

Deputy Ridgway shook his head, glanced at his boss, and said, "Here he goes again, Sheriff. I think John would pay the whole world's bills if he knew how much everybody owed."

Langan nodded, smiling. "The man's generous to a fault."

"Mind if I ask you something, John?" Ridgway said.

"Nope."

"Well, I've been terribly curious since I first came to Denver and heard about all the people you bail out of financial problems. Since you're from an undisclosed far country…do you own a diamond mine in Africa? Or is your father a fabulously wealthy European aristocrat?"

John gave him a tight grin, glanced at Langan, then looked back at the deputy. "That's for me to know and you to wonder about."

Ridgway picked up his coffee cup, blew on the hot liquid, and said, "And that's the only answer I'm going to get, isn't it?"

Stranger grinned.

"But you didn't mind that I asked?"

"I told you I didn't. You can ask the same question again some time. I don't mind."

"But I'll not get an inch further."

Stranger shrugged his wide shoulders.

Ridgway turned to his boss. "The man really is a mystery, isn't he?"

"You might put it that way," Langan said.

The three men talked about various other subjects while the sheriff and deputy ate their meal. When they were finished, they excused themselves and left.

Lila Clark saw John Stranger sitting alone once again, and went to him. "Looks like I have a few minutes, Mr. Stranger. You said you wanted to talk to me."

"Where does Eric work, Lila?"

"Denver Lumber and Supply over on Champa Street."

"And you're having some financial difficulties since he's drawing no pay?"

"A…a little."

"He still has the job, though?"

"Oh, yes. Mr. Furley said Eric's job would be waiting for him once he can work again."

"But there's something that's got you worried, isn't there?"

Lila looked at the floor, then met Stranger's gaze. "Well, Mr.

Stranger, it's like this. Eric and I put money down on a house two days before his accident. We've been renting a room in a boarding house, but we really wanted to have our own home."

"Can't blame you. Nothing wrong with that."

"Well, the man who sold us the house was going to carry the loan for us. But now that Eric won't be able to work for several weeks, we can't even make the first payment. According to the contract we signed, if we back out, we forfeit the three hundred dollars we put down on the house. That three hundred was our life's savings, Mr. Stranger."

John pulled absently at an ear. "Lila, how much are the monthly payments?"

"Twenty dollars a month," she said, her lips trembling.

He reached into a pocket and pulled out several twenty-dollar gold pieces. He counted out twelve and dropped the rest back in his pocket.

"These will make your payments for a year. Open your hand, Lila."

Tears filled her eyes. "Oh, Mr. Stranger, I can't take those."

"Why not?"

"Well…you don't even know us. I appreciate what you're trying to do, but it's not your responsibility to pay our bills."

John reached down, took hold of her hand, pressed the dozen gold pieces into it, and closed her fingers around them.

"Just take these as a gift from the Lord."

Lila wiped tears with the back of the hand that held the gold and asked, "Just who are you, Mr. Stranger?"

Without a word, John produced a silver medallion the size of a silver dollar from another pocket and laid it in her other hand.

Stranger noticed a huge man come into the café and make his way toward the table closest to his. His hat was greasy like his shaggy hair, and the smell of him assaulted Stranger's nostrils.

Blinking against her tears, Lila dropped the gold pieces into the pocket of her apron and studied the medallion. It was centered with a raised five-point star, and inscribed around its edge in raised letters were the words: *THE STRANGER THAT SHALL COME FROM A FAR LAND*—Deuteronomy 29:22.

"The stranger that shall come from a far land," she whispered, raising her eyes to his. *"What* far land?"

John smiled and looked around. "You have customers needing attention, Lila."

She blinked and looked around. "Oh, I forgot where I was for a moment! I...I don't know how to thank you. Eric is going to be so surprised!" Looking at the man who had just come in, she said, "I'll be right back to take your order, sir."

"Well, make it snappy! I'm hungry!"

Lila smiled at Stranger and said, "I'll take these back and put them in my purse."

Stranger decided to stick around for a few minutes. In addition to the man's foul body odor, he also smelled of trouble.

More customers came in. Lila emerged from the kitchen with cups and hot coffee. She took orders, then hurried back to the kitchen. She glanced at John as she went, then vanished through the kitchen door. The drifter was shifting his weight on the chair in an agitated manner and mumbling something to himself.

Lila returned, carrying the coffeepot and a cup. She smiled at John Stranger as she paused at his table, and asked, "May I warm up your coffee?"

"Sure," he said, extending it to her.

"Hurry up, woman!" the drifter said. "I told you I'm hungry!"

Lila turned to the man, poured his coffee, and said, "I'm sorry, sir. Would you like our normal breakfast, or would you like to see a menu?"

"I have no idea what your normal breakfast is!"

"Fried eggs. Fried potatoes. Beef or pork sausage. Pancakes."

"Bring me a large portion of all of it."

"How do you want your eggs?"

"Over easy."

"All right."

"And make it snappy! I'm in a hurry!"

The man had the attention of everyone in the café. They watched as John Stranger leaned toward him and said, "Pardon me, Mr.—?"

The man glowered at him. "Bowron. Jules Bowron."

"Mr. Bowron, the young lady is going through some deep troubles in her life right now. She's been very upset. I'd appreciate it if you would lower your voice and be courteous when speaking to her."

Bowron frowned at Stranger, sharp hostility in his eyes, but did not reply.

Lila emerged from the kitchen, carrying a tray of food to a man and woman at a table near the front. She then took an order from two men who had come in right after Bowron. When Lila returned to the kitchen, John saw Bertha Clements, the café's owner and cook, at the kitchen door, looking at Bowron. Then she looked at Stranger. John gave her an assuring smile, then set his eyes on Lila as she drew up to Bowron's table.

"Coffee's weak," Bowron said as Lila set the heaping platter of steaming food before him.

Lila glanced at Stranger, then said to Bowron, "I'm sorry, sir. No one else has complained."

"Well, bring me some more and stiffen it up! I hate weak coffee, and I hate poor service!"

Lila's lower lip quivered. "I'll go make you some stronger coffee, sir."

"Well, hurry it up!"

Bowron emptied the small pitcher of syrup on his stack of pancakes, then salted and peppered his meat and potatoes. He ate like a pig, chewing with his mouth open and smacking his lips. Food spilled onto his beard, and he made no attempt to clean it off.

Lila came from the kitchen and said, "Sir, your coffee will be ready in about ten minutes."

"Ten minutes! I'll be done eatin' by then! Besides, I didn't ask for no beef sausage. And what's more, this food is cold. I ain't payin' for no cold food!"

"Sir," Lila said shakily, "I told you that with our regular breakfast, we offer beef or pork sausage. You said to bring you a large portion of all of it. So I did. I brought you both beef and pork. And I can see steam still coming off your plate. How can you say the food is cold?"

Bowron's fist came down hard on the table and he swore vehemently. "Take this food away and bring me some that's hot! And I want that strong coffee right now!"

Lila burst into tears and covered her face with trembling hands. John Stranger rose from his chair and motioned for her to leave.

"You know what I think of a man who uses profanity in front of ladies, Mr. Bowron?" Stranger asked.

"I don't really give a flip what you think, pal."

The whole place was quiet as a tomb. Every eye was fixed on John Stranger as he bent over Jules Bowron.

"You may not care what I think, but you might want to care that you've got me angry. Not only for the language you used in front of all the ladies in here, but for being so rude to Miss Lila."

Bertha was now out of the kitchen, standing next to Lila. She stepped up beside Stranger just as Bowron shoved his chair back and rose to his feet.

"Funny, we ain't had no complaints this mornin' at all until you came in, mister," Bertha said. "You get up on the wrong side of your bedroll, did you?"

"Maybe your regular customers don't mind eatin' cold hog slop, woman, but I do."

"You know where the door is, Bowron," Stranger said. "Nobody's making you eat here. Soon as you apologize to all the ladies in here for your foul mouth—and to Miss Lila for your rudeness—you can leave and pick you out another place to eat."

Bowron let out a string of profane words and told Stranger he should mind his own business.

The muscles in Stranger's square jaw rippled beneath the skin. "It *becomes* my business when someone with a mouth as foul as yours comes into a place where I'm eating and acts as disgustingly as you have. Now you apologize as I told you a moment ago."

Jules Bowron hitched at his gunbelt, burned Stranger with angry eyes, and said, "Just who's gonna make me apologize?"

"I am!"

Bowron guffawed, swore again, and said, "You ain't man enough, hotshot!"

Stranger moved so close to Bowron that their noses were only inches apart. "I'm telling you one more time. Apologize to the ladies for your dirty mouth and to Miss Lila for your rudeness."

"Make me."

CHAPTER

SEVEN

———◆◆◆———

John Stranger lashed out with a backhand blow that caught Jules Bowron on the mouth and took him by surprise. The impact of the blow whipped the huge man's head back and all but made him fall.

Before he could right himself, hands like spring steel seized him by the collar and began dragging him toward the door. Bowron tried to break the hold John had on his shirt, but found it impossible. He was amazed at the man's strength.

People on the boardwalks looked on as John dumped Bowron in the dust of the street. Bertha, Lila, and the Bluebird Café customers crowded at the door, watching.

John stood over him and said, "We can do this the easy way or the hard way, Jules. It's up to you."

"I ain't apologizin' to nobody!" Bowron said, rising to his feet and going for his gun.

Stranger kicked the gun out of his hand. It flew halfway across the street and clattered against the spokes of a passing wagon.

Bowron lowered his head and came at Stranger. John evaded Bowron's huge fists and landed a powerful punch to his jaw. Bowron went down, but the shock of the blow sent fiery streamers all the way up Stranger's arm. It was like punching a charging Brahma bull.

Traffic had stopped on Tremont Street as occupants of wagons, buggies, and surreys looked on. People were coming out of stores and shops to watch the fight. An elderly man told a boy to go find Sheriff Langan.

Bowron rolled onto his knees, breathing hard, then rose to his feet, fists clenched. John connected with a roundhouse right, but so did Bowron. Bright lights flashed in John's head as he landed hard on his back.

Bowron dived for him, but John rolled out of his way. Bowron hit the street's hard surface and swore. Stranger rose to his feet, blinking and shaking his head. He caught a glimpse of Lila and Bertha standing together at the edge of the boardwalk in front of the Bluebird's door. They both looked worried.

John's dizziness was beginning to clear, but he had to strike out at Bowron almost blindly through the fog that clouded his brain. It worked. He caught the man flush on the nose and heard a pop. Bowron's eyes widened when he saw bright crimson on the back of his hand. His nose was bleeding profusely. With an oath, he went after Stranger again, and was clipped on the nose another time. Enraged, he fought the harder.

They traded blows, moving in a circle, and soon were halfway through the wide doorway of the blacksmith shop next door to the café. A solid blow sent Stranger staggering against the frame of the big door. Bowron came after him and swung his right fist at Stranger's face. Stranger ducked, and Bowron's fist cracked against the hard wooden frame. He howled and grabbed the fist with his other hand. Blood oozed from the torn skin of his knuckles as he sucked air through clenched teeth.

Snarling, Bowron threw his weight against the smaller man, who was still a bit unsteady. John felt himself wrapped in a vise. His feet were off the ground. Bowron had John Stranger in a deadly bear hug, gripping him under the arms. Stranger felt the breath leave his lungs. Bowron was behind him, breathing hotly into one ear, and bearing down with all his might.

Suddenly John threw his hands back and jabbed a thumb in each eye. Bowron screamed and threw John ten feet through the air. He rolled hard against a buggy that stood near the flaming pit. The impact knocked the wind out of him.

Jules Bowron staggered toward John Stranger, rubbing his burning eyes. As he drew up, he saw a single-tree lying next to the wagon tongue. Stranger was getting up when Bowron came at him, wielding the heavy, metal-tipped single-tree like a club. He swung it in a wicked arc, intending to crush John's skull.

John ducked as it cut air over his head. The metal rings in the ends made a ringing sound. John spun around, placing his back to the buggy. Bowron chopped at his head, and the single-tree slammed the side of the buggy with a deafening bang, showering splinters in every direction.

John leaped at Bowron and grasped for the single-tree. They stumbled, twisted, and fell, with Bowron on top. He jammed the single-tree downward at John's throat. John met it with both hands, pressing against the giant's weight and strength. Bowron was breathing hard, spraying blood into John's face.

The wooden instrument quivered between them. Bowron grunted, forcing it downward. John met him strength for strength.

The spellbound crowd formed a large half-circle in the street. Those who knew the boy had gone after Sheriff Langan wondered where the lawman was. This fight needed to be stopped.

Bowron moved himself forward to force the single-tree against John's throat. John's keen senses told him the big man had moved too far. John flung his knees upward, catching Bowron on the rump. The top-heavy man peeled over, head-first. Whirling around, John wrung the single-tree from Bowron's grasp.

Both men came to their feet, and Bowron attacked. John brought the single-tree up in both hands and cracked Bowron hard just above the eyebrows. The blow knocked him down. As Bowron struggled to get up, John threw the single-tree into the buggy and prepared to finish the fight with his fists.

Jules Bowron's glassy eyes were fixed on John Stranger as he lunged toward him. John put every ounce of strength he had left into one right-hand punch. His fist struck Bowron so hard it lifted him off his feet and laid him flat on his back. The giant did not move. He was out cold.

John was breathing hard as the blacksmith and some other men moved toward Bowron. "Don't...don't let him move when he comes to. I'll be right back."

The crowd applauded and cheered John Stranger as he stepped out into the sunlight and headed for the closest water trough, which was next to the hitch rail in front of the blacksmith shop.

He eased down to his knees and buried his head in the water. When he pulled it out, Lila Clark was beside him.

"Oh, Mr. Stranger!" she gasped. "Are you all right?"

"Will be with one more dip," he said, submerging his head again. He held it there a moment, then came up, spitting water.

Lila took his hand and helped him stand. Her eyes were swimming with tears.

"Mr. Stranger, you sure went to a lot of trouble just for me and the women in the café. We've heard men swear before."

"I'm sure of that," he said, "but no man is going to do it and get away with it if there's anything I can do about it. And he's about to tell you how sorry he is."

Sheriff Curt Langan and Deputy Steve Ridgway came running up the street. Stranger saw them, then re-entered the blacksmith shop where Jules Bowron was now sitting up and holding his head. Harry Wagner and a half-dozen men stood close by.

Stranger looked down at Bowron and said, "You ready to make your apologies?"

Before Bowron could reply, the two lawmen pushed their way past the half-circle of men.

"What happened, John?" Langan asked.

Stranger briefly explained the reason for the fight.

Langan knelt down in front of Bowron and studied his bloody face. Blood was still trickling from his nose. "Both his lips are split pretty bad, John," Langan said. "He'll need stitches. Doc Goodwin's office is closer than Doc Wakeman's or Doc Stratton's."

"Fine," Stranger said. "He can go to Doc Goodwin's just as soon as he makes his apologies."

Langan nodded. "Okay." Then looking Bowron in the eye, he said, "You heard the man."

Bowron gave Stranger a pained look, then nodded. "All right," he said.

Harry Wagner and another man hoisted Jules Bowron to his feet and helped him move outside. Lila was at the front of the crowd with Bertha Clements.

When Bowron was face to face with them, Stranger looked toward the Bluebird and called out, "If the ladies who were in the café when this man filled their ears with foul language will step up close, please, Mr. Bowron has something he wants to say to you."

Though it galled Jules Bowron to tell the women he was sorry, he did so.

Then Stranger said, "All right, Jules, now tell Miss Lila that you're sorry for how you treated her."

Bowron looked at the ground and muttered, "I'm sorry, ma'am."

"Sorry for *what,* Jules?" Stranger said.

Bowron looked Lila in the face. "For treatin' you bad, ma'am."

"You're *real* sorry, aren't you?" Stranger said.

"Yes."

"Tell *her* you're real sorry."

Bowron licked his split lips and said, "I'm *real* sorry, ma'am."

"Fine," Stranger said. "Now, gentlemen, take him to Doc Goodwin."

While Langan and Ridgway helped Jules Bowron down the street, the women who had been in the café thanked John Stranger for coming to their defense. When they had turned away, Lila Clark stepped up to John and said, "You're shirt is dirty and blood-spattered, Mr. Stranger. I'd be happy to wash and iron it for you."

"Thank you, but that won't be necessary. Breanna is in town right now. When she and I are here at the same time, she does my laundry."

Lila nodded with a smile. "I...I don't know how to thank you for the money, Mr. Stranger. Eric will want to try, too."

"No need, m'lady. Like I said, just take it as a gift from the Lord, and thank Him."

"Nonetheless, He used you to give it to us. Thank you so much."

Lila embraced John Stranger discreetly and headed toward the Bluebird.

John looked down the street and saw that the lawmen and Jules Bowron were almost to Dr. Goodwin's office. Then he remembered his hat. He dashed into the café, grabbed it off the chair by the table where he had been sitting, and hurried down the street.

At Dr. Lyle Goodwin's clinic, Breanna Baylor was in a discussion with Goodwin and his regular nurse, Letha Phillips, at the desk in the front office.

"You ladies do know, I assume," Dr. Goodwin said, "that the medicinal qualities of water have been known since God first put man on the earth. During the middle ages of Europe, however, physicians decided that immersion in water was not good for one's health."

"You're kidding, doctor," Letha said.

"No, I'm not."

"I've read that, too," said Breanna, who, like Letha, wore a white pinafore apron over her cotton, ankle-length dress. "Didn't they use spit-baths during the middle ages, Doctor?"

"Yes. Then about 1650, they began to change their minds. Soon Europeans were bathing themselves in streams, lakes, and bathtubs again. About a hundred years later, in the English seaside village of Brighthelmstone, a prominent British physician named Richard Russell decided to go swimming in the warm waters that washed the shore. Dr. Russell had a glandular disease, and quickly found that the warm salt water eased his pain and discomfort."

"He wrote a book about it, didn't he?" Breanna said.

"Mm-hmm. *Sea Water and Diseases of the Glands*. People flocked to Brighthelmstone—which later became known as Brighton—and soon the village was transformed into a fashionable health spa. The idea of saltwater bathing spread over England. Soon, people were bathing themselves in the warm mineral springs at Epsom, a village in Surrey County. The Epsom springs, though inland from the sea, were naturally salty. This is where Epsom salts come from."

"I recall reading that somewhere," Letha said.

"But we must always tell our patients who bathe in Epsom salt water to keep it warm," Goodwin said. "Hot is even better. They should never bathe in cold salt water."

"That's what killed the Scottish poet Robert Burns, wasn't it?" Breanna asked.

"Indeed," Goodwin said. "Burns was suffering from a glandular disorder. His physician told him to stand up to his armpits in the freezing salt waters of the Solway Firth for two hours a day. Shortly thereafter, Burns died. It was the cold salt water that killed him. He was only thirty-seven."

"Mrs. Chastain will be in at two this afternoon, Doctor," Letha said. "When I give her the powders for her rheumatism, I'll be sure to tell her about keeping her Epsom saltwater baths warm."

Heavy footsteps were heard on the boardwalk, and Sheriff Langan and Deputy Ridgway appeared at the open door with the battered drifter between them.

Dr. Goodwin took one look at the man and said, "Let's take him back to the examining room, Sheriff. Who is this man, and what happened to him? He looks like he ran into a stampede."

"His name's Jules Bowron, Doc. He's just passing through town. But it wasn't a stampede he ran into. It was John Stranger."

Jules Bowron's head snapped up. He had not heard before the name of the man he had just tangled with, but he had heard of John Stranger. Few people west of the wide Missouri had not heard of John Stranger and of his skillful use of fists and firearms.

Breanna's eyes widened. "Is John—?"

"He's fine, Miss Breanna," Langan said. "I noticed a couple small cuts on his face, but that's all."

"Oh, thank the Lord," Breanna said, observing the size of Jules Bowron.

The nurses followed Dr. Goodwin and the other three men into the examining and work room. Dr. Goodwin gestured toward the examining table.

"What started the fight, Sheriff?" Breanna asked.

"Seems Bowron here used some bad language in the Bluebird and talked pretty rough to Lila Clark. Your Mr. Stranger told him to apologize. Mr. Bowron refused. Need I explain the rest?"

Breanna smiled. One of the things she loved about John Stranger was his respect for women. In John's presence, Breanna always felt as if she were on a pedestal, and this was exactly where John wanted her. She loved him for it.

"Jules, if you were from around here, you'd have known better than to get into a fight with John Stranger," Langan said.

Letha was starting to clean Bowron's face with alcohol, but through his split lips, he said, "I didn't know he was Stranger. I just took the measure of 'im and figured I could handle 'im."

"If you're going to take the measure of a man," Langan said, "you'd better take the full measure of him."

Bowron wondered if John Stranger could survive a bullet in the back.

EIGHT

A man's footsteps were heard by all in Dr. Lyle Goodwin's outer office.

"Do we have an appointment at this time, Letha?" Breanna Baylor asked.

"Sure don't. Next one is Barton Simms at nine-thirty."

"I'll see who it is."

When Breanna opened the door that led to the outer office, she saw John Stranger smiling at her. She closed the door and rushed into his arms.

"O John, I'm so glad you're all right! Curt and Steve told us what happened."

"Thought I might have you put a little iodine on these cuts," John said.

Breanna drew back and examined his suntanned face. There was a cut on the bridge of his nose and two on his left cheekbone. None were deep enough to require stitches.

"Sit down here at the desk, darling," she said. "I'll be right back."

When Breanna returned, Deputy Sheriff Steve Ridgway came with her. Ridgway was about to head back to the sheriff's office, but as Breanna started working on John, she thanked him for the generous contribution he had just made toward Denver's new hospital. Ridgway was interested in the new hospital and paused to pick up any new information he could get.

"Dr. Goodwin wasn't supposed to tell you it was me who gave it," John said.

"He didn't have to." Breanna dabbed at John's cuts with alcohol-soaked cotton. "When I heard the amount, and I was told it came from someone who called Denver home, I guessed who the donor was. You wouldn't want Dr. Goodwin to lie, would you?"

"Of course not."

"And by the way, Dr. Goodwin told Letha and me just this morning that another physician is coming to Denver. His name is Eldon Moon."

"Is he the one who's going to head up the hospital?" Ridgway asked.

"No. He'll be setting up his own private practice."

"Then who they going to get to run the hospital?"

"Well, I'm praying and hoping it will be a certain very special somebody."

"Excuse me?"

Breanna smiled. "About a month ago, Dr. Goodwin told me that he and the other two doctors were considering making an offer to a man on the west coast to come as chief administrator of the hospital. His name is Matthew Carroll. He's both a medical doctor and a psychiatrist, and he's currently administrator of City Mental Asylum in San Francisco and a staff physician at San Francisco's City Hospital. He'd be perfect as head man at the hospital here."

Breanna was applying iodine to the cuts as John said, "Not to mention, Steve, that Breanna's sister, Dottie, is about to marry Dr. Carroll."

Ridgway's eyebrows arched. "Oh, really?"

"Yes, not to mention that!" Breanna grinned and poked one of the cuts on John's cheek with a cotton ball.

"Ow, that hurt!"

"It was supposed to," she said in mock anger.

"So has Dr. Carroll been presented with the offer?" Ridgway asked.

"I don't know. I don't feel I can say anything to Dr. Goodwin about it without appearing to be pushy. You know, seeing as how it'll soon be a family matter."

"I can see why you'd be reluctant to bring it up to him," Steve said. "How soon are Dr. Carroll and your sister getting married?"

"In two weeks."

"That soon?"

"Mm-hmm. And if Matt is offered the job and takes it—which I'm praying hard about—it'll give them a little time to get adjusted before making the move to Denver. According to Dr. Goodwin, construction will begin on the hospital about the first week of August, if not a little before."

"Sounds like they've really got things rolling."

"Yes, thanks to a certain tall, handsome man's contribution."

John looked puzzled, "Who could she be talking about, Steve?"

"Beats me," Ridgway said. "I don't know anyone who fits that description. So, Breanna, when does Dr. Goodwin think the hospital will be ready for patients?"

"He's shooting for the first week of October. He says it will be done in sections so they can begin to use part of it while the rest is being completed."

"You still planning to go to San Francisco for the wedding?" John asked.

"I'm afraid that's changed. I just got a new assignment about thirty minutes ago that'll keep me from going."

"That's too bad."

"I know, but it can't be helped. Remember I told you back in April that they're building a new hospital in Billings? Well, it's done, and the doctors there wired Dr. Goodwin to see if I could come and help them for a few weeks when they open."

"How soon are you leaving?"

"Tomorrow."

"So soon?" John said.

"They need me as quickly as I can get there. I'll take the eight-thirty train in the morning for Cheyenne City, and ride stagecoaches from there to Billings. I'll wire Dottie later this morning and explain. She knows this kind of thing is part of my work, so she'll understand. It won't be quite so hard knowing that in a few weeks she and her family will be coming here to live."

"That's something to look forward to all right," John said. "I'm eager to get to know them myself."

"Well, I've done all I can for those cuts," Breanna said, picking up her materials. "They should heal up just fine in a few days."

"Unless you jab them again," John said.

Breanna's eyes glinted. "Watch what you say around me, Mr. Stranger, and you won't get hurt!"

Steve Ridgway laughed and left to return to the sheriff's office.

John took Breanna in his arms, held her close, and said, "I love you, Breanna."

"And I love you," she said, laying her head against his chest.

"Looks like I'll be leaving soon myself," John said.

"Oh?"

"Chief Duvall left a message for me at the hotel that he needed my help. Couple of outlaws he wants me to chase down. His deputies are being run ragged trying to catch all the outlaws running around this part of the country. He has a couple of appointments this morning. Asked if I would come by the office about eleven o'clock."

At 8:25 the next morning, John Stranger stood with Breanna Baylor on the platform beside the Cheyenne City train at Denver's Union Station.

"I'll miss you terribly, as always," Breanna said, looking up at him.

"And I'll miss you, sweetheart," he said, folding her in his arms.

"I'll be praying for your safety as you go after those outlaws."

"Thank you. I don't know when I'll see you again. I hope it won't be too long."

"The Lord will take care of that," she said.

The voice of the conductor came loud and clear: "All abo-o-ard!"

John and Breanna kissed tenderly, then he walked her to the steps of her coach, carrying her overnight bag, and helped her onto the platform. The conductor repeated his call, the engine's whistle blew, and the train lurched forward. Breanna wiped tears as she stood on the coach's platform and waved good-bye. John waited till Breanna passed from view, then turned and walked out of the depot, missing her already.

On the day that Jules Bowron received his whipping from John Stranger, he left Dr. Lyle Goodwin's office with the help of Sheriff Curt Langan. Since Bowron was weak and unable to ride, Langan guided him toward the Colorado Hotel, a short distance down Tremont Street from the clinic. Bowron was to return to Dr. Goodwin in five days to have the stitches removed from his lips.

His own assessment of the situation was simple. He would take a couple of days to gain his strength back, then work out a plan to kill John Stranger. When that was done, he would ride hard out of Denver and have the stitches removed by a doctor in another town.

Two days passed. Feeling stronger, Bowron went to the stable where Sheriff Langan had taken his horse. He saddled the animal, then slowly rode the streets, looking for Stranger. Nobody beat up on Jules Bowron and got away with it.

After nearly four hours of riding about town, Bowron decided to start asking questions. It was a hot summer day, and the cool inside the Brass Rail Saloon felt good as Bowron entered and halted just inside the door to let his eyes adjust to the dark. The smell of tobacco smoke, along with the bitter scent of whiskey and the odor of unbathed bodies, assaulted his nostrils.

When he could see better, he let his gaze roam around the place. It was midmorning, and less than half the tables were occupied. Two men were standing at the bar, whiskey glasses in their hands. The bartender was a heavy-set woman with close-cropped hair. She looked like she could whip the average man. She wore bib overalls, a man's shirt, and had a live cigarillo stuck between her teeth.

Bowron approached the closest table, where four men were playing poker. "Pardon me, fellas," he said, drawing up. "I just rode into town and—"

"Looks like you got yourself into a scratchin' contest with a wildcat, pal," one of the men said.

"I'd like to see what the wildcat looks like!" another said.

His card-playing partners laughed. The other patrons and the bartender all heard it and laughed, too.

When the laughter died down, Bowron said so that all could hear, "I'm lookin' for a fella calls himself John Stranger. Anybody here know where I might find 'im?"

"You don't look like his type," one of the men at the bar said. "You a friend of his?"

"Just an acquaintance."

"What do you want with John Stranger?" the barkeep said.

"Just a little business 'tween him and me," Bowron said.

"He travels a lot, mister," a man at a far table said. "I heard yesterday he's outta town."

"I don't suppose you have any idea when he might be back?"

"Nope. Don't seem to be any pattern about his comin' and goin'. He...uh...he does some work for the U.S. Marshal's office. I suggest you check there."

Bowron thanked the man for the information, left the saloon, and rode back to his hotel. He was determined to wait in Denver until Stranger returned.

Bowron returned a couple of days later to Dr. Goodwin's office to have his stitches removed. An hour later, he was slouching on a chair at the window of his hotel room, which overlooked Tremont Street. The second story of the hotel was hot, and there was no breeze. He chewed on a wad of tobacco and spit periodically into a spittoon. He could see his horse tied at the hitch rail below, in front of the hotel, with the Winchester .44 rifle in the saddleboot.

Suddenly Bowron sat up straight, his gaze fixed on a rider on the dusty, sun-struck street below. Amid the slow-moving traffic was John Stranger aboard a big black gelding. In Stranger's hand were lead ropes, tied to the reins of two horses that trailed behind him. In the saddles were two rough-looking men with hard-set faces. Their hands were cuffed behind their backs.

Jules Bowron's heart raced. Clapping his hat on, he spit his entire wad in the spittoon and headed for the door.

The man-in-black rode slowly down the street with his prisoners in tow. Jules Bowron swung into his saddle to follow him. Stranger guided his black horse, Ebony, to the sheriff's office and jail. Bowron reined in a half-block away and watched as Stranger took his prisoners inside.

Five minutes later, Stranger emerged, swung into the saddle, and rode off down the street. As he guided Ebony up to the hitch rail in front of the Federal Building, he said, "Well, big boy, I'll make my report to Chief Duvall, then take you to the hostler so you can get a good meal and a rubdown."

Ebony nickered, bobbing his head as if he understood.

In the alley directly across the street from the Federal Building, Jules Bowron slid from his saddle, looking both ways. There was no one in sight.

He tied his horse to a fence behind a vacant building, slipped the Winchester from the saddleboot, and made his way toward the street between the vacant building and a clothing store next door. Both structures were two-story with false fronts facing the street.

Bowron neared the front of the buildings, staying in the deep shade they provided. Across the street, John Stranger had just touched ground with his broad back toward Bowron.

Bowron levered a cartridge in the chamber, braced the rifle against the building, and took aim between Stranger's shoulder blades. He was squeezing down on the trigger when a man yelled, "Hey! What're you doing!" from a second-story window in the clothing store next door.

The sudden noise startled Bowron a split second before the hammer slammed down on the firing pin, spoiling his aim. The Winchester barked, and the bullet struck Ebony in the hip. As the big black screamed and shied to one side, John Stranger spun around and drew his Colt .45. His eye caught sight of the shadowed form behind the puff of blue-white smoke across the street, and the Colt roared...once...twice...and a third time.

People on the street looked on in amazement as the man between the buildings went flat on his back, the Winchester clattering to the ground. John Stranger turned his attention to Ebony while two or three men hurried to the spot where the man had fallen.

Ebony was frightened and in pain as John laid a hand on his back side and said, "Steady, boy. I want to see how bad you've been hit."

People were collecting on both sides of the street. Two deputy U.S. marshals came charging out of the Federal Building, followed by Chief U.S. Marshal Solomon Duvall.

Sheriff Langan and Deputy Ridgway came on the run. They stopped to ask a few questions of the people standing around the lifeless form of Jules Bowron. Then they hurried across the street to where John Stranger was patting Ebony and trying to calm him down. A trickle of blood was running down the big black's rump.

"Bowron's dead, John," Langan said. "Folks over there said he tried to kill you. Got your horse instead."

John nodded, swinging his gaze to Edgar Donaldson, who stood with them. "Was that you who hollered at him, Ed?"

"Yes, sir. I was upstairs in the storeroom. I opened the window to let some of the hot air out and happened to see this guy taking aim toward the street with his rifle. I didn't realize who he was aiming at until after I shouted at him."

"Well, I'm glad you did it," Stranger said.

"You know him, John?" Duvall asked.

"Sort of." Stranger gave a full explanation of his fight with Bowron five days previously.

"Guess he's been planning to kill you since then," Deputy Ridgway said.

"I'd say so," replied Stranger, turning back to Ebony.

"How bad is he hurt, John?" Donaldson asked.

"The slug plowed a furrow about eight inches long and an inch or so deep. High on the left hip, here, as you can see. Passed on through, though. I'm thankful for that. I'll take him over to Doc Goodwin and have the wound stitched up."

Sheriff Langan cast a glance across the street and said, "John, that was some kind of shooting, to take him out like you did."

"He must've been hard for you to see from over here," Donaldson said. "The shade is pretty deep between the buildings. I just barely saw him, myself."

"I fired at the smoke from his rifle, mostly. Didn't have time to look for him."

"Most men would never have got him," Ridgway said.

"Most men aren't John Stranger," clipped Solomon Duvall.

"Let's go see to the body, Steve," Langan said. "Glad you weren't hit, John."

"Thanks. Me too."

As sheriff and deputy crossed the street together, Steve said,

"I've heard about the many times John Stranger has cheated death. He must have a guardian angel watching over him."

Langan, who had come to know Christ a short time earlier through Breanna Baylor's witness, said, "The Lord has probably assigned six or seven angels to watch over that man, Steve. But give John a little credit, too. He's something else with that Peacemaker he wears on his hip."

"He's pretty good with his Bible, too. At least he sure used it to show me where I was headed."

The lawmen pushed their way through the crowd where Jules Bowron lay dead. He had been drilled three times in the heart.

Sheriff Langan looked down at the dead man and said, "You should've gotten out of town while the getting was good. I told you, if you're going to take the measure of a man, you'd better take the *full* measure. You flat underestimated John Stranger."

John Stranger's main concern was Ebony, but before he led him away, he said to Duvall, "Chief, I brought Cox and Myers in. They're at the jail."

"Great! Have much trouble taking them?"

"A little. No bullet holes in them, though. Just a few knots on their heads."

Duvall smiled. "Good job, John. As always." He paused, then said, "You go ahead and take Ebony to Doc Goodwin. Soon as Doc's done fixing him up, come on over to the office. We'll talk about the next place I need you to go."

"Will do. Come on, big boy. Let's get you to the doctor."

NINE

I n the alley behind the Goodwin Clinic, the big black gelding stood in a narrow enclosure made of horizontal split rails bolted to heavy posts while Dr. Lyle Goodwin worked at stitching up the laceration made by Jules Bowron's bullet.

John Stranger stood in front of Ebony, holding his bridle with one hand and stroking his long face with the other. Heavy timbers at Ebony's chest and rump kept him from moving either direction. He nickered periodically and tried to lunge forward when he felt the punctures of the needle. His ears stood straight up most of the time, but when the pain was the worst, he laid them back and snorted.

"Maybe by the turn of the century, John, this town will have a veterinarian," Dr. Goodwin said.

"That's almost thirty years away, Doc."

"Well, it'll probably be that long."

"I've been told that the United States now has a veterinary school. Back East somewhere. I can't recall where."

"Actually there are two now," Goodwin said. "One in Chicago and one in Kansas City. They both were founded since the Civil War ended."

"The one in Chicago is the one I heard about, now that you mention it."

"The one in Chicago was first. Started in '67. The one in Kansas City opened its doors to students in '69."

"Guess it will be a while before some of the graduates come out West."

Ebony snorted and tried to bolt, eyes bulging. Stranger held his head firm and stroked his long face. "I know it hurts, boy, but you'll just have to endure it." He looked back at the silver-haired physician and said, "Haven't there been veterinary schools in Europe for quite some time?"

"Better than a hundred years. About a hundred and ten, in fact. First one was established in France in 1761. Now Germany has one, as do Spain, England, and Switzerland. Very few veterinarians have crossed the Atlantic to make their fortune in this country, however. I know of one in Maine and one in Virginia. Might be some more that far east, but if there are, I don't know of them."

"Well, I guess until we get some out here on the frontier, you M.D.s will have to take care of the animals, too."

"Not that I mind, of course," Goodwin said with a clever grin. "After all, I charge by the pound. Today I'm working on a horse that'll go a couple of thousand—"

"Wait a minute, Doc, you'll bankrupt me! Besides, Ebony doesn't weigh a ton!"

"Well, let's go by height. He's what—sixteen hands at the withers? That's about sixty-four inches. Let's say my fee is a hundred dollars an inch. You'll owe me sixty-four-hundred dollars when this job is finished! See why I don't mind doing a little veterinary work now and then?"

"Larcenist!"

Both men had a good laugh as Dr. Goodwin was finishing. "There," he sighed. "All done."

"What do you think?" Stranger asked. "How long till I can ride him again?"

"You mean on long rides, like you usually go?"

"Yes."

"Couple of months."

"That long?"

"Afraid so. You have to give the wound time to heal without putting any strain on it."

"Okay, Doc. I'll just have to leave him with Jed Oaks at the stable till then. Can I pay you the sixty-four-hundred a dollar a month?"

"No, I want it all right now."

"Okay, Dr. Goodwin. Seriously...how much do I owe you?"

"Nothing."

"Now, look, Doc. I want to pay you."

"After your generous contribution for the new hospital? Are you kidding? Get out of here and take this beautiful animal to the stable!"

Ebony was released from his narrow confinement. As Stranger led him out, he said, "What about the stitches, Doc? When should they come out?"

"Week or so. Bring him back at that time, and I'll take a look at him."

"I may be leaving town. I have a meeting with Chief Duvall yet this morning. He has a job for me, and no doubt it'll involve traveling. That being the case, I'll leave Ebony with Jed. You can look in on him there, if you don't mind."

"Fine. I'll do it."

"I'll be glad to pay you for—"

"Will you hush up about paying me?"

"Looks like ol' horse doctor did a good job," hostler Jed Oaks said as he examined the stitches on Ebony's hip. "Just come on back and let me know about this next trip before you leave. Okay, John?"

"Will do. Give him a good rubdown, will you? He just carried me for quite a spell without much rest."

"Consider it done."

"Okay, Chief, what can I do for you?" John asked as he sat in front of Chief U.S. Marshal Solomon Duvall's desk.

"The name Wade Kyger mean anything to you?"

"Yes. Last I heard, he was leading a gang of robbers and cutthroats up in Dakota Territory. Why?"

"I received a wire yesterday from Yellowstone County Sheriff Mack Jensen up in Billings. Seems Kyger and his bunch have moved into eastern Montana Territory. They're robbing and killing all over Yellowstone County, and in some places farther north and east. Jensen says there are so many other outlaws running rampant in his county that he and his deputies are spread so thin they can't begin to handle them all. They can't spend all their time chasing Kyger and his bunch."

"So he wants me to add some weight to his force. Free them up so they can chase the other desperadoes."

"That sums it up."

"As far as you know, he isn't aware of my butting heads with Wade Kyger in the past?"

"He didn't mention it. I don't even know about it. When I asked if Kyger's name meant anything to you, I figured you might've heard about him. So fill me in."

Stranger laid his hat on the chair next to him. "A few years ago—almost six to be exact—I tracked Kyger through the northern part of New Mexico for Chief U.S. Marshal William Stone in Santa Fe. Did you know him?"

"Only about him. I never met him. He's dead, isn't he?"

"Yes. I'll get to that. Back when I went after Kyger, he was a lone outlaw, but vicious as a rabid wolf. Loves to shed blood.

Especially lawmen's blood. I tracked him up Raton Pass and was able to corner him. He found himself on the lip of a rocky ledge with a five-hundred-foot drop to some jagged rocks below. There was a sheer rock wall behind and above him, so climbing was out of the question. It was jump over the edge, or surrender. So he surrendered. While I was taking him to Marshal Stone at Santa Fe to be hanged, he said if he ever saw me again, he'd kill me."

"Why didn't they hang him?"

"I don't know. Next thing I heard, he'd managed to escape from the prison there at Santa Fe. He boldly walked into Stone's office, shot him dead, and got away. I heard later that he'd formed a gang—which included his younger brother, Wilson—and was terrorizing, robbing, and killing people in Dakota Territory. I'm not surprised to learn that they're now in Montana."

"So can I wire Jensen back and tell him you'll come?" Duvall asked.

"Do it. I'll take the morning train to Cheyenne City. Tell Sheriff Jensen I'll be there on Monday and will need to get my hands on a good horse. It'll be stagecoaches from Cheyenne City to Billings. Breanna just headed for Billings to help open a new hospital there. She said it takes four days from Denver to Billings, according to the schedule. I assume the stages run at night, too."

"I would think so if the trip can be done in four days."

A smile spread over Stranger's face. "Maybe I'll even get to see Breanna a little."

"That would be nice. I hope so."

Stranger left the marshal's office with Duvall's sincere thanks and went to the stable. He paid Jed Oaks a month's board in advance, then spent a few minutes with Ebony. Stranger told his horse he would be gone for a while, but that Ebony would be in good hands.

He then went to the Goodwin Clinic and explained the situation to the physician. Dr. Goodwin assured him that he would remove Ebony's stitches when they were ready to come out, and he would instruct Jed Oaks on the horse's exercise.

From there, Stranger went to the train station and purchased his tickets for both the trip to Cheyenne City and the stage ride to Billings. Then he headed for the hotel.

Deputy Sheriff Steve Ridgway was cleaning one of the rifles that stood in a rack in the sheriff's office when he heard the sound of someone running up the street. Suddenly a young man Ridgway knew well bolted through the door.

"Steve!" Larry Kenyon said. "Is Sheriff Langan here?"

"No. He's east of town settling a dispute between a couple of farmers. Is there something I can do for you?"

Larry pointed to one of the wanted posters on the wall next to the rifle rack. "It's him, Steve! That Vennard dude! I just saw him go into the Buckhorn!"

"What? You just saw Jason Vennard?"

"Yes! He stood next to his horse at the hitch rail and looked around for a few seconds before entering the saloon. I got a good look at him!"

Steve laid the rifle aside, stood up, and went to the wall. Studying the poster, he said, "You're sure?"

"Yes! I've been in here enough times to memorize the faces of every man you've got pinned up there. It's Vennard! I'm positive."

Jason Vennard was wanted in five western territories for bank and stagecoach robbery. There was a $1,000 reward offered by authorities in Montana for his capture. His initial crime spree had begun in Montana Territory, where he had shot and wounded a stagecoach driver and his shotgunner two years earlier.

Ridgway pulled his revolver, broke it open, and spun the cylinder, making sure it was fully loaded. He slid it back into the holster and headed for the door. Larry followed and drew up beside the deputy as he raced up the street.

"Maybe you ought to get some help, Steve. Vennard won't be easy to take."

"Can't endanger private citizens," Steve said. "I'm the guy wearing the badge. It's my responsibility to arrest him."

"I've got a gun at home. I'll go get it!"

"No you won't! I'm the lawman here, and it's my job to handle Vennard! I want you to stay outside when I go in there."

"Which horse is his?" Steve asked as they drew near the Buckhorn Saloon.

"The piebald mare."

The deputy stopped a few steps from the saloon door and said, "Do me a favor. Take the piebald and the rest of the horses tied here around back. Just a little precaution I learned from Sheriff Langan."

"Will do," Larry said, heading for the horses.

Steve Ridgway took a deep breath and let it out through his nostrils as he headed for the door. He pushed his way through the batwings and paused for a moment, allowing his eyes to adjust to the dark interior. The low murmur of men's voices met his ears.

He ran his gaze around the smoke-filled room and saw a man at the bar who resembled the picture on the poster. Ridgway's heart was banging his rib cage as he cautiously approached Jason Vennard from behind.

Vennard was standing at the bar with a whiskey glass in his hand. One foot was resting on the brass rail. Next to him was Benny Cumberland, a small, toothless man who was trying to make conversation. Vennard only grunted now and then.

A whiskey bottle stood on the bar in front of the outlaw. He was filling his glass for the third time when movement in the long mirror behind the bar caught his attention. He saw Steve Ridgway moving toward him in the reflection.

Ridgway had not yet pulled his gun, and Vennard would have paid no further attention to him, but at that instant sunlight caught the badge on Ridgway's chest. Vennard threw an arm around Benny

Cumberland's neck, drew his Colt .44, and whirled around to face the surprised deputy.

"Make like a statue, lawman!" Vennard yelled, pressing the muzzle of his gun to Cumberland's head.

The old man whimpered, his eyes bulging with fright.

"Make a false move, and I'll splatter this old chatterbox's brains all over the place!"

Steve froze, and the bartender and all the other patrons looked on with bated breath. Who was this man, and how dangerous was he?

"Me and this old duffer are goin' outside," Vennard said. "Anybody makes a move, the old duffer dies! And you, lawman, drop your gunbelt! You're goin' out with us!"

Steve hesitated, and Vennard pressed the muzzle harder against Cumberland's head. "I mean it, tin star! Drop it and get those hands in the air!"

Ridgway unbuckled his gunbelt and let it fall to the floor. The sound of it seemed like the shot of a cannon in the silence.

"All right, let's go. You step out in front of us so I can keep an eye on you. I want those hands kept above your head. Just don't try anything stupid, and I'll be long gone. Be stupid, and after I kill this old man, I'll kill you!"

John Stranger was walking briskly toward his hotel, which was still almost three blocks away. He was some twenty yards from the door of the Buckhorn when he saw Steve Ridgway emerge through the batwings with his hands held high and his gunbelt missing. Stranger leaped into the doorway of a ladies' ready-to-wear shop, pulled his gun, and cocked it.

He recognized Jason Vennard from the poster he had seen dozens of times in lawmen's offices. It took him only a couple of seconds to figure out what was happening.

"Hey, where's my horse!" Vennard yelled, staring at the empty space at the hitch rail. Vennard was swearing and demanding in a blind rage to know where his horse was.

Stranger hurried toward the three men until he was some forty feet from them. Steve saw him coming but did not let on. Stranger lined his cocked revolver on Vennard's head, steadying it with both hands, and yelled, "Drop the gun, Vennard!"

The outlaw's head whipped around. When he saw the tall man pointing the gun at him, he spat angrily, "You want me to kill this old duffer?"

"Is it worth dying for? You pull that trigger, you're a dead man. I don't miss!"

People were lining the street on both sides, looking on.

"Even if you shot me," Vennard said, "reflex will pull this trigger and kill the old man!"

"Not if I hit you an inch above the bridge of your nose. There will be no reflex to your trigger finger. And I've got a perfect bead on just that spot!"

"Please, John," Benny Cumberland said with quavering voice, "don't let him kill me!"

"He's not going to kill you, Benny. But he's going to be buried before sundown if he doesn't drop the gun!"

A thin thread of panic lanced through Jason Vennard. He had been backed into a corner he had not foreseen. He licked his lips and turned the gun away from Benny's head. "Okay, mister. You got me."

There was a sigh of relief along the street as the outlaw released Benny, eased down the hammer of his .44, and let it drop to the wooden slats at his feet.

There was cold sweat on Jason Vennard's face as Deputy Ridgway yanked the handcuffs from his hip pocket and quickly shackled his hands behind him. The bartender emerged from the Buckhorn and handed Ridgway his gunbelt.

Vennard glared at John Stranger while Ridgway strapped on

the gunbelt. When the deputy had his own gun out and pointed at the outlaw, Stranger holstered his and said, "I take it Curt's not around."

"Not at the moment," Ridgway said, "but I'll have Mr. Vennard all packaged up and waiting for him in a cell when he returns late this afternoon."

Benny Cumberland gave Stranger a toothless smile and said, "John, for a preacher, you really know how to handle yourself."

Vennard scowled hard at Stranger. "You're a *preacher?*"

John let a lopsided grin curve his mouth. "Among other things."

"You wouldn't really have shot me, would you?"

"Sure would've."

"You're a preacher, and you'd have shot me?"

"There's nothing in the Bible that says because a man's a preacher, he can't protect innocent citizens from outlaws. What kind of man would I be if I hadn't stopped you? If you'd pushed me to the point that I thought you were actually going to kill Benny, I'd have dropped you where you stood."

"And…and that bullet-an-inch-above-the-bridge-of-the-nose business was really true?"

Stranger gave him another lopsided grin. "That's for me to know and you to wonder about."

TEN

It was a warm Sunday night in mid-June. Baxter Beaumont and his nineteen-year-old son, Mason, were at the kitchen table in the *Box Double B* ranch house, playing poker. The ranch hands were in the bunkhouse doing the same thing. Lillian, Cory, and Joline were in town at church.

Baxter puffed on a cigar and said, "Things haven't been so good around here on Sundays since the rest of the family got religion, Mason."

"Yeah, I miss 'em. Too quiet without Ma and Joline always talkin' and fixin' good stuff to eat. Seems those fanatics at that dumb ol' church are more important than us."

"All religion has ever done for mankind, son, is cause trouble. It splits up families and causes all kinds of conflicts. I've read enough history to know that if Jesus Christ hadn't tried to change the Jews' religion, He wouldn't have got Himself nailed to that cross."

"I suppose. For sure, religion has done its job in our house. Seems to me all that goin' to church stuff is a waste of time."

"Yeah. Don't make any difference whether you go to church or not. When you die, you're dead like a dog, anyhow. Might as well enjoy life while we're here."

Mason studied his cards, then looked at his father. "Funny thing is that Ma, Joline, and Cory say they're havin' a big ol' time singin' hymns, listenin' to preachin', and all that. Sure seems boring to me."

"Well, you just keep thinkin' like that, son. Your ol' pa won't steer you wrong. The way I see it, a man's gotta get all he can while he's alive and breathin' on this earth. There's nothin' but the grave ahead."

After a while, father and son grew tired of poker. They put the cards away and just sat at the table and talked.

"I will have to say that your mother treats me better than she did before she became one of them born-again types," Baxter said.

"Yeah, and it's made my brother and sister easier to live with. Only thing is, I get sick of hearin' that Jesus talk."

"Well, we gotta admit that they don't hammer us with it. At least they're decent about it. I hear it ain't always like that in some families."

"I know, but it gets to my gizzard, all that prayin' before we eat and the like. And…and all three of 'em quotin' Bible at us every once in a while."

"I don't care for that either."

Mason grew suddenly quiet. His father puffed on his cigar and eyed him suspiciously. "Somethin' botherin' you, son?"

"Not really. I was just thinkin' about a talk Cory and I had yesterday."

"About what?"

"Well, he was tellin' me what the Bible says about it not bein' all over when we die. Like a dog, as you said. He really believes there's a heaven and a hell."

"Well, don't let that worry you, boy. My pa taught me the same thing I've taught you. He was a good, hard-workin' man. Never hurt nobody. Never cheated nobody. If there is a heaven, he went there."

"But Cory was quotin' Scripture and tellin' me that when

Jesus arose from the dead, it was proof there is life after death. He didn't stay dead. He came back and told people they needed to believe in Him, or they'd go to hell...not just the grave."

"Nonsense. Jesus Christ didn't come back from the dead. That's just a fairy tale, Mason. You stick with your ol' pa. Grab everything you can while you're here. That's all that counts."

"You mean like grabbin' the land those squatters are on once you've scared 'em off?"

"Yeah. Like that."

"How come you don't let those outlaws you hired just kill a few of those squatters? That'd put the fear into the rest of 'em."

Baxter tilted his chair back a little. "Now, son, your grandpa did teach me the value of human life. You kill somebody, you've taken somethin' you can never put back. It isn't for us to go around killin' people."

"Even to grab more for ourselves?"

"No. And don't you ever forget it. Murder is an awful thing, Mason. You don't murder to gain more for yourself. You gotta have respect for human life."

"Is this because there's a possibility that there really is a God, and because *He* gave us life?"

Baxter took the cigar from his mouth and stubbed it out in an ash tray. "Well, maybe. But even if there is a God out there somewhere, He didn't send no Son to die on a cross for us. He made the world and forgot it. But human life is important because it's different than animal life."

"So you don't hold to that Darwin fellow's teaching that we came from apes?"

Baxter rose from his chair. "I gotta go to the bunkhouse and talk to a couple of the boys. See you later."

Just then they heard thundering hoofbeats in the yard. Baxter sent a glance toward the dark windows. "That'll be Wilson and his gang. I thought they'd be a little later than this."

"You sent for 'em?"

"Yeah, we got some business to discuss."

Mason joined his father as he headed out the door; they watched the eight gang members ride up by the light of a half-moon. They dismounted and stepped up on the porch.

"C'mon in, fellas, and take a seat," Baxter said.

Baxter sat at one end of the table, and Wilson Kyger took a seat at the other end. The others pulled up chairs.

Kyger tilted his hat to the back of his head and set dark eyes on Beaumont. "Well, Baxter, I got word in town this mornin' that three more squatters pulled up stakes."

"That's good. Who?"

"The Watermans, the Bonners, and the Zimmermans."

"I'm glad, but it ain't happenin' fast enough. Looks like the rest of 'em need heavier proddin'. Ted Sullivan is our biggest problem. He's better than two weeks past the deadline you put on him, Wilson."

"I'm aware of that," Kyger said. "Is he what you called us here about?"

"Him and Zach Meadows."

"I want 'em both gone. The rest will give in and pull out when Sullivan and Meadows are outta the picture. You done anything to Meadows lately?"

"Not since we hanged his dog." Kyger looked Beaumont square in the eye. "You know, Baxter, if you'd let us kill a few, the rest of 'em would run like scared rabbits."

Baxter Beaumont set cold, piercing eyes on Wilson Kyger. The silence that fell over the room was so palpable that Kyger felt he could whack it with a hammer.

"We went over that when I hired you, Wilson," Baxter finally said. "I'm a rock wall when it comes to murder. You told me when I offered you and your boys this job that you could get rid of the nesters without killin' anybody."

Kyger felt pinned to his chair by Beaumont's piercing gaze. There was a strange tingle in his blood.

"Well, didn't you?"

"Yeah, I did."

"Then Wilson, let's get it done."

"But there's a new element, now," Wilson said. "Both sheriffs and their deputies are ridin' the valley with posses every night. We're havin' to be real careful."

"I know that, and I want you to be careful. But it's big country, and those posses can only cover a small portion of it at a time."

"Right, but in being careful, we've stayed away from Sullivan's place and Meadows's place because we figure the posses will probably be waitin' for us. We did make some heavy threats, you know."

"Okay, I understand," Beaumont said. "But don't drag your tails on Sullivan and Meadows too long. I want 'em out of here. I don't care what you do to 'em, just be sure there's no killin'."

A tight grin curved Wilson Kyger's lips. "I figured you'd stick to your guns on the murder bit, Baxter, so I've come up with an idea what to do to Sullivan. I'll work on Meadows later if he stays when Sullivan goes. What I'm gonna do is—"

"I ain't interested in hearin' what you're gonna do. Just go do it. I want results. Come back and tell me what you did *after* Sullivan has vacated his land."

Late the next afternoon, some of the Kyger gang were lounging around on the porch of the cabin high in the Montana Rockies. Wilson Kyger, along with A. J. Titus, Roy Coulter, and Fred Vogel, were a hundred yards or so below the cabin, sitting on the bank of a small stream.

Clete Sarno sat next to big Jake Ransom on the porch steps and watched a bird wheeling in the sky overhead. He could tell by the wingspread that it was a bald eagle. Many hawks were seen in the area, but rarely did one catch sight of the small family of eagles that nested somewhere in the crags of the surrounding mountains.

"You know, boys," Sarno said, his eyes squinted against the sun, "maybe we oughtta just slip when we deal with Ted Sullivan and kill 'im. We could tell Baxter it was an accident. He'd get a little upset, maybe, but who can fault an accident?"

"No way, Clete," Bill Arkin said. He was sitting in a rocking chair on the porch. Leo Davey sat in a straight-backed chair next to him. "Even if we made Baxter believe Sullivan died by accident, there'd be the devil to pay. Baxter would go mad. He'd make it plenty rough on us...and we wouldn't get another penny."

Jake Ransom was testing the sharpness of his hunting knife on the ball of a dirty thumb. "Bill's right, Clete," he said. "We don't want to agitate the Big Bull. We'll just have to do what we told Baxter we'd do—scare off the squatters without killin' anybody."

"Anybody got an inkling as to what this fancy plan is that Wilson mentioned to Baxter?" Davey asked.

To a man, they shook their heads.

"Guess he'll tell us when he's ready," Sarno said.

Ransom left the porch step long enough to pick up a fist-sized rock, then sat down again and began running the blade of his knife over it. He glanced down the slope and noticed Wilson Kyger and the others climbing toward the cabin. "Maybe we're about to find out," he said.

Kyger came and stood in front of the steps while Coulter, Titus, and Vogel sat down on the edge of the porch. Kyger let his eyes sweep across their faces and said, "Well, boys, the sun'll be down in another couple of hours. I want to tell you what I've got in mind for Mr. Hardnose Ted Sullivan."

The sound of steel scraping against rock had become a monotonous thing as Ransom continued honing the blade of his knife.

"Jake, you got that knife about sharp enough?" Kyger said, looking down at Ransom.

Ransom dropped the rock. "Yeah. Sharp enough."

"Here's what I want you to do, Jake," Kyger said as Ransom slid the knife back into the sheath he wore on his belt.

"I'm listenin'."

"Take one of the ropes and make a hangman's noose. Use that knife of yours to cut the rope down to a few threads right next to the spiral knot at its top. Make it close enough so the cut can't be seen. Understand?"

"Yep."

"We'll remind Sullivan that he's way past the deadline we gave him…and we'll remind him that we promised to hang him if we found him there when we came back."

Ransom grinned. "Then we'll make him think he's really gonna hang this time, and put the noose on him."

"Right. We'll put him on your horse and let him sweat for a few minutes. Roy and Fred, I'll depend on you to make sure Sullivan's wife doesn't interfere." Both men nodded.

Kyger swung his gaze back to Ransom. "Jake, you'll slap your animal's rump when I give you the nod. Sullivan will get his scare, but no more than a little rope burn on his neck."

"That oughtta be enough to scare the livin' daylights outta that squatter and his wife!" Titus said. "No doubt they'll be packin' their bags before midnight!"

"I'll give 'em forty-eight hours to clear out," Kyger said. "And they'll get a solemn warnin' that if they ain't gone by then, we'll hang Sullivan for real!"

"So let's say Sullivan decides to buck us, even on this one, boss," Vogel said. "What will we do if they ain't gone by the new deadline? I mean, since Baxter insists there be no killin'."

Wilson Kyger's features hardened. "I'll have to think on it, Fred. But whatever we do, it'll be severe. Maybe we'll kill off his whole herd, burn down the house and every building…and break both his arms and legs."

Night had fallen as Ted Sullivan sat at the kitchen table talking to Myrna while she finished putting the dishes away. His Bible lay on the table before him.

"I'm sure glad the Hathaways and the Nelsons have stuck it out," Myrna said. "They got pretty rough treatment."

"Yes, they did. But like us, they've made up their minds nobody's going to run them off."

"Those poor little Hathaway girls, having to watch those dirty scoundrels shoot up their dolls."

"Mighty lowdown thing to do."

"I wonder how far west the Zimmermans, Bonners, and Watermans are by now?"

"I'd say they ought to be at the Continental Divide, or mighty close. They'll probably make the Idaho border by the first of next week."

Myrna turned around with a dishcloth in her hand. "I hope they find happiness in Idaho."

"Me, too. They sure didn't find it here. Thanks to Baxter Beaumont and his hoodlums."

"You really think none of the other big ranchers are in on it?"

"No. And neither does the majority of our group. I was talking to Zach about it when I ran onto him in town yesterday. He thinks maybe Beaumont has hired a gang of outlaws to harass us. Makes sense to me. I don't think Beaumont's got eight hard-nosed ranch hands who would or could do what these masked riders are doing. Men who work with cattle don't slaughter them needlessly."

"Makes sense to me, too," Myrna said. "Ted, they've let us go way past the deadline they set. But they'll be back. You know that, don't you?"

"Yes. I have a feeling they may have been watching the place and saw the posses here."

"They might have. But the posses can't always be near. What are we going to do when those hoodlums come back?"

"Well, honey, I don't know. We've prayed about it since the last time. The Lord knows I can't fend off eight men by myself. But I don't believe He would have us to run from them. This is our ranch, and the Lord wants us to keep it." Ted picked up his Bible. "You remember what I read you from Ecclesiastes about God wanting us to enjoy the portion of what He's given us in this life?"

"Yes."

"And we agreed to stay and fight because God gave us this ranch."

"Yes, we did."

"Now let me read you something the Lord gave me this morning in Psalm 56: 'Mine enemies would daily swallow me up: for they be many that fight against me, O thou most High. What time I am afraid, I will trust in thee. In God I will praise his word, in God I have put my trust; I will not fear what flesh can do unto me.'"

Myrna laid the dishcloth on the cupboard, went to the table, and stood behind her husband, placing a hand on his shoulder. "That's beautiful, Ted. I especially like, 'What time I am afraid, I will trust in thee.'"

"Yes, and I like it when David says, 'I will not fear what flesh can do unto me.'" Ted flipped further back in the Psalms, stopping near the end. "Look here, honey. This tells me that while there are many who fight against me, I'm to trust the Lord in the battle and fight back. Look here at Psalm 144:1: 'Blessed be the LORD my strength, which teacheth my hands to war and my fingers to fight.' We aren't going to let them drive us off our land. We'll stand against them as best we can and trust the Lord to deliver us. We've got to resist them till they give up trying to run us off."

Suddenly pounding hooves were heard outside. The Sullivans looked at each other.

"It might be one of the posses," Myrna said, her throat tightening.

Ted closed the Bible and rose to his feet. "And it might not."

A strong, familiar voice roared, "Ted Sullivan! Outside! Right now!"

Myrna felt a shudder course through her. She gripped her husband's arm. "Ted, don't go out there. The Lord can make them go away."

"We've been expecting them, Myrna," Ted replied, licking his lips. "In all this harassment, they haven't actually killed anybody. I won't say I'm not afraid, but like David, 'what time I am afraid, I will trust in thee.' My hands and fingers are ready to fight. I won't back down, but I won't try something foolish, either. We've got to trust the Lord in this, honey. If I don't go out there, you know they'll break down the door."

"Sullivan! We know you're in there!"

Myrna followed as Ted headed toward the front of the house. He picked up the Winchester, worked the lever, and handed it to her. "Like I said before…if they try to come in, shoot through the door."

Trembling, Myrna wrapped an arm around Ted's neck and squeezed hard. "Please, darling. Stay in here with me. *You* shoot through the door if they try to come in!"

"I can reason with them, honey. They aren't going to kill me. We've got to stand firm and let them know we aren't going to be robbed of our good life here…nor of our land."

Myrna fought tears as she gripped the rifle and watched her husband step out onto the porch, closing the door behind him. She slid the bolt in place with a shaky hand, then hurried to the nearest window to watch.

Carefully, she pulled back the curtain and peered out. The sky was clear, and there was enough moon to allow her a good view. She flinched, and her face twisted in disbelief. A noose was dangling from the same tree limb as before, and one masked man was in his saddle near the swaying rope. But this time, there was a riderless horse beneath the noose.

Outside, Ted Sullivan saw the dangling noose and the rider-less horse before he had even closed the door. His mouth went dry.

All the masked men except the one in the saddle by the noose were on the ground in a semicircle, facing him. Jake Ransom stood at the bottom of the porch steps, his revolver lined on Ted's heart.

As Ted moved toward him, Ransom growled, "You didn't take my warnin', mister! Didn't I tell you if you were still here when we came back, we'd hang you?"

"That's what you said."

"You think I was kiddin'?"

"If you hang me, it will be cold-blooded murder! The law will track you down, and *you* will hang!"

Ransom glared hard at Sullivan, then turned and shouted, "Let's hang 'im, boys!"

The six men in the semicircle quickly moved in. Roy Coulter and Fred Vogel stationed themselves near the porch to make sure Sullivan's wife didn't try to interfere. The door was shut. They glanced at the windows, but the house was now dark, and they couldn't see anything there.

Clete Sarno, Bill Arkin, A. J. Titus, and Leo Davey seized Ted and started dragging him toward the tree. He was a strong man and fought them tenaciously, digging his heels into the ground and making them struggle to hold onto him.

As they forced him closer to the tree, the horse became skit-tish. Ransom hurried to it and took hold of the bridle, speaking in low tones to quiet it.

When the masked men had finally forced Ted Sullivan within a few steps of the tree, they flung him to the ground and began tying his hands behind his back. When the cord that held his wrists was knotted securely, they jerked him to his feet and pushed him toward the horse.

David's words kept racing through Ted's mind as he tried to fight them off: *What time I am afraid, I will trust in thee. I will not fear what flesh can do unto me.*

Jake Ransom's horse danced about with its hind legs, eyes bulging, as the struggle continued only a few feet away. Ransom bore down hard on the bridle, and the horse soon stood relatively still, breathing hard through flared nostrils.

At the porch of the house, Coulter and Vogel stood with their backs to the door, watching the scene with keen interest. Ted Sullivan was giving them a scuffle they would not soon forget.

As they lifted Ted's feet off the ground and were about to hoist him into the saddle, a woman's voice cut the night air. "Let go of him!"

Every head turned to see Myrna Sullivan standing on the porch with the Winchester .44 aimed at Coulter and Vogel, who were standing shoulder to shoulder. The moonlight revealed the determination in the set of her jaw.

Ted's feet were once again on the ground. He looked back at Myrna as she yelled, "You there on the horse! Tell them to let my husband go, or I'll kill these two men in front of me!"

ELEVEN

———◆———

Myrna Sullivan's face was deathly pale as she stepped off the porch, wielding the Winchester. Her eyes were bulging with the shine of fear and the fire of anger. "I mean it!" she screamed at the men who held Ted. "Let him go!"

Roy Coulter and Fred Vogel exchanged cautious glances, then Coulter ventured a step closer to Myrna, saying calmly, "Now, Mrs. Sullivan, you don't want to get yourself hurt."

"Get back!" She pointed the rifle at his chest. "Or I'll kill you!"

Coulter took another step. "You can do that, Mrs. Sullivan. But before you can lever another cartridge into the chamber, these other men will gun you down. Then they'll hang your husband, anyway. Now, is it worth getting yourself killed just to put a bullet in me?"

While Coulter kept Myrna's attention fixed on himself, Vogel inched his way closer to her.

"Is it worth it to you to get killed trying to take this gun from me?" Myrna said.

Coulter took another step. He was almost in arm's reach of the Winchester's barrel. "Put the rifle down, Mrs. Sullivan. You're gonna get yourself killed."

"Get back, or I'll shoot you!" Myrna said, shaking the weapon at him.

"And get yourself killed?"

"Myrna!" Ted called. "You can't stop them! Go back inside! Please!"

Tears filmed Myrna's eyes. "Ted, I can't! I've got to put a stop to this! They'll—"

Coulter lunged for the Winchester and jerked it from her hands. The gun roared, sending the bullet into a clump of bushes at the end of the porch.

Vogel leaped at Myrna, but she eluded him and ran toward the spot where the four outlaws were struggling to hoist a kicking, writhing Ted Sullivan into the saddle.

"Somebody get her!" Wilson Kyger shouted from his saddle.

Vogel reached for Myrna, but he stumbled and fell. Coulter fell on top of him.

Myrna jumped on A. J. Titus's back and dug her fingernails into his eyes. Titus howled and grabbed her wrists. Clete Sarno left Ted to Leo Davey and Bill Arkin and yanked Myrna off Titus's back, throwing her to the ground.

Davey and Arkin continued their attempt to hoist Ted onto the horse's back, and Wilson Kyger left his saddle to help them.

Myrna was a wildcat. She bounded off the ground and clawed at Sarno's face. Her fingers hooked into the round holes of the mask. Cloth ripped as Sarno swore and sent a punch to her stomach, doubling her over. He followed with a blow to her jaw, knocking her down.

Myrna lay flat on her back, rolling her head from side to side. She could hear the neighing of the frightened horse and the grunting of the men struggling to lift her husband, but her head was spinning and her eyes were clouded.

Ted's boot heels scraped against the black Mexican saddle, and he dislodged one of the silver ornaments. No one noticed it fall to the ground.

Suddenly Ted was in the saddle, and Wilson Kyger slapped the horse's rump with the palm of his hand. The startled animal bolted.

Ted's body lifted out of the saddle. He stared at the star-studded sky with bulging, horror-filled eyes. Only when his full weight came down on the remaining threads of rope did they snap. Hands bound behind his back, Ted Sullivan fell to the earth and lay still, eyes closed.

Wilson Kyger looked at the lifeless form of the rancher and swore. "Jake, you idiot! You didn't cut the threads thin enough! I heard his neck snap!"

Myrna was working herself to a sitting position. Kyger's angry words filtered into her foggy brain, and she lashed out. "You murderers! You filthy murderers! You'll hang for this! You will, I tell you! You'll hang!"

Suddenly the rumble of pounding hooves filled the night.

Wilson Kyger's head whipped around. He saw a band of riders no more than two hundred yards away coming at a full gallop. "It's one of the posses!" he cried. "Let's get outta here!"

The masked men swung aboard their mounts as Jake Ransom ran toward his horse, which had darted some thirty yards and stopped. With Wilson Kyger in the lead, the gang galloped toward the nearby forest.

Sheriff Lloyd Gross shouted for them to halt, but his words were swallowed up in the thunder of pounding hooves. Shots were fired at the fleeing outlaws, but they were soon in the dark forest, and gone.

Wilson Kyger and his gang charged full-speed into the deeply shadowed forest. Kyger looked back and saw the posse heading toward the ranch house. He quickly slowed to a trot, and his men followed suit. They rode deeper into the forest, then Kyger signaled for them to stop. When they drew up in a bunch, he wheeled his mount about and jerked off his mask.

"Jake, you fool! Do you realize what you've done?"

"I cut that rope plenty thin. How was I to know the threads were that strong?"

Kyger swore and said, "Baxter Beaumont's gonna be hoppin' mad when he hears of this! You know how he feels about murder!"

"But it wasn't murder, Wilson! It was just a…a mistake in judgment."

"Well, Baxter ain't gonna see it as any mistake in judgment. He's gonna see it as murder! And he'll probably fire the whole bunch of us without payin' us what he owes us! We had a big pay-day comin', but your stupidity has done us all in!"

Jake Ransom, left to himself with Wilson Kyger, would have pounded the man into the dirt for speaking to him like that. But he was outnumbered, and he knew the other men would side with Wilson. He went silent and looked at the ground.

"Well," Kyger sighed, "let's get on back to the hideout. We'll meet with Baxter in the mornin'…and take the consequences."

The possemen left their saddles and made for Ted. The first one to reach him knelt down, and after a close glance, said, "Looks like they cut him down for some reason, Sheriff. He's dead."

Sheriff Gross rushed to Myrna and helped her up. "Mrs. Sullivan, I'm…I'm so sorry about Ted. If only we had gotten here sooner."

Myrna nodded, sniffed, and looked toward her husband, who was surrounded by the possemen.

"Sheriff, would…would you let me have a few minutes alone with Ted?"

"Would you rather we carried the body into the house first, ma'am?"

"No. Please, I just want a few minutes alone with him."

"Certainly." The sheriff motioned his men away from Ted, then helped Myrna to the spot. Whimpering, she thanked the sheriff for his kindness, then knelt beside the motionless form.

The sheriff moved away, joining his possemen where they had left their horses.

Myrna wiped tears from her eyes with the back of one hand and stroked her husband's cheek with the other. "O Ted, I tried to stop them! I—"

She sucked in a breath when Ted's head moved, and he moaned. Her heart leaped in her breast. "Sheriff! He's...he's alive!"

The men rushed to Myrna's side. As Sheriff Gross bent down beside her, she said, "Look! He's moving his head!"

"Oh, thank God!" Gross said.

Myrna slid her arms around Ted's neck and wept for a long moment. Then she looked into his eyes, wiping tears, and said, "Come on, darling, can you sit up? Sheriff Gross and his posse are here. They'll help me carry you into the house."

Ted focused on Myrna's face, then said in a weak voice, "I...can't."

"You can't what, Ted?"

"I...can't move. I can only move...my head. I...I can't even feel my arms...or legs. It's like they aren't there."

"O dear God in heaven!" Myrna cried. "No! Please Lord, don't let it be!"

"It may not be permanent, Myrna," Gross said. "We'll use your wagon to take him into town to Doc Sutton."

Myrna searched the sheriff's face. "Do you really think so, Sheriff? Oh, let's hurry! Quick—the wagon's in the barn!"

Gross quickly sent four men to the barn to hitch up the wagon. Myrna stayed with Ted, stroking his face and speaking words of encouragement.

"Sheriff..." One of the posse stepped up to Gross with a coiled rope in his hand. "I just took this down from the tree. Look."

Gross took hold of it and held it so he could see it by the moon's light. "It's been cut. Let's get the noose off Ted. I want to look at it."

Myrna helped them remove the noose from Ted's neck, and when Gross compared the two ropes, he said, "They didn't really mean to hang him."

"What?" Myrna said.

He showed her the cut ends. "See here? It was cut before they ever put the noose on him. This was another scare tactic. The threads were supposed to break the instant the rope went tight. Whoever cut the rope didn't cut deep enough."

"I don't understand all of this, Sheriff," Myrna said. "I just don't understand."

"Well, whoever is heading this pack up is greedy enough to want to frighten all of you out of the valley. But he's got enough fiber to him that he's not willing to murder to get what he wants."

"Baxter Beaumont," one of the possemen said.

Gross glanced at him. "My first choice for a suspect. But not a shred of evidence."

"We'll get the evidence one of these days, Sheriff," another said. "Sometime, somewhere, somebody will make a mistake."

"I've got to believe that," Gross said.

Ted Sullivan was placed in the bed of his wagon, and Myrna sat beside him. Sheriff Gross drove the wagon with his horse tied to the tailgate and the posse riding on three sides.

As they rode toward town, Gross asked Myrna for the details of the assault. Myrna told him as much as she could recall, even that she had torn the mask of one of them, but not enough to reveal his features.

"Can you think of anything at all that might give us a clue as to who they are? I mean…a limp, or a scar on a hand, something that was said?"

Myrna thought for a moment. "I'm sorry, Sheriff, but I can't think of a thing."

"Well, if something should come to mind later, please let me know."

Myrna Sullivan and Sheriff Lloyd Gross sat in the waiting room, talking in low tones while Jefferson City's Dr. Hal Sutton went over Ted in the examining and surgical room. The possemen had gone to their homes for the night.

They had been waiting for nearly an hour when the door came open and Dr. Sutton, a stately looking man in his mid-fifties, stepped into the room. His face was somber. Myrna stood up, as did Gross.

Sutton moved up to them and cleared his throat. "Mrs. Sullivan...I'm sorry. Your husband will never move anything below his neck again. He is paralyzed for life."

Lloyd Gross put an arm around Myrna's shoulder as she placed her hand to her mouth. She closed her eyes and tears coursed down her cheeks.

"Doctor, have you told Ted?" she asked.

"Yes. He wants to see you. I thought it best to let the impact of my news pass before you went in."

She dried her tears and took a deep breath, then straightened her back and shoulders. "All right. I'm ready."

Myrna's heart pounded as she drew up to the examining table with the two men flanking her. She took hold of Ted's hand and said, "The Lord...has some purpose in all of this, darling."

"You're right." Ted managed a weak smile. "He could have kept this from happening, but He didn't. I...I was thinking of Romans 8:28. This is part of 'all things.'"

"Yes. 'All things work together for good,'" she said in a low tone. "We must cling to that truth now."

"And I thought of another Scripture we've talked about many times—Psalm 18:30."

"Yes." Myrna nodded, fighting to control her emotions. "'As for God, his way is perfect: the word of the LORD is tried: he is a buckler to all those that trust him.'"

Ted looked Myrna straight in the eye. "His way *is* perfect. He let this happen, and now we must believe this is His perfect will for us. And we must let Him be our shield."

Myrna leaned over and kissed her husband. "You're such a wonderful man, darling. I'm so glad I married you."

"Still?"

"Of course. This doesn't change anything. There'll have to be some other changes, though. We'll have to sell the ranch and move into town. I'll find a job and earn us a living."

"Maybe that won't be necessary, ma'am," Lloyd Gross said.

"What do you mean, Sheriff?"

"I mean, I heard some of the men in the posse talking. They're going to see if they can raise enough money to help you stay on the ranch. I'll have your pastor here first thing in the morning. I'm sure your fellow church members will help. So don't make any decisions just yet. Give us all a few days to work on it."

"And there'll be no charges for my work in this," Dr. Sutton said.

The Sullivans were pleasantly stunned. They thanked both men for their kindness.

Myrna returned to the ranch the next morning. She pulled the wagon into the yard and stopped the team close to the cottonwood tree where the horror had taken place the night before. She slid down out of the wagon, held onto the front wheel a moment, then took a deep breath and walked a bit unsteadily to the spot where Ted had hit the ground. Somehow the bright sunlight seemed to ease the pain of it all.

"Lord," she said, "those awful men must be caught. They must pay for what they've done. And so must Baxter Beaumont...or whoever is behind them. You can't let them get away with it. After all, you are a God of justice and—"

Suddenly a flash of reflected sunlight stabbed Myrna's eyes, coming from the trampled ground where Jake Ransom's horse had stood.

"What's this?" She bent over and picked up what appeared to be a silver saddle ornament.

The memory of last night's tragedy welled up in her and brought her to tears. While she wept, something kept picking at the back of her mind. What was it? Something the man—apparently the gang leader—had said in his moment of panic and anger.

Jake, you idiot!

That's it! Jake! He called him Jake!

Myrna fed the ranch's animals, then entered the house. She bathed, brushed her hair, and headed for town.

Sheriff Lloyd Gross and Deputy Jerry Zeller eyed the silver ornament carefully.

"Mrs. Sullivan," the sheriff said, "I appreciate you bringing this to me...and I'm sure glad you remembered hearing the name *Jake.* I'll ride over to Deer Lodge City and show the ornament to Sheriff Hawkins. He and I will spread the word. Somebody will spot that black Spanish-style saddle, and we'll get the guy who owns it!"

"And we'll ask around about the name *Jake,* ma'am," Zeller said. "We'll get him, too."

"Oh, I pray so," Myrna said. "This whole thing has to be stopped, and the guilty men punished!"

Myrna went to the doctor's office and found Ted in good spirits. Their pastor had just been there, and he was going to call a special meeting at the church that night to lay the Sullivans' plight before the church members. Help was on the way.

The next day, Dr. Sutton gave Myrna instructions on how to care for Ted, and allowed her to take him home. Women from the church had volunteered to work in shifts and stay with Myrna for a few days until she was accustomed to handling things by herself.

The pastor came to the ranch with money donated by members of the church, and Sheriff Gross brought money collected from other townspeople and small ranchers. The Sullivans were encouraged by these displays of support.

For a while, at least, they could stay on their ranch.

TWELVE

J ake Ransom sat sullenly on the porch of the cabin watching the rest of the Wilson Kyger gang prepare to go on another night ride.

It was now the third day after the gang had met Baxter Beaumont in a secret ravine some ten miles from the *Box Double B Ranch*. The meeting had taken place the day after the Ted Sullivan tragedy.

Ransom's mind went back to that eventful morning when Beaumont rode into the secret ravine alone. Beaumont had noticed the solemn looks on their faces and asked what was ailing them. Nervously, Wilson Kyger told him that Ted Sullivan had died of a broken neck. Beaumont acted like a madman. He ranted and raved, swearing at the top of his voice, demanding to know what had happened.

When Beaumont learned that the death was Jake Ransom's fault, he stormed at Jake, calling him every vile name he could think of. He told Kyger to get rid of Ransom, threatening to fire the whole gang without paying them another red cent if he didn't.

Kyger waited until Beaumont calmed down, then told him that he and Jake were good friends, and he would not put him out of the gang. Beaumont started to act like a madman again, but Kyger calmed him by saying that Jake would no longer ride with the gang at night. Beaumont had bristled at first, but Kyger told him that if he insisted Jake be thrown out of the gang, they would all leave, and Beaumont could find somebody else to do his dirty work. Kyger also demanded that the gang be paid the same amount agreed upon at the beginning.

Beaumont quickly capitulated, as Kyger figured he would, and even said that maybe Ted Sullivan's death would send the rest of the small ranchers packing. Ridding the valley of the squatters must be done soon, Beaumont had said. One of these days Gross or Hawkins was going to learn who the gang was, and who they were working for, and close in. Every man involved—even Baxter Beaumont—could be hanged for murder.

Jake's thoughts were interrupted when Wilson Kyger came out of the cabin in the dim twilight and said, "Well, Jake, sorry you can't come along, but I need to keep my word to Baxter."

"I understand," said Jake, rising from the chair he was sitting on. "But it's hard to just sit here and know you and the boys are out there ridin' together." There was a silent moment, then he laid a hand on Kyger's shoulder. "Boss, I want to say again that I appreciate you standin' by me in this thing. I made a serious mistake, and I know it. You could've sent me on down the road, and I couldn't have blamed you. Thanks for stickin' with me."

"I was plenty upset at you, as you know, but I got to thinkin' of all the good you've done this gang. Fella shouldn't let one mistake ruin the good points a man has built up."

"So it's Zachary Meadows's place tonight?"

"We know Zach and his family always go to church Sunday mornin' and night, so that's where we're goin'. Those squatters will come home to a big surprise tonight."

"What're you gonna do?"

"Torch the house."

Jake grinned, though Wilson could hardly see it. Suddenly

rapid hoofbeats were heard from near the stream down the slope.

"Just one rider," said Jake, listening intently.

Soon the dark form of horse and rider drew near, and a familiar voice called, "Wilson, that you on the porch?"

"Mason Beaumont," Jake said.

"Yeah, Mason!" Kyger answered.

Baxter Beaumont's youngest son pulled rein and drew up to the porch. "Got some good news for you!"

"Well, get off and tell it."

Mason's feet touched ground, and as he stepped up on the porch, he said, "You want all your boys to hear this at the same time, or you want to hear it and tell 'em later?"

"This is big news, you say?"

"Yeah. Big news."

Wilson Kyger called the rest of the men to the house. When they were gathered at the porch, Kyger said, "Okay, kid, let's hear it."

"Ted Sullivan is alive!"

"How do you know?" Kyger asked.

"Some of our ranch hands were in town and heard people talkin' about it. One of them walked into Dr. Sutton's office and flat asked, saying he was a cowhand from a neighboring ranch and wanted to know if what he heard was true. The doc himself told him that Ted is paralyzed from the neck down. Will be for the rest of his life."

"He sure looked dead!" Kyger said.

"But since he ain't, Pa told me to ride up here and tell you that you should restore Jake to his place in the gang."

Kyger chuckled. "Go back and tell your pa thanks for lettin' us know."

When the youth was gone, Jake Ransom laughed and said, "Let's go, guys! I can hardly wait to burn down Zach Meadows's house!"

At the *Diamond M Ranch,* sixteen-year-old Steve Meadows lay on his bed in his second story bedroom as darkness blanketed the land. A lantern burned on the bedstand. He heard light footsteps in the hallway, then the door opened and his sister came in.

Sage Meadows leaned over her brother, felt his brow, and said, "You don't have a fever, Steve. It has to be something you ate."

"You sound like Mom. We all ate the same thing for Sunday dinner. How come the rest of you didn't get sick?"

"Because we didn't eat *as much* as you did, son," came Wanda's voice as she entered the room with Zach behind her. "I don't know what it is about teenage boys, but all three of my brothers were just like you when they were in their teens. Filled their stomachs till they got them upset."

"Didn't seem like I was eating that much," Steve said.

Wanda brushed past her daughter and laid a palm on her son's brow. "Still no fever. Well, hopefully you'll feel better by morning...but I really think I should stay home with you."

"I'll be okay, Mom. You're right, I'm sure. I just made a pig of myself at dinner. I'm sorry. I won't eat so much after this."

"Sure," Sage said. "I know how you teenage boys are. You eat one meal a day—all day long!"

Zach laughed. "She's got your number, son, I can see that!"

Steve shook his head. "Sisters!"

"You wouldn't know what to do without me!" Sage said.

"At least I'd have some peace."

Wanda turned to her husband. "You really think he's in no danger from the masked riders if we leave him here while we go to church?"

"Those skunks know we're in church on Sunday night. They can't harass us if we're not here. If by some remote chance they should come by, they'll move on when they see we're not home.

We'll douse this lantern, and Steve can just go to sleep. Nobody will even know he's home."

"Sounds good to me, Pa," Steve said.

"Well, okay," Wanda sighed. "I guess you're right."

Zach patted Steve's shoulder and said, "See you after church, son."

Wanda kissed Steve's forehead and told him she loved him.

All the lanterns in the house were put out, and the three of them climbed in the wagon and headed for Jefferson City, Bibles in hand.

Upstairs in the dark bedroom, Steve quickly fell asleep.

The moon was bright, and the Kyger gang headed toward the *Diamond M* at a steady trot. Jake Ransom rode beside Wilson Kyger and said, "Well, even though my blunder didn't kill Ted Sullivan, there's no way he can run the ranch now. They'll have to pull out."

"For sure. Bax oughtta be glad for that, at least."

Soon they were on Meadows property and riding toward the ranch house and outbuildings. At Kyger's signal, the gang reigned in about thirty yards from the house and dismounted.

"Place is in total darkness, boss," Clete Sarno said. "No need to put on the masks, is there?"

"Nope. Let's just torch the place and get outta here. Jake... Leo..."

Jake Ransom and Leo Davey struck matches, and the kerosene-soaked burlap torches they were carrying burst into flame. Ransom and Davey ran toward the house, smoke billowing off the flaming torches. When they reached the darkened house, Ransom pitched his torch through a parlor window. The glass shattered and the curtains immediately caught fire.

Davey dashed toward the rear of the house and slung the blazing torch through a kitchen window. It crashed through the glass and flared bright, setting the curtains afire and knocking a kerosene lantern off the cupboard. The glass bowl of the lantern shattered, spreading kerosene across the floor.

"You bring the sign I told you to make?" Wilson Kyger asked Clete Sarno.

"Sure did, boss." Sarno hurried to his horse and returned with a large square of cardboard that had been folded up in his saddlebags, along with a hammer and some nails.

"Nail it to the barn door," Kyger told him.

"Hey, what's it say?" Bill Arkin asked.

Grinning from ear to ear, Sarno held it up so everyone could see: *Get out before it gets worse!*

"I sure hope Steve is feeling better," Sage Meadows said as they neared home.

Wanda chuckled. "If he's feeling much better, he's probably already found himself something to eat."

"I wouldn't put it past him," Zach said.

Sage was sitting between her parents on the wagon seat. Wanda turned toward her in the gloom and said, "Pastor Bayless outdid himself tonight, don't you think?"

"I'll say. When he described John at Patmos hearing Jesus say three times that He's coming quickly, the chills ran down my back! And then when he pictured John saying, 'Even so, come, Lord Jesus,' I wanted to stand up and shout the same thing!"

"So did I," Zach said. "I almost expected to hear the trumpet right then and there!"

The wagon rounded a bend in the road where the *Diamond M* property began. Wanda gasped and pointed across the dark fields toward the flames flickering against the night. Zach saw it too and snapped the reins, putting the team to a gallop.

When the wagon fishtailed to a stop, the moon passed from behind a cloud bank, revealing the blackened stone foundation of the ranch house. The stone fireplace where the parlor had been stood like a charred sentinel over the smoking ruins. Red-tongued flames still licked at what wood remained.

"No, dear God, no!" Sage wailed.

Zach held his wife and daughter. Together, they wept for several minutes.

Zach's line of sight happened to drift to the cardboard sign on the barn door. He climbed down from the wagon and hurried to the barn. Wanda and Sage were close behind.

Zach ripped down the sign and began tearing it into small pieces, but not before the two women had read what it said. He threw the pieces on the ground, then took his wife and daughter into his arms again.

It was Sage who first caught movement at the toolshed a short distance from the barn. The door had come open, and a dark figure stepped out.

"Steve!" she cried.

All three ran toward the sixteen-year-old, who was staggering their direction.

There was a happy reunion with tears, sobs, and hugs as parents and sister thanked God Steve was alive. Suddenly the loss of the house and its contents faded in importance.

When their emotions had calmed, Steve told them he had awakened to the smell of smoke and heard the flames roaring downstairs. Sick as he was, he made it down the blazing stairs and outside. He stumbled to the toolshed and watched the house collapse in flames and smoke, then he lay down to wait for his family to come home. He had dozed off and awakened when he heard them weeping.

Zachary Meadows pulled his wife and children close and said, "Let's thank the Lord right now that He spared Steve's life."

Clinging to each other, and more aware than ever how much they loved each other, Wanda, Sage, and Steve bowed their heads while Zach led them in prayer and praise.

When the "Amen" came, Zach said, "We'll go into town and stay at the hotel for the night. I want Sheriff Gross to know what's happened here. That gang almost killed Ted Sullivan, and now, but for the hand of God, they would have killed Steve. Something must be done to catch them before they actually do kill someone. We need to let Pastor Bayless know, too."

Sheriff Lloyd Gross arose from bed on Monday morning, having slept little. Allison sat across the breakfast table from him and watched him pick at his food.

"You'll get them, dear," she said. "Now that you know the first name of one of them and have that silver ornament off one of their saddles, something will turn up to let you make your arrest."

"I sure hope so. I want my hands on those scum-buckets so bad I can taste it…and whoever is behind them."

There was a knock at the front door. Allison started to get up, but the sheriff shoved his chair back and said, "I'll get it."

Gross found Zach Meadows at the front door and was pleased to learn that already people of the town were rallying to help him. Gross knew that Zach and his family had gone to their pastor's home upon first arriving in town late last night. While Zach was at the sheriff's house telling him about the fire, Reverend Robert Bayless was making the rounds of the church members, letting them know what had happened at the *Diamond M Ranch*. The Baylesses would not hear of the Meadows staying in the hotel. They were invited to stay the night with them in the parsonage.

Zach told Gross and his wife that they already had offers of many homes to stay in until their house could be rebuilt. In addition, over sixty men had volunteered to help them begin building a new house. Money was coming in to help pay for the building materials.

The Grosses rejoiced with Zach, saying they also would put money toward the new house.

It was almost noon when Cory Beaumont galloped into Jefferson City. The news of the *Diamond M* fire had reached the *Box Double B Ranch* by mid-morning, and Cory wanted to see Sage and her family.

As Cory rode down Main Street toward the church and parsonage, he noticed Sheriff Lloyd Gross in front of the general store. Gross was talking with two young ranchers, whose wagons were loaded with furniture and personal goods. Josh Bentley and Martin Gilliam were leaving the valley.

Cory reigned in, dismounted, and approached the three men.

"Howdy, Cory," Gross said.

"Morning, Sheriff. Morning, Josh…Martin."

Both ranchers greeted Cory warmly.

Cory glanced to the two wagons and said. "You're not doing what it looks like, I hope."

"They are," Gross said. "I'm trying to talk them into staying, but I'm getting nowhere."

"I hate to see this," Cory said.

"We hate it, too, Cory," Josh Bentley said. "But our wives and children are terrified. They can't stand living with the threat that something like what happened to Ted Sullivan or the Meadows family is going to happen to us."

"I can't blame them for being frightened," Cory said. "But it isn't right that you should have to give up your homes because of some bad apples. I'm sure the sheriffs will find a way to stop them soon."

"I know they're trying," Martin Gilliam said, "but we can't

wait any longer. We're on our way."

At that moment, the wives and children of the two families emerged from the store and began climbing into the wagons. Cory and Sheriff Gross watched helplessly as the two men climbed aboard.

Gilliam looked down at young Beaumont and said, "Cory, in no way am I blaming you, but it's my opinion, and the opinion of most everybody in this valley, that your father's the one financing this harassment."

"He swears he's not behind it, Martin."

Taking reins in hand, Gilliam said, "You mark my word, Cory. Whenever the law gets to the bottom of this, your father's hand in it will be exposed."

Martin Gilliam then snapped the reins and drove away, followed by the Bentley wagon.

The sheriff laid a hand on Cory's shoulder and said, "I'm sorry, but I've made it no secret that I think your father's behind all of this. Maybe some of the other big ranchers are in it with him, but he's the Big Bull. I know you love him. He's your pa. But I believe Martin's right."

Cory scrubbed a shaky hand over his face and adjusted his hat on his head. "Sheriff, the Bible tells me to honor my mother and father. Because Baxter Beaumont is my father, I will honor him. But, just between you and me, I think you and Martin are right, even though Pa has sworn to us that he's clean."

"I don't mean to put you in a bad position, Cory, but I just need to ask you—have you seen anything at all that would tell you your pa's involved in this?"

"Nothing, Sheriff. My feelings about it come from the attitude I know he has toward these people he calls nesters and squatters. And I know the power he holds in this valley."

"Let me ask you this... In your own mind, do you think there are other big ranchers in on it?"

"It's possible. There are a few who might go along with Pa."

"Do you think this masked gang is made up of ranch hands?"

"No. I think they're outlaws who've been hired to come in here."

"My thoughts exactly," Gross said. "And, Cory, let me say that if your father is guilty, I hate it for your family's sake that I'll have to take him down all the way. He'll go to prison. If someone is killed before we can catch the gang and get proof that he hired them, he'll hang with them."

"I understand, Sheriff. I wouldn't want you to do anything but your sworn duty. Mom and Joline would feel the same way. With Mason, it might be different because he and Pa are so close."

Gross nodded. "Well, these posses who are riding the valley every night are going to stay at it until we catch that bunch in the act, like we almost did at the Sullivan place."

"I hope you catch them soon, Sheriff, no matter who they are or who's behind them."

Cory rode on to the church parsonage. Sage Meadows ran to him as he was dismounting and embraced him. Wanda was not far behind her.

"I just wanted to come and tell you I'm sorry about what happened at your place last night," Cory said to them both.

"Thank you for coming," said Sage, holding onto his arm.

"I just don't understand how these masked riders and whoever's behind them can be so cruel."

"We don't either," Wanda said, "but they are."

"On my way here, I stopped and talked to Sheriff Gross. He was trying to persuade Martin Gilliam and Josh Bentley not to leave the valley, but they wouldn't listen. Their wives and children are terrified after what happened to Ted Sullivan and to you people. They're on their way out of the valley right now."

"Oh, I'm so sorry to hear it, Cory," Wanda said.

"Are Mr. Meadows and Steve inside?" Cory asked, looking toward the house.

"No, they're somewhere on Main Street buying some new clothes. Sage and I have already bought some material to make us some new dresses. Zach also is going to the sheriff's office to tell Sheriff Gross that he wants to ride in one of the posses."

"Well, God bless him," Cory said. "I'd ride with them too, but Pa wouldn't let me have the time...even at night."

Sage and Wanda looked at each other, and their hearts went out to Cory. He and his family were going to suffer terribly when Baxter was caught by the law.

C H A P T E R

THIRTEEN

O n Jefferson City's Main Street, Sheriff Lloyd Gross watched
Cory Beaumont ride away, then turned to head for his
office.

"Sheriff!" came a voice from behind him.

Gross turned and saw two well-dressed men coming out of
the general store. Royce Hayland and Web Moore were Jefferson
City businessmen. Hayland owned the town's hardware store and
gun shop, and Moore was proprietor of the Jeff City Boot and
Saddle Shop. Both men were posse volunteers.

Hayland and Moore asked about the fire at the *Diamond M
Ranch*. While Sheriff Gross was answering their questions, Jake
Ransom rode onto Main Street, having come to town from the
gang's hideout in the mountains.

Sheriff Gross was facing the door of the general store, and as
he talked to the two businessmen, his attention went casually to the
rider who hauled up in front of the store. When the big man swung
from the horse's back, Gross noticed his black Spanish-style saddle.

His heart lurched in his chest when he saw the silver ornaments. They looked like the one he carried in his shirt pocket. He
waited till the rider withdrew two burlap sacks from his saddlebags

and entered the store, then excused himself to Hayland and Moore, saying he had a man to see.

Gross hurried to the chestnut gelding that bore the black saddle and counted the ornaments on the right side. There were four—two at the front and two at the back. Rounding the rear of the animal, he looked at the ornaments on the left side. One was missing. He pulled the ornament from his pocket and laid it next to the single one at the front of the saddle. It was exactly the same.

From behind, a familiar voice said, "Sheriff, could I talk to you for a moment?"

The sheriff turned to see Zachary and Steve Meadows. Steve was clad in new Levis, shirt, hat, and boots.

"Zach, look! I told you about the saddle ornament Myrna Sullivan found in her yard. Well, this is it! This is the saddle! We've got our break!"

"Where's the rider?" Zach asked.

"He's in the general store."

"You going to take him…or follow him?"

"Take him! I want his hide behind bars right now. I'll find out where the rest of the gang is once I've got him where I want him."

"Sheriff," Steve said, "you want I should go get Jerry?"

"He isn't at the office. I've got him on an errand to a ranch ten miles south."

Zach hitched at his gunbelt. "I'll help you. Steve, you get on the boardwalk."

"Better yet, Steve," said Gross, pulling his gun, "you go clear the people off the street as fast as you can. Okay?"

"Sure."

"Go to it!"

Next door to the general store was Smith's clothing store. As Steve hurried off, the sheriff said, "Zach, step back into Smith's doorway so you'll be out of sight. If this guy gives me trouble, you move in from behind him. I told you we also have a name, didn't I?"

"Yeah. Jake."

"Well maybe we've got Jake, too. We'll soon find out."

Gross backed up to the front wall of the general store on the opposite side of the door from Smith's, and waited.

Two women came out, chatting merrily, carrying grocery sacks. When they saw Gross, he put a forefinger to his lips and whispered, "Move fast, ladies!"

Without asking why, the women scurried away.

A middle-aged man came out carrying a cardboard box full of groceries and headed toward his wagon, which was parked near the hitch rail in front of Smith's. Zach Meadows stepped out and whispered, "Mr. Deckert! Sheriff Gross is about to make an arrest! Put your box in the wagon and hurry down to the end of the block!"

Deckert did as he was told.

The next three or four minutes seemed like hours. Then heavy boots sounded on the floor of the general store. Jake Ransom emerged, carrying the bulging burlap sacks over his shoulders.

The sheriff let the man reach the edge of the boardwalk, then with cocked gun in hand, moved up behind him and said, "Hey, Jake! How you doing?"

The man turned and his head bobbed when he saw the gun aimed at him and the badge behind it. "How'd you know my name, Sheriff? And what's that gun aimed at me for?"

"One of the masked riders was called Jake by his leader the other night when Ted Sullivan was hanged."

"I don't know what you're talkin' about, Sheriff. I don't know any Ted Sullivan. I live up in the mountains. Some coincidence if you're lookin' for a man named Jake, but you've got the wrong Jake."

"Oh, really?"

"'Fraid so."

Gross lifted the silver ornament so Jake could see it. "Some coincidence that the Jake who helped hang Ted Sullivan lost this ornament off his saddle at the Sullivan place, and yours is missing too."

"Wha—?"

"Your under arrest, Jake. Put the sacks down and see how high you can reach."

"Ain't no one man can take me, Sheriff."

"How about two?" came a steady voice from behind him.

Ransom looked around to see Zachary Meadows. Meadows had his revolver trained on Jake's face, the hammer in firing position.

"Do like the sheriff said, Jake."

Cursing under his breath, Jake Ransom lowered the burlap sacks to the boardwalk and raised his hands over his head. Lloyd Gross stepped up and pulled Jake's revolver from its holster and stuck it under his belt.

"Now, what's your last name, Jake?"

"I ain't tellin' you nothin', tin star."

"Zach," the sheriff said, "go look in his saddlebags and see if you can find anything with his name on it."

Zach went to the chestnut gelding and started rummaging through the saddlebags. He came up with a small bundle of envelopes with string tied around them. He looked at the one on top and said, "His last name's Ransom, Sheriff. R-A-N-S-O-M."

Gross grinned. "And I've got a feelin' we'll find him on the wanted list. Right, Jake Ransom?"

"I ain't tellin' you nothin'."

Gross pulled a pair of handcuffs from his belt and commanded Jake to put his hands behind his back. The ratchets made their staccato clicking sound, and the sheriff said, "Okay, big boy. The jail's that way."

The people who had gathered at both ends of the street closed in. As Gross and Meadows ushered Ransom up the street, there were jeers and hisses aimed at Ransom, along with fierce accusations. Some in the crowd called for him to be hanged immediately.

Deputy Jerry Zeller rode up and dismounted in front of the sheriff's office as Gross and his troupe arrived. He eyed the prisoner and said, "Who you got there, Sheriff?"

"His name's Jake Ransom," Gross said as they filed inside the office.

"This is the Jake Mrs. Sullivan told us about?" Zeller asked.

"You got it. And the silver ornament is from his saddle." Gross holstered his gun, pulled a straight-backed chair from next to the wall, and placed it in the center of the floor. "Sit down, Jake!"

Ransom dropped onto the chair, visibly uncomfortable with his hands cuffed behind his back.

Gross tossed his hat on the desk, then stood in front of Jake and said, "Okay, I've got some questions, and I want some answers. Who's the gang workin' for, and where are they hidin' out?"

"I ain't tellin' you nothin'."

"Look, Ransom, as sure as I'm standin' here, you're a wanted man. I'll get confirmation on it shortly. Now, I can see that things don't go so hard for you if you cooperate. If you don't, you're gonna take a big fall...all by yourself."

"You deaf, Sheriff? I said I ain't tellin' you nothin'! You got that? Nothin'!"

Gross sighed, his breath going out heavily.

A red flush was slowly crawling up Deputy Zeller's neck and face. He took a step closer to the prisoner and said, "Let me have him for a while, Sheriff! I'll make him glad to answer your questions!"

"You talk real tough when I've got my hands shackled behind my back, little man," Ransom said. "Take these cuffs off and we'll see who's the real man!"

Zeller's anger mounted. "Sheriff, a few needles under his fingernails would loosen his tongue. And if that doesn't work, how about a cracked kneecap or two?"

Gross eyed his deputy. "I've never seen you like this, Jerry."

"And I've never seen people treated the way this scum and his pals have treated the ranchers around here," Zeller said. "It gets under my hide. Just lock me in a cell with him. His size doesn't scare me."

"Jerry, I'm as angry about this whole thing as you are, but if we resort to those kind of tactics, we'd be just like him. You don't want that, do you?"

"No, I sure don't want to be like *him.* "

A sneer curved Jake Ransom's lips. "You dudes are nothin' but talk. You can carry on all you want. Call me names if you want to. I don't care. Threaten me if it makes you feel better. But like I said, I ain't tellin' you nothin'."

"Take him and lock him up, Jerry!" Gross said. "Or I'm liable to forget the sermon I just preached to you!"

Three days later, Circuit Judge Chadwick Singleton held trial for Jake Ransom, whose criminal record had been wired to Jefferson City from the office of Chief U.S. Marshal Solomon Duvall in Denver. The trial had been publicized all over both counties, and the courtroom was jam-packed. There were more people outside the building than inside.

Ted Sullivan was there in a wheelchair, with Myrna sitting next to him. The Meadows family sat in the same row. Cory Beaumont was beside Sage, and Reverend Robert Bayless sat next to Zach. The rest of the Beaumonts were there, as were some of the other big ranchers and a large number of the small ranchers. Sheriff Hank Hawkins was also in attendance.

Though he did not show it, Baxter Beaumont was furious at Jake Ransom for getting himself caught. When Jake had failed to return to the hideout, Wilson Kyger had sent Leo Davey into town to find him. It didn't take Davey long to learn that one of the mysterious masked riders named Jake had been arrested. Davey had ridden like the wind to inform Kyger of Jake's arrest. Kyger, in turn, had relayed the message to Baxter Beaumont.

Now, Kyger and the rest of the gang waited for word of Jake's fate. Baxter had promised to send Mason on a fast ride to the cabin with news of the trial's outcome as soon as it was over.

Sheriff Gross presented the saddle ornament to the court, along with the saddle itself, to prove that Jake Ransom had been one of the men who hanged Ted Sullivan. Myrna Sullivan testified that she heard the gang's leader call the big man *Jake* in a moment of anger. She also told of finding the silver ornament on the ground where the horse stood when her husband was hoisted into the saddle with the noose on his neck.

It took the jury of twelve men less than ten minutes to return to the courtroom with the verdict. *Guilty.*

Judge Singleton ordered the defendant to approach the bench. Jake Ransom was in handcuffs and flanked by Gross and Zeller as he stood before the judge. He showed Singleton a stone face.

"Jacob Ransom," the judge said in a solemn tone, "you have been duly tried in this court of law and found guilty of having a part in the hanging of Mr. Ted Sullivan. I want you to turn around and look at Mr. Sullivan."

Ransom set his jaw and kept his eyes on the judge.

A flush of crimson darkened the judge's face. "You're in contempt of court, Mr. Ransom! You do as I told you, or the sheriff and his deputy will turn you around!"

Reluctantly, Jake made a half-turn and looked at Ted Sullivan.

"Because of you and the rabble you company with, Mr. Ransom," Judge Singleton said, "that man will never move any part of his body below his neck for the rest of his life. Do you not feel any remorse for what you've done to Ted Sullivan?"

Jake turned back to the judge. "I…uh…we…we didn't mean to harm him, Judge. The rope was supposed to be cut so when his weight hit it, it would snap and no harm would come to him. It was only meant to frighten him. But somebody didn't cut the threads thin enough. I…uh…I'm sorry he's paralyzed."

"If Mr. Sullivan had died," Singleton said, "your execution by hanging would be tomorrow morning at sunrise. You are very fortunate, Mr. Ransom, that your victim is still alive. But since you doggedly refuse to give Sheriff Gross any information as to who is behind your gang's harassment of the ranchers of these two counties, I am going to be more severe in sentencing you." Singleton paused, adjusting himself on the chair. "However, before passing sentence, I will give you one more opportunity to give us that information."

Jake stared blankly at the judge, his silence speaking loudly.

Singleton drew a deep breath through his nostrils and let it out slowly. "Very well then, I will now pass sentence. Jacob Ransom, the files on you in Denver say you are thirty-seven years of age. If you outlive your sentence, you will be sixty-seven when you are released from prison...for I hereby sentence you to thirty years confinement in the Montana Territorial Prison at Deer Lodge City. You will be transported there under the authority of Jefferson County Sheriff Lloyd Gross."

The gavel banged on the desk, and the trial was over.

The crowd cheered the judge's sentence, and the cheers changed to jeers, boos, and hisses as Ransom was escorted from the courtroom. When the guilty man reached the street, many voices taunted him.

Mason Beaumont left the courtroom, filtered his way through the throng on the street, and rode hard toward the mountains. When Lillian and Joline asked where Mason had gone, Baxter told them he had no idea. This did not alarm the women, for Mason often went riding without saying where he was going.

Wilson Kyger and his six men were lounging on the front porch of the cabin when they saw a rider plunge out of the forest, jump his mount over the small stream at the bottom of the slope, and charge upward toward them.

"Mason, boss," said A. J. Titus.

As young Beaumont thundered to a skidding halt at the

porch, they all rose to their feet. Mason stayed in the saddle and spoke to the gang leader. "They convicted him, Wilson. The judge said if Ted Sullivan had died, Jake would be hanged tomorrow morning at sunrise. Before he pronounced sentence, he told Jake that if he'd cooperated and told Sheriff Gross who was behind this, he'd've given him a lighter sentence."

"Good for Jake," Roy Coulter said. "He's stickin' by you, boss."

"And he's stickin' by your pa too, kid," Bill Arkin said.

"So what was his sentence?" Kyger asked.

"Thirty years."

"Thirty years!"

"Yep. At the new prison in Deer Lodge City."

"When they gonna take him there?" Clete Sarno asked.

"I don't know."

"If you're thinkin' about us tryin' to bust him loose, Clete, forget it," Kyger said. "I happen to know that when they take convicted felons to that prison, they go with a virtual army. There ain't enough of us. Besides, we've got more squatters to lean on."

The Wilson Kyger gang did not let up. The small ranchers continued to suffer under the gang's atrocities. Both sheriffs had their posses riding with them and their deputies every night, but they were never at the right place at the right time. The two counties were simply too large, and there were still over ninety small ranches to try to cover.

Ranch houses, barns, and outbuildings were burned, and horses and cattle were killed.

When three weeks had passed without even one posse catching sight of the masked riders, Sheriff Gross hopped on his horse early one morning and rode for Deer Lodge City.

Sheriff Hank Hawkins and Deputy Murray Hill were just

returning to the office from the cell block when Sheriff Gross came through the open door from the street.

"'Mornin', gentlemen."

"Hello, Lloyd. What brings you to our fair town?" Hawkins asked.

"I've got an idea to discuss with you that just might end this gang business."

"Well, I'm ready to listen to any idea that might end this thing."

"I'm sure you've heard of a mysterious man who roams the West—calls himself John Stranger."

"Sure have. He's got quite a reputation for handling outlaws."

"I've heard of him, too," Hill said. "They say he's faster'n greased lightning with his gun and good with his fists. No nonsense type."

"You got it," Gross said. "I've never met the man myself, but I've talked to many lawmen who have. The man's tracked down countless outlaws for Chief Duvall, has even brought entire gangs to justice. His success has been uncanny."

"Same way I've heard it," Hawkins said. "So I take it your idea is to bring this John Stranger here and turn him loose on the masked riders."

"Yes. What do you think?"

"If we're taking a vote, you've got mine."

"Good. There's no way to tell how long it'll take to get him here, but I wish I'd had this idea a month ago. I'll wire Chief Duvall soon as I get back to Jeff City. From what I understand, he usually knows Stranger's whereabouts."

CHAPTER

FOURTEEN

B illings, Montana, was dozing in the hot July sun as Yellowstone County Sheriff Mack Jensen left his office and strolled down the block toward the Montana Stagelines office, wishing for a breeze. It was 2:30, and the sun was at its hottest. What few people were on the street greeted Jensen or waved to him.

Jensen wore a tied-down Colt .45 on his slender waist and gave the impression he could use it adeptly. He had a hard-boned face, tight through the cheeks and red-brown from sun and wind.

The sheriff drew up to the office door and stepped inside. Agent Lou Flagg was behind the counter selling tickets to a middle-aged couple, whom Jensen recognized as Faye and Elmer Simpson, owners of the Big Sky Hotel in Billings. Jensen knew they also owned hotels in Worland and Sheridan, Wyoming. He greeted them, then said to the agent, "Stage going to be on time, Lou?"

"Far as I know, Sheriff. No wire saying otherwise. You expecting someone on it?"

"Yes."

"Family member?"

"No."

"Friend?"

"Not exactly. I've never met him, but we'll probably become friends. He's coming here to help us take down the Wade Kyger gang."

"Oh, a lawman. What? Federal marshal?"

"Not exactly. He's being sent here by the U.S. marshal's office in Denver, but he doesn't wear a badge. You ever hear the name John Stranger?"

"John Stranger?" Elmer Simpson said. "Faye and I know him! He did us a mighty good deed when we lived down in Worland."

"Saved us from financial disaster," Faye said, digging in her purse. "Left us a memento, as he put it, so we wouldn't forget him. As if we could." She took a shiny silver disk from the purse. "This is it. A silver medallion. He put it in my hand just before riding away after giving us enough money to rebuild the hotel when it was gutted by fire. Wonderful man! Like to see it?" Faye asked the sheriff, extending the medallion toward him.

"Sure."

Lou Flagg leaned across the counter. "Looks like a star in the center."

"Mm-hmm." The sheriff turned the medallion in his fingers. "Has Scripture inscribed around the edge. 'THE STRANGER THAT SHALL COME FROM A FAR LAND—*Deuteronomy* 29:22.' I wonder what far land?"

"From what we've heard about him," said Faye, "nobody knows where he's from, and he won't tell."

"He's a mystery, all right," Elmer said.

The sheriff handed the medallion back to Faye. "Are you two taking this incoming stage when it turns around?"

"Yes," Elmer answered him. "As you know, our two sons manage the hotels in Worland and Sheridan for us. We go a couple of times a year to check on the hotels and spend time with our children and grandchildren."

"You sure have a hot, dry trip ahead of you this time."

"Sure wish we'd get some rain," Elmer said. "If we don't get some pretty soon—"

His words were interrupted by the sound of the stagecoach coming down the street. Mack Jensen moved outside with the others on his heels. The six-up team trotted down the broad street, sending up clouds of dust that seemed to float in the breezeless air.

"Oh, Elmer," Faye said, "it'll be so good to see Mr. Stranger again!"

"That it will, honey. If it weren't for him—"

"We'd be in the poorhouse," Faye finished for him.

The stage rolled to a halt as the driver pulled rein and climbed down. The shotgunner made his way to the rack on top. The door came open, and a tall, broad-shouldered man dressed in black except for his dusty white shirt stepped out. Mack Jensen knew the man was John Stranger by the description he had heard from many sources.

Stranger helped three ladies out, then an elderly gentleman. Each thanked him, then stood on the boardwalk, waiting for their luggage to be unloaded by the crew. Lou Flagg moved up to help remove luggage from the rack.

Elmer and Faye Simpson were eager to speak to Stranger, but held back as Sheriff Jensen stepped up, extended his hand, and said, "Mr. Stranger...Mack Jensen."

Jensen felt the power in John Stranger's grip as they shook hands. They were exchanging a few words when from atop the coach, the shotgunner said, "Mr. Stranger, here's your gear."

Stranger took the two pieces of luggage and set them down. Before Jensen could say another word to him, the eager couple moved in, and Elmer said, "Mr. Stranger, do you remember us?"

John studied their faces for a few seconds. "Why, yes! You're out of context, so it took me a minute. Elmer and Faye Simpson... Worland, Wyoming. Bless your hearts, how are you?"

Elmer shook Stranger's hand, and when Faye offered hers, Stranger bent at the waist and lightly kissed it.

"We were just purchasing tickets when we learned from Sheriff Jensen that you were on the stage," Elmer said. "Faye and I were so happy to learn of it. We...we want to tell you what your generous gift did for us."

"Well, tell me!" John said, smiling broadly.

"Well, the hotel we rebuilt in Worland did so well that we built one in Sheridan...and it's done so well, we built one here in Billings and moved here. Our two sons manage the other hotels for us."

"Wonderful!"

"You'll be staying at the Simpsons' hotel when you're in town, Mr. Stranger," Jensen said. "It's called the Big Sky, and it's the nicest one in town."

"So he's booked with us?" said Elmer, his eyes shining.

"Yes. The county's footing the bill since he's here to help rid us of the Kyger gang."

"No, no!" Elmer said, waggling a forefinger. "There will be no bill for Mr. Stranger."

"But—"

"No buts about it, Sheriff. I'll write you a note to take to Michael. Any meals Mr. Stranger eats in the restaurant are to be without charge, and if he stays for a year—or longer—the room is free."

Stranger shook his head. "Now, Mr. Simpson, this isn't necessary."

"Oh, yes it is. The Big Sky wouldn't even be there if it weren't for you. This is the least we can do to thank you for what you did for us."

"No sense arguing with him," Jensen said. "Elmer's a stubborn man."

"How well I know!" Faye said. She laughed as Elmer scurried inside the stagelines office to find a piece of paper. "Please, Mr. Stranger, let us do this." As she spoke, she lifted the silver medallion and said, "See? We've always kept it."

Stranger smiled. "I'm glad you still have it. And since you both insist, and I wouldn't want to insult your generosity, I'll let you put me up at the hotel."

"Thank you for letting us return your kindness," Faye said.

Elmer returned from the office, handed the scribbled note to Jensen, and said, "Just give this note to Michael."

Jensen nodded, slipped the note into his shirt pocket, and said, "Well, Mr. Stranger, we'd better be going."

Good-byes were said, and the two men headed down the street, carrying Stranger's luggage. As they walked, Jensen filled Stranger in on the robberies and killings being done by the Wade Kyger gang all over southeastern Montana. He and his deputies, Herb Doud, Bob Harmon, and Larry Slocum, were spread so thin chasing other outlaws, they didn't have time to concentrate on the Kyger gang.

They were nearing the Big Sky Hotel when Jensen said, "I've got three crack deputies, Mr. Stranger."

The tall man held up a palm. "You can drop the *Mister,* Sheriff. Just call me John."

"Well, all right. If you'll call me Mack."

"It's a deal, Mack. Now, you were telling me about your deputies."

"Yes. They've made a dent in Wade Kyger's gang. They apprehended four of Kyger's men six weeks ago, and those four have already been hanged."

"Four less outlaws in this world is always good news."

"Unless Wade has added new men since, this brings his gang down to eleven men, including Wade. That's still a sizable bunch. You think you can bring them to justice?"

"I'll do my dead-level best." Stranger said.

"I hear that's what you always do, and that's enough for me."

"Where can I buy a good horse, Mack? I'll need bridle and saddle too, of course."

"I'll take you to the *Flying R Ranch* just west of town. Fella named Fred Ryal owns it. He raises excellent saddle horses and is quite reasonable on his prices. He specializes in producing bays with white blazes and four white stockings. Has some magnificent animals."

"Good. Any idea which way I should ride to catch scent of the Kyger bunch?"

They were at the hotel. "Let's get you checked in, then we'll talk about it," Jensen said. He gave Elmer Simpson's note to Michael Brett at the desk, and Stranger was assigned room 201, the best room on the second floor, which overlooked the street.

Stranger and Jensen climbed the stairs, entered the room, and laid the luggage on the bed. Stranger gestured toward an overstuffed horsehair chair. The sheriff settled into it, and John sat on the edge of the bed.

"The gang moves around a lot," Jensen said. "Recently they've been pulling stagecoach and bank robberies in the towns along the Yellowstone River northeast of Billings. Only a few of the larger towns are able to afford a town marshal. Some of the small ones have marshals who serve only part-time."

"So there's nobody to chase the bunch when they pull their robberies," said Stranger, "be it stagecoaches or banks."

"Right. There are a couple of army forts in eastern Montana, but the troops are too busy dealing with hostile Sioux and Blackfeet to give any time to chasing outlaws. So, John Stranger, my friend, we need your help desperately."

"That's what I'm here for. I'll just ride the Yellowstone then till I sniff a repugnant smell, and I'll know I've hit Kyger's trail."

"Yes, sir."

"I'll be out of Billings at first light, Mack. It just so happens that my fiancée is here in town at the moment."

"Really?"

"Yes. She's a certified medical nurse. Works out of Dr. Lyle Goodwin's office in Denver. She's here to help establish your new hospital."

"Your fiancée wouldn't by chance be Miss Breanna Baylor?"

"Sure is. You've met her?"

"Day before yesterday. I had to clonk a drunk on the head to subdue him. Took him to the hospital to get him patched up. It was your Miss Baylor who did the patching. I recall that she told me she's from Denver. She's quite a lady, John. You're a fortunate man."

"Don't I know it?"

"When's the wedding?"

"We haven't set a date, yet. Circumstances in both of our lives."

"Well, congratulations when it happens," Jensen said, rising from the chair.

"Thank you."

"So you'll get to spend the evening with her?"

"Unless they have her tied up at the hospital. Either way, I'll be in the saddle and riding up the banks of the Yellowstone at first light. Speaking of the saddle…maybe we'd better head for the *Flying R.*"

Sheriff Jensen let John Stranger ride double with him to the *Flying R Ranch*. Stranger looked the herd over and found many outstanding, well-bred horses. He especially liked the looks of the bays with white blazes and four white stockings. He picked out a bay gelding, along with saddle and bridle.

When the sheriff explained Stranger's mission, Fred Ryal told John he would buy horse, saddle, and bridle back from him when he returned them. He would keep enough money to make a reasonable profit, but he would treat John right. Stranger paid him, then saddled and bridled the bay. He and the sheriff rode back to town together.

The sun had already gone down when John Stranger neared Billings General Hospital on foot. A welcome, cool breeze was picking up. He passed through the door into the reception area and approached the desk. A teenage girl wearing wire-rimmed glasses smiled up at him.

"May I help you, sir?"

"I believe so. You have a nurse here from Denver. Her name is—"

"Miss Baylor. And unless I'm mistaken, you are Mr. John Stranger."

"Well, you're not mistaken. How did you know?"

"Because Miss Baylor has talked a lot about you and told us what you look like. You really are almost as tall as a cottonwood tree, aren't you?"

John grinned.

"I'm Betsy McCall."

"Glad to make your acquaintance, Betsy."

"I don't recall Miss Baylor saying anything about you being here, sir."

"That's because I just came in on the stage today, and she didn't know I was coming. Do you know if she is where I can see her?"

"The last I knew, she was helping one of the doctors do an appendectomy," Betsy said, rising from her chair. "Let me check."

While Betsy was gone, John looked around the reception area. Part of it was still unfinished. Bare studs showed, and the windows had not been completely framed. When he heard footsteps returning down the hall, he turned toward the desk again. Betsy appeared, smiling.

"I didn't get to speak to her, Mr. Stranger, but the doctor told me she's just washing up. If you'd like to wait outside the washroom, you're welcome to do so."

"All right."

Betsy led him down the hall. They turned a corner, where John saw a sign that said *Surgery,* and just beyond it was a door marked *Ladies' Washroom.* Apparently there were doors open that he could not see, for the evening breeze was creating a welcome draft in the hall.

"Miss Baylor is right in there, sir. She should be out shortly."

"Thank you, Betsy."

Betsy scurried back to her place, leaving Stranger alone in the hall, which was lighted by kerosene lanterns. John could hear Breanna humming Stephen Foster's *My Old Kentucky Home* as she neared the door, turned the knob, and stepped into the hall. Her back was toward John, and she saw another nurse cross the hall at the far end and wave. Breanna waved back.

She resumed her humming and started walking away from John. He hurried up behind her on tiptoe and said, "You've never had a home in Kentucky, lady."

Breanna spun around, surprise showing on her face. "John! What are you doing here?"

He took her into his arms. "I'll tell you that after I get a smooch!"

They kissed tenderly, then John held her close and said, "I'll explain it while I walk you to wherever you're staying. Then I want to take you to dinner. Can you go with me?"

"I'm off as of right now."

"So, where are you staying?" he asked.

"At the Big Sky Hotel."

"Hey, that's where I'm staying! How about we eat at the hotel's restaurant?"

"Sounds good to me. Do you mind if I change into a fresh dress before we eat?"

"Not at all. I expected that."

As they walked toward the hotel, John explained his mission, then told Breanna about Ebony being shot. Breanna loved the black gelding and was glad to know he would be all right.

Later, following a leisurely dinner, John and Breanna held hands as they climbed the stairs to the second floor of the hotel. Breanna's room was a few doors down the hall from John's. When they arrived at her door, he took her in his arms and told her he would be leaving just before dawn. He said he would be back as soon as possible, but if she had returned to Denver by then, he would see her there.

John kissed her long and sweet, then said, "I love you more than life itself, Breanna."

Tears filled Breanna's sky-blue eyes. Holding onto his fingertips, she whispered, "And I love you with all my heart, John."

"See you as soon as the Lord wills it."

She nodded and, reluctantly, let go of his fingers, backed into the room, and slowly closed the door.

John Stranger was up, shaved, and ready to go before the first hint of dawn was on the horizon. He strapped on his gunbelt, picked up his Henry .45 rifle, and stepped into the hall.

John was surprised to see Breanna standing there by the light of a lantern that hung on the wall. She was in a freshly ironed solid blue cotton dress with white pinafore, and her hair was brushed and ready for the day.

He smiled and asked, "Miss Baylor, how long have you been waiting out here?"

"Long enough to be sure I would be here when you came out, Mr. Stranger. I just had to tell you that I love you one more time before you left."

John took her in his arms. "You make it hard for me to leave you."

"I plan on making it harder each time."

He kissed her soundly, then said, "You need to go back to your room and lie down till time to go to the hospital. Don't neglect your rest."

"I'll be fine. May I walk you down to the lobby?"

He gave her his arm, kissed the tip of her nose, and said, "You may."

John Stranger heard from residents of the small towns that lined the Yellowstone River how the Wade Kyger gang had been robbing and terrorizing people, killing anyone who even looked like they were going to resist them. Bank employees and customers, stagecoach crews and passengers had been shot down in many of the robberies.

Stranger soon picked up the gang's trail. Five days after leaving Billings, he was able to find their present lair. They were hiding out in an old log cabin about three miles north of the Yellowstone and some forty miles from Billings. The cabin was in a low spot on the Montana prairie and had a few cottonwood trees to one side of it, next to an old barn and corral.

It was late in the afternoon when Stranger hunkered down on the crest of a hill, some ninety yards south of the hideout. As the outlaws moved about the yard and the corral, he counted eleven, including Wade Kyger, whom he recognized easily, even from that distance.

The next morning, as the gang was sitting down to breakfast, Kyger looked around and said, "Where's Borden?"

The gang members exchanged glances and shrugged.

"I ain't seen him since he left the cabin this mornin' to go to the privy, Wade," Art Coglin said.

"Well, the rest of us have been out there since then," Kyger said. "You boys go find him."

Wade Kyger was fit to be tied by the time his men came filing back in and reported that Borden Karsh was nowhere to be found.

"Is his horse in the corral?"

"All the horses are there," Jack Okerman said.

"Well, why would he just up and walk away?"

"I don't know, boss, but apparently he did."

"The only thing I can assume is that he's deserted us," Kyger said.

"That don't make sense, boss," Fletcher Braund said. "If Borden was gonna do that, he'd at least get on his horse and ride. Surely he'd know if he's on foot we can catch up to him in no time."

"Well, what else could it be?"

"Maybe he's been captured by the law," Tony Cook said.

Wade Kyger looked at Cook as if seeing him for the very first time. "The *law?* What're you talkin' about, Tony? If the law knew we were here, they'd try to take all of us!"

"Not if some lone sheriff, or even one with a deputy or two, has found us. It'd be safer to take us out one at a time."

Just then heavy footsteps were heard on the porch, and Sherman Wood came through the door, carrying Borden Karsh's hat.

"Found this out behind the privy, boss," Wood said. "You'll see the crown has been caved in. Looks like somebody conked Borden and hauled him away."

Wade Kyger cursed. "Then it is the law!"

"Not necessarily," Les Fenton said. "Maybe the Sioux or the Blackfeet got him."

"I don't know, Les. If the Indians wanted to kill us, wouldn't they just come whoopin' in here with a hundred warriors and wipe us out?"

"Maybe not. They might like to do it one at a time to unnerve us."

"Well, it's workin' with me," Coglin said. "I don't like the thought of bein' abducted by red savages and tortured to death."

"Best thing for us to do, boss," Braund said, "is to stick close together."

"And that's exactly what we'll do. Let's keep our eyes open and not let whoever it is get any more of us."

The next morning, the gang was preparing to ride out and pull a stagecoach robbery. Art Coglin had hit the bottle pretty heavy the night before, and he had a hangover. Coglin had done this before, and Kyger was miffed.

"Art, I told you last night you should cork that bottle," Kyger said, standing over the ailing gang member, who lay on his cot. "But no, you had to go ahead and polish it off. Well, you ain't sharin' in what we take off that stage today, y'hear?"

Moments later, Art Coglin heard the pounding hooves as the gang galloped away. He clutched his throbbing head and cursed his weakness toward alcohol.

The Kyger gang galloped into the yard of the old cabin and dismounted. They led their horses into the corral and began to remove saddles and bridles. Art Coglin's horse stood looking on.

The first man to enter the cabin was Jack Okerman. It was a one-room affair, with cots on one side and kitchen on the other. When he didn't see Coglin, Okerman headed back out the door. The others were just approaching the porch when Okerman said, "I'm checkin' the privy. If Art ain't there, we got another man missin'."

Moments later, Wade Kyger stood before his men with Art Coglin's gunbelt in his hand. It had been found on the bank of a small creek some forty yards from the cabin.

The outlaw leader was furious. *Who was doing this?*

At sundown that same day, the majority of the men lounged on the porch while two of them cooked supper. Chatting casually, they watched Fletcher Braund pass through the corral gate and enter the barn. It was Braund's turn to feed the horses.

A half hour later, the cooks called for the men to gather in the kitchen for supper. As the men filed into the cabin, Les Fenton shouted toward the corral, "Hey, Fletch! Suppertime! Better hurry or you won't get anything!"

Braund's place at the table was still empty as the gang began to wolf down their food. Wade Kyger looked at Tony Cook and said, "Go see what's keepin' him, will you?"

A few minutes later, Cook entered the kitchen carrying Fletcher Braund's gunbelt. No words were necessary.

"That does it!" Kyger said. "From this minute on, nobody goes anywhere alone, not even to the privy! Understand? I want no less than three men together at all times! Somebody's takin' a toll on us, and it's got to stop!"

C H A P T E R

FIFTEEN

⟞◆⟝

Sheriff Mack Jensen sat at his desk and chatted with two of his deputies, who had just returned from chasing down four outlaws that had robbed the Billings Bank a week previously. One of the robbers had been killed, and another wounded. The wounded one was in the town's new hospital, being guarded by Deputy Bob Harmon, and the other two were locked up in a cell.

Deputies Herb Doud and Larry Slocum were telling their boss how they had tracked and captured the robbers when Jensen's attention was drawn outside to the street. John Stranger was reining in the bay gelding at the hitch rail, and he had three horses in tow. Aboard each horse was a sullen-looking man with his hands tied behind his back.

A wide grin spread over Jensen's face as he rose to his feet.

"What is it, Sheriff?" Doud asked, looking through the open door toward the street.

"I told you fellas that John Stranger was on the trail of the Kyger gang. Well, here he is with three of them."

The deputies filed out the door behind Jensen into the hot sunlight. John Stranger was pulling the second outlaw out of the saddle as Jensen said, "Well, John, looks like you found some of them!"

"I found them all, Mack," Stranger said as he stood the second one on the ground and reached up for the third. "There are eight more, including Wade."

When the third outlaw's feet touched ground, Stranger said, "Sheriff Mack Jensen, I want you to meet Fletcher Braund, Art Coglin, and Borden Karsh."

"I know the names. All three are wanted on murder charges, as well as robbery. They'll face the judge and the gallows."

Jensen introduced Stranger to Doud and Slocum, and the prisoners were taken to the cellblock behind the office and locked up.

Stranger sat down in the office with the lawmen and explained how he had captured each man. He had kept Karsh and Coglin tied up in a brush-covered ravine. When he captured Braund, he decided to bring those three in before proceeding to capture more. He had borrowed the three horses from a ranch near the hideout and would return them on the way back.

"I've got assignments for my deputies, John," Jensen said, "but if you want, I'll postpone one assignment and send a man with you."

"No need. Let them go ahead and do what else is needed."

Jensen nodded. "So they apparently haven't added any more men to the gang."

"No. I was able to coerce the names of the rest of the gang from those three. I figured you might like to know which of the rest of them are wanted on previous charges."

"Sure would," said Jensen, picking up a pencil and pulling a sheet of paper from a desk drawer.

"Ready?"

"Shoot."

"Okay, let's see...there's Sherman Wood."

The sheriff didn't bother to write the name. "He's wanted for murder, too."

"Lester Fenton."

"Murder."

"Marty Madden."

"Murder."

"Tony Cook."

"Same."

"Everett Kincaid."

"Same."

"Jack Okerman."

"Bad dude. Murder."

"And...ah...Guy Reese."

"Yep. Murder."

Jensen hadn't written one of the names; they were all familiar.

"That makes eight with Wade, I believe," John said.

"Yep."

"Well, three down, eight to go," Stranger said, standing up. "I need to get back at it."

The sheriff thanked John, then watched him as he rode eastward with the three horses in tow.

Early the next morning, John Stranger led the bay gelding to a spot behind a grassy knoll some thirty yards from the barn and corral of the hideout. A stiff wind was blowing across the prairie. He eased his way to the crest of the knoll and saw one of the gang members working the lever of a well pump at the water trough inside the corral. He decided to move in and take him before he headed back for the cabin.

Bending low, Stranger started over the crest of the knoll. A gust of wind caught his hat and blew it off his head. A second outlaw came out of the barn, followed by a third. Everett Kincaid, his head bent against the wind, was working the pump hard and had not looked up at his companions. Marty Madden was headed toward him, and Guy Reese was fighting the wind, trying to close the barn door.

Madden's attention was drawn toward the tawny field of wind-thrashed grass by a small black object bounding down the side of the hill that led to the knoll.

John Stranger backtracked toward the top of the knoll and plunged over the top, trying not to be seen. But it was too late. Madden shouted above the whine of the wind, "I just saw some dude spyin' on us up there on the hill! Let's get him!"

All three whipped out their guns, vaulted over the split-rail fence, and ran in Stranger's direction. The wind took off their hats as they ran. When they were within thirty yards of the knoll's crest, Stranger suddenly stood up with the Henry .45 pointed at them and shouted, "Hold it right there! Drop those guns!"

Madden swore and fired at Stranger on the run. The bullet buzzed past Stranger's ear as the other two started blasting away at him. Stranger shot from the hip, dropping Everett Kincaid. He worked the lever rapidly and shot Guy Reese as another slug hissed close by, then took out Madden just as the outlaw was about to fire another shot.

Stranger dashed to the lifeless form of Marty Madden, stuck a silver medallion between his lips, then ran to a clump of sagebrush where his wind-blown hat had lodged. He picked it up and ran over the top of the knoll.

Wade Kyger and the rest of his gang bolted out of the cabin bareheaded, guns in hand, and scurried toward the spot where Kincaid, Madden, and Reese lay sprawled.

Kyger commanded his men to follow him up the hill. When they topped the crown of the knoll, there was no one in sight. Kyger found evidence of only one horse having been stashed on the backside of the knoll. He swore and wondered who the lone gunman could be.

They returned to their fallen colleagues and found that all

three were dead. Jack Okerman pointed to the silver disk between Marty Madden's lips, and Kyger leaned over and took the medallion in his fingers. At first he thought it was a silver dollar, but when he looked at it closely, his head bobbed with shock and his eyes widened. He threw the medallion down and ground it into the dirt with his heel. He began to curse the name of John Stranger, swearing that he would find him and kill him an inch at a time with his bare hands.

Kyger's men quietly waited for him to calm down. When he did, they asked him why he had so much hatred for this man named Stranger.

Kyger, still breathing hard, wiped saliva from his mouth and said, "Let's get these bodies in the ground. I'll tell you about him while we dig the graves."

They dug the graves with old shovels they had found earlier in the barn, and Wade Kyger told his men the story of how John Stranger had captured him at Raton Pass. He had dreamed while in prison of getting even with Stranger, and continued to do so after his escape. A day had not passed in the past six years that he had not thought of Stranger and his desire to make him pay. Now that desire was stronger than ever.

They covered the bodies with dirt, filling in the graves. Kyger told his men they would have to pull out in a hurry and find another hideout. John Stranger would be back. They must be gone before then.

"But if he found us this time, boss," Okerman said, "he'll find us again. We've got to fortify ourselves and take him out."

"It won't work," Kyger said. "The man's too good at what he does. I'd heard about him long before he cornered me at Raton Pass. It's almost like he ain't human. We can't match wits nor guns with him. If we meet him on his own ground, he'll wipe us out completely. You saw what he did to the three men we just buried."

"But you were carryin' on about killin' him real slow with your own two hands a while ago, Wade," Sherman Wood said.

Kyger gave him a petulant glance. "Well, I was just spewin' off at the mouth and not thinkin' clear."

"What're we gonna do if we can't match wits or guns with him?" Tony Cook asked.

"Somethin' just came to mind, Tony. I've got an idea how to get rid of that stranger from a far land without havin' to match wits or guns with him. I'll explain it while we ride outta here."

With bedrolls tied behind their saddles and spare clothing stuffed in the saddlebags—along with cookware and utensils—what was left of the Wade Kyger gang rode west. Kyger knew of an abandoned cabin in a hidden ravine about seven miles to the north of Billings.

While they rode, Wade said, "Okay, boys, here's what I've got in mind for Mr. John Stranger. I've got a friend in Miles City used to be a top-dog gunfighter."

"What's his name, Wade?" Okerman asked.

"Rick Dane."

"Rick Dane! I know that name. He was a top dog, all right. Haven't heard anything about him in years. I figured he met up with the wrong guy and got himself killed."

"Wasn't he also arrested for murder, Wade?" Wood asked.

"Three or four times. But they were never able to prove anything. Course, I happen to know of eight men and a woman that he murdered. Could be a lot more, knowin' Rick. He's heartless. Has no conscience, and he's the greediest dude I've ever met. He'll be perfect for what I've got in mind."

"Certainly you ain't gonna send him to draw against Stranger?" Fenton said. "I just remembered it was Stranger who took out Tate Landry down in Lander, Wyomin'…the top-dog gunfighter, himself."

"No, no, no!" Kyger said, throwing up his hands. "That's not it at all. I doubt Rick could outdraw Stranger even if they squared off when Rick was in his heyday."

"So what's this Rick doin' now?" Wood asked.

"Actin'."

Wood's eyebrows arched. "Actin'?"

"Yeah. He's workin' at the Miles City Playhouse. Rick's cousin on his ma's side, Emerson Wheeler, owns the place. Wheeler's payin' Rick as best he can, which really is pretty good, but Rick's not satisfied with the money he's makin'. He's been sayin' he might go to San Francisco and see if he can get into one of the big playhouses there."

Sherman Wood cocked his head. "So if you're not thinkin' of sendin' Dane up against Stranger for a shootout, what you got in mind?"

"Rick Dane is a dead ringer for John Stranger. Same height and build. Same color hair and mustache. They could easily pass for brothers. Even look a whole lot alike in facial features. Eyes are a little different—Stranger's are gray and Rick's are pale blue. But Rick can pass for him easily...and he's not known in Billings."

Okerman shook his head, looking at Kyger blankly. "You've lost me, boss."

Kyger smiled. "Rick's makin' fifty dollars a week at the playhouse. Just think if I offer him two thousand for a couple weeks' work. Greedy as he is, he'll jump at the chance."

"To do what?" Okerman asked.

"To come here dressed exactly like John Stranger and start brutalizin' and killin' people. All he has to do is make people think he's Stranger. When he kills somebody, he has to be sure to leave an eyewitness who'll swear he was John Stranger. The law will take it from there. You and I can stay in hidin' and let Sheriff Jensen and his deputies take care of Stranger."

"But what if they grab Dane instead?" Cook asked.

"They won't. Rick'll make this idea work. Once Stranger's been shot to death or hanged, we'll add some new members to our bunch and go on about our business."

The Kyger gang found the well-hidden old cabin unoccupied and moved in. The next day, Wade Kyger rode to Acton, a small town some 18 miles north of Billings, and wired a message to Rick Dane in Miles City, 150 miles to the east. He offered him two thousand dollars for "a couple weeks' work" without disclosing what the job was.

Kyger had no doubt his friend would be interested. He told the Western Union agent he would wait at one of Acton's saloons for a reply.

The reply was on the telegraph receiver in less than thirty minutes. Kyger responded with a second message, telling Dane to meet him in three days at a certain spot along the Yellowstone River.

John Stranger returned to the Kyger hideout and found the freshly dug graves. The hideout itself was deserted. He followed the gang's trail for a ways, but Kyger had ridden the middle of a shallow creek for several miles. There was so much rock and shale along the creek bank that Stranger could not find where they had left it for dry ground. He would have to scour the area to find them.

In the evenings, he spent time with Breanna, enjoying every minute of it. He had moved about Billings enough that nearly every citizen of the town knew him by sight and understood what he was there to do. They all were pulling for him, hoping he could find the rest of the Kyger gang and bring an end to their robbing and killing.

Day after day, Stranger rode the open range of Yellowstone County, searching for some sign of the gang or for someone who had seen them.

Three days after receiving the telegram, Rick Dane rode up to the place on the river that Wade Kyger had designated and dismounted. While he was tying the reins to a bush, his attention was drawn to a dark speck on the northwestern horizon that soon evolved into horse and rider. Another five minutes showed him that the rider was Wade Kyger.

"Howdy, Rick," Wade said, reining in with a broad smile.

"Same to you, Wade."

Kyger slipped from the saddle, shook Dane's hand, and said, "Well, pal, I'll get right down to business."

It took Kyger only a few minutes to tell his friend about John Stranger's efforts to destroy his gang, and what he wanted Rick to do. The actor in Rick Dane responded quickly to the challenge. The avarice in him responded to the two thousand dollars.

"So you think we can have this Stranger fella in the hands of the law within a couple of weeks?"

"If you do your job right, probably in less time than that," Kyger said. "You have any problem with your cousin? Gettin' off to do this job, I mean?"

"Naw. Emerson's aware I might be heading for San Francisco one of these days, anyhow. All I told him was I needed to be gone for a couple weeks. He's got my understudy playing the part."

"Good." Wade shook his head and chuckled. "Lookin' at you makes me even more amazed at how much you resemble that rat. Skin the same texture. Posture the same. Even the way you walk."

"I'll need to learn how he talks too, wouldn't you say?"

"Hadn't thought about that. It would be good if you could sound like him." Kyger scratched his head. "I guess the only thing you can do is disguise yourself and hang around Billings a few days. No way of knowin' for sure at this point, but I'll bet he's workin' with the law there, so he'd be in and out of town. He's probably got

Borden, Art, and Fletcher in Mack Jensen's jail. Anyway, maybe you could spot him and get a chance to listen in on some of his conversations. His voice is rather deep, and mainly he speaks in soft tones."

"It's worth a try. As long as I'm going to work this masquerade, I just as well do it right."

"There's a tailor at Acton. I'll have you outfitted exactly like Stranger, all the way to the gun on your hip."

For the next three days, Rick Dane appeared in Billings dressed like a farmer, straw hat pulled low. Skulking about town with a limp and shoulders stooped, he caught glimpses of John Stranger from time to time. Twice he sat near John and Breanna at the Big Sky Hotel restaurant so he could hear John's voice.

On the fourth day, Dane rode up to the hideout and dismounted. It was almost midmorning, and the sun was beating down on the prairie unmercifully. Wade Kyger and his four remaining gang members were huddled in the shade of the old, rickety front porch.

"Well, Rick," said Kyger, rising from the chair he'd been sitting on, "did you see him enough?"

"I did. And I think if you listen to me talk, you'll know I did."

"Hey, that's great! You picked up real good on his voice!"

"Thanks. You got my clothes and boots?"

"Picked 'em up a couple hours ago. They're inside." Kyger paused, then asked, "You get the face paint you needed?"

"Right there in my saddlebags. I want you to watch me as I paint those scars on my cheek...make sure they look exactly like Stranger's."

"All right. Let's go to the mirror inside."

Rick Dane sat in front of the warped old mirror in the cabin and began carefully making fake scars on his right cheek.

"Lookin' good, lookin' good," Wade Kyger said. "You're gonna pull this thing off, Rick. I know it!"

"This will be my greatest challenge as an actor—putting a noose around Stranger's neck without even touching him."

Ten minutes later, Rick Dane stood before Wade Kyger clad in flat-crowned black hat, white shirt with string tie, black trousers, and black boots. When he strapped on the black gunbelt that held a Colt .45 Peacemaker with bone-white handle grips, Kyger laughed, clapped his hands together, and said, "Rick, you're beautiful! Stranger's own mother would think you're him...if she didn't look too close!"

Kyger crossed the room to the cot where his saddlebags lay, pulled out a brown envelope, and handed it to Dane.

"There you are, Rick. One thousand dollars. Once Stranger's in the hands of the law or dead, you'll get the other thousand."

"Sounds fair enough. Now for Act One, Scene One."

Because he had not been successful in tracking down the Kyger gang anywhere near Billings, John Stranger told Breanna Baylor and Sheriff Mack Jensen he was going to begin covering more land in a bigger circle. He would not return to town each evening. He would return only when he had results.

It was nearing August, and there had been no rain—according to local residents—since early spring. The ground was thirsty, evidenced by the way it was cracked just about everywhere one looked. The grass was brown and dry, and the trees lifted their leaves toward the brassy sky, begging for moisture.

Day after day, Stranger rode the hills and valleys in spite of the heat and the dust. He was determined to find the rest of the Wade Kyger gang and bring them in, dead or alive.

At the Billings General Hospital, Breanna Baylor was helping Dr. Jacob Farner splint the broken leg of a teenage boy when the door to the hallway burst open. Two medical attendants rushed in, supporting a middle-aged man under the arms. His feet were dragging the floor. Blood streamed down his face from his scalp and from lacerations on his forehead, nose, and cheeks.

Dr. Farner recognized the man as Lance Garcy, one of the town's hostlers. Right behind Garcy and the attendants who were hoisting him onto an examining table came another staff physician, Dr. Glenn Hackman.

Dr. Hackman looked over his shoulder and said, "Dr. Farner, the other nurses are in situations they can't leave. It looks like you're about finished there. Could I please borrow Nurse Baylor?"

"Of course. Breanna, I can finish up here. How about giving Dr. Hackman a hand."

Breanna nodded and hurried to the examining table as the attendants left the room. She took one good look at the bleeding man, then turned to the counter and medical cabinets and began gathering instruments and materials she knew Dr. Hackman would need. She placed them on a small stand next to the table.

"What happened to him?" she asked, looking at the doctor.

"Pistol-whipped. Sheriff Jensen's on his way here to take his statement."

Breanna returned to the cupboard, poured water into a shallow pan from a pitcher, and began washing the blood from Garcy's hair and face. She noticed that Garcy was scowling at her.

"Sorry if I'm hurting you, Mr. Garcy," she said. "I'm being as gentle as I can."

"It isn't what *you're* doin', ma'am. It's what your boyfriend did. It was him who did this to me."

Breanna's eyes widened. "Pardon me?"

"You heard me. It was your John Stranger who pistol-whipped me. He's been keepin' his horse at my stable. Haven't seen him in over a week. Then he pops in twenty minutes ago, swearin' at me for no reason. Pulls that bone-handled Peacemaker of his and starts beatin' me on the head and face with it."

Breanna was shaking her head. "No. No, Mr. Garcy, you're mistaken. John doesn't swear, and he would never do a thing like that. It couldn't have been him."

"Well, believe me, lady, it was!"

Dr. Hackman moved in and said, "No more talking, Mr. Garcy. I need to go to work on you now."

Breanna assisted the doctor, but her mind was on the man she loved. What was going on?

SIXTEEN

———◆◆◆———

The next day, Sheriff Mack Jensen was standing at the door of his office talking to two townsmen when suddenly a stagecoach came charging down Main Street at full speed. The shotgunner was driving, the regular driver slumped over on the seat next to him.

"Sheriff!" shotgunner Dale Anderson shouted as the bounding, swaying coach drew near without slowing. "We were robbed! Come to the hospital!"

Jensen broke into a run, following the stage up the street. People looked on wide-eyed. Someone dashed to the Montana Stagelines office to alert the agent.

Sheriff Jensen came running up as two hospital attendants carefully eased driver Lenny Bean down from the seat. Jensen saw that Anderson had also been shot. There was blood on the front of his shirt at the left shoulder. He remained on the seat, leaning against the rack behind him.

Dr. Jacob Farner was inside the coach, examining passengers. The sheriff peered over Farner's shoulder. Three men and two women were slumped in their seats, and he could see no movement.

"Looks bad, Doc," Jensen said.

"It is, Sheriff," Farner said, backing out slowly. "They're all dead."

The attendants had Lenny Bean down now. The elderly driver's shirt was soaked with blood, and he was barely breathing.

"How is it in there, Doctor?" one of the attendants asked.

"All dead," Farner said solemnly. "Get him inside. I'll help Dale down. Looks like he's lost a lot of blood, too."

"I'll get him, Doc," Jensen said.

"All right. How about going to Chet O'Dell for me? I don't know any of those people in the coach. He'll have to go ahead and bury them. We'll locate their next of kin as soon as possible, but in this heat, those bodies will begin to decompose in a hurry."

"I'll take care of it just as soon as I talk to Dale," Jensen said.

The doctor followed the attendants as they carried Lenny Bean into the hospital. Jensen moved up to the front of the coach, just below the box, and lifted his arms.

"Here, Dale. Let me help you down."

Ten minutes later, Dale Anderson was in surgery.

Sheriff Jensen stood before the reception desk in the lobby talking to Betsy McCall. "I've got to take those bodies out there to the undertaker, Betsy. I'll be back in half an hour or so. Will you tell Nurse Baylor it's important that I talk to her as soon as possible?"

"I sure will, Sheriff. It may be quite a while though. She's working with Dr. Farner on Mr. Bean."

"I understand. I'll check back soon as I deliver the bodies to Chet."

Lou Flagg was coming on the run as the sheriff stepped out into the hot sunlight.

"Sheriff, how is it?"

"Not good, Lou. Five passengers dead. Lenny shot up real

bad. Dale shot too, but not so bad."

The Stagelines agent nodded and hurried into the hospital.

Breanna Baylor and Betsy McCall were talking at the reception desk when the sheriff returned.

"Through already?" he asked Breanna.

The nurse's features were somber. "Lenny died during surgery, Sheriff."

Jensen looked away, then closed his eyes and heaved a sigh. "Do you know how Dale's doing?"

"Dr. Hackman is still working on him. I don't know any more than that. Betsy said you wanted to talk to me."

"Yes. Is there a private place?"

"We can use Dr. Hackman's office."

There were two chairs in Dr. Glenn Hackman's office besides the one behind the desk. Breanna and the sheriff sat down, then he looked her square in the eye and said, "Ma'am, you weren't here by the time I arrived to take Lance Garcy's statement last evening, but I understand he told you who it was that pistol-whipped him."

"Yes, but it can't be true, Sheriff. I know John too well. He would never do a thing like that."

"Well, I had a pretty high opinion of him too, ma'am, or I wouldn't have asked for him to come here and help me take out the Kyger gang."

"Sheriff, there's something wrong, here. Lance said John swore at him before he started beating him. John doesn't use that kind of language. I'm telling you, whoever beat him up, it wasn't John. The only thing I can think of is that Lance's mind was affected by the beating, and he just *thinks* it was John."

"He described John's clothing to a T, ma'am, and said he whipped him with that bone-handled Peacemaker. Sounds to me like his thinking is clear."

"Well, it isn't. If he's not mistaken, then he's lying."

Jensen removed his hat and laid it on the desk. He ran his fingers through his hair, looked at the floor, then brought his gaze up to meet hers. "What would you say if I told you Dale Anderson told me it was John Stranger who held up the stage, robbed everybody on it, then shot them in cold blood?"

Breanna stared at him, unable to speak.

"John was on Lenny and Dale's stage when he came to Billings, Miss Breanna. They got to know him pretty well. Dale told me it was John who stopped the stage four miles outside of town. He held his Peacemaker on them and made them throw their weapons on the ground. After he'd taken the cash box, he relieved the passengers of their valuables, then shot Lenny and Dale and blasted away at the passengers with both guns. He rode away laughing."

"No! It can't be, Sheriff. Dale's mistaken. Somebody's impersonating John."

"Somebody with the exact same clothing and hat and gun? Somebody his exact height and build...with two jagged scars on his right cheek?"

Tears filled Breanna's eyes.

"I've got to arrest him, Miss Breanna. He'll hang for sure."

One of the tears slipped to Breanna's cheek, and her lips quivered. "I...I can't explain it, Sheriff. But I'm telling you, there is some mistake."

"The mistake was John Stranger's, ma'am," Jensen said, rising to his feet. "He killed six people today. I'm sorry. I know you were going to marry him."

"I still am," she whispered.

"Pardon me? I didn't understand what you said."

Breanna looked up at the lawman through a wall of tears. "I still am going to marry him. The man I love did not do this horrible thing."

Mack Jensen shook his head. "I've got to send my deputies after him, ma'am. He's been positively identified by two responsible men. Again…for your sake, I'm sorry."

Breanna watched the sheriff pass through the door and head up the hall. She felt as though she was in a horrible nightmare from which she could not awaken. She leaned over, placed her arms on the desk, and rested her forehead against them.

"O Lord God in heaven, You know who this person is that's impersonating John. Please…please let the culprit be caught before they catch John and hang him!"

Wade Kyger emerged from the gun shop in Acton carrying a fresh supply of cartridges. A burlap sack that contained supplies he had purchased at the general store hung from his saddlehorn. He added the cartridges to the sack, then swung into the saddle and rode south toward the hideout.

An hour later, he veered off the road that led to Billings and dipped into a grassy draw. He rode the draw for several minutes, pulled out and trotted the horse over undulating prairie for about two miles, then crested a gentle rise and looked down into the brush-laden ravine where the cabin was hidden.

"Not too much longer in this place," he told himself. "Once the law has removed John Stranger from the face of the earth, me and the boys can add a few to the gang and go back to makin' good money."

Kyger headed down the slope toward the cabin. Moments later, he pressed the horse through a thicket of trees, and the cabin came into view. What he saw in front of the cabin caused him to quickly draw rein.

At first he thought it was Rick Dane's back he was looking at, but then he saw a gun in the hand of the man-in-black and his men with their hands in the air. Panic arose in the outlaw leader. John Stranger had killed or captured every man in his gang. His only thought was to get away fast.

Where would he go?

That question had a quick answer. He would ride west and join Wilson's gang. In the cabin was a letter from his brother, containing a map of how to find Wilson's hideout in the Rockies near Jefferson City. Wade had an open invitation to visit anytime he wanted to. He would more than visit. He would move in.

Wade wheeled his mount and rode to a low spot. He left his horse there and crawled to the crest and looked back toward the cabin. He cursed John Stranger under his breath as he watched the man bind the hands of the four outlaws behind their backs, then hoist them into the saddles. In another minute, Stranger was headed south on his own mount, leading the others.

Kyger knew Stranger would be back looking for him. He would get his hands on the map and hightail it out of there.

Deputies Herb Doud and Larry Slocum rode at a steady pace under the hot summer sun in search of John Stranger. They realized, as did Sheriff Mack Jensen, that finding Stranger and capturing or killing him would be no easy task.

They figured first to ride the road that led to Sheridan, Wyoming. This was the road where Stranger had waylaid the stage and killed six people. Maybe he would plan to do the same thing to the next stage that came from Sheridan.

The stage from Miles City rolled into Billings and halted in front of the sheriff's office. A short, fat man on the boardwalk noted that the driver was alone in the box, then looked through the windows of the coach and saw three men doubled over and a woman leaning back in the seat, holding a bloody cloth to her left shoulder.

People were looking on and shouting to others that another stage had been robbed, and there were dead people aboard it. The message traveled quickly, and people were soon in a hubbub, milling about.

The driver noted that the door to the sheriff's office was closed. He looked down at the short, fat man on the boardwalk and said, "We've had a robbery and a shooting, sir. Would you see if you can find the sheriff and send him to the hospital? I've got a wounded lady back there. My name's Seth Porter. He knows me."

"Will do," said the man. "He's gotta be around town somewhere."

Forty minutes after arriving at the hospital, Seth Porter looked up to see Sheriff Mack Jensen and his deputy, Bob Harmon, come through the lobby door.

"Sorry we took so long getting here, Seth," Jensen said, "but we were a ways out of town trying to settle a fight between a couple of ranchers. Herb and Larry are on a manhunt at the moment. What happened?"

Seth Porter told of a lone gunman who waylaid the stage at a spot where it had to slow down to cross a creek some ten miles east of Billings. The tall man-in-black robbed them, then shot and killed the shotgunner. When two male passengers railed at him, he gunned both of them, hitting a woman passenger as well. Both men died instantly. The woman was in surgery at the moment. She had taken a slug in the left shoulder.

"Give me a full description of this man," Jensen said.

When Porter had done so, the sheriff said to his deputy, "I thought so."

"You've had this guy hold up other stages, Sheriff?" Porter asked.

"One two days ago. Stage from Sheridan. The same man killed six people on the stage."

"You got any idea who he is?"

"I know exactly who he is. He's the one Herb and Larry are hunting."

"Well, I hope they catch him. I want to see him hang!"

"He will," Jensen assured him.

"Oh, Sheriff…I know Darla Case personally. Her husband's a wealthy merchant in Miles City. Name's Myron. Myron Case."

"Yes?"

"Darla rides my stage quite often. She has a sister in Bozeman and travels to visit her periodically. Since I'm sort of responsible for her, as a passenger, I don't want to leave the hospital till I know how the surgery went. Could I get you to wire a message to her husband and let him know what's happened?"

"Of course."

"Be sure to tell him it's only a shoulder wound. Her life's not in danger."

"Sheriff, I'll go send the wire," Bob Harmon said. "That way you can stay here with Seth."

"Okay. Thanks, Bob."

"That's what deputies are for," Harmon said, heading for the door. "To run errands for the big cheese!"

"Aw, get outta here!" Jensen said in mock anger.

Twenty minutes later, Dr. Glenn Hackman entered the lobby and told Porter and Jensen that Darla Case had come through the surgery all right. The slug had chipped bone in her shoulder. She would wear a sling for a long time, but she would be fine.

At that moment Breanna Baylor appeared.

"He did it again, Miss Breanna," Jensen said.

"You mean the man who's impersonating John shot Mrs. Case?"

"She didn't tell you?"

"She was unconscious when they brought her in. She's under ether now."

"Sheriff, Miss Baylor told me the story," Dr. Hackman said. "From what she says, there's somebody impersonating the man she's engaged to marry. Is this not possible, in your thinking?"

Jensen scratched at an ear. "Well, Doc, how would it be possible to come up with a man exactly the same size and build as John Stranger, who has hair the same color, and looks exactly like him?"

"Maybe it's an identical twin brother nobody knows about."

"With the exact same scars John has on his cheek?"

Hackman scrubbed a hand across his mouth. "That *would* be pretty close to impossible, wouldn't it?"

"Sheriff," Breanna said, "I can't answer your questions. But I'm telling you, the man who's doing these horrible things is not John Stranger."

"I'd love to know it isn't him, ma'am, but I don't know who else it could be."

"No! John is not an outlaw! And he's not a killer!"

The sun was almost down when Sheriff Jensen and Deputy Harmon walked together toward the office. Harmon had sent the wire, and an answer had come back that Myron Case would catch the morning stage. He would be at his wife's side in two days.

The two lawmen were almost to the office when they halted dead in their tracks. Coming up Main Street from the opposite direction were five horsemen. The one in the lead was aboard a bay gelding with white blazed face and four white stockings. In tow were four men with their hands bound behind their backs.

"Sheriff, are we both in the same dream?" Bob Harmon said.

"Must be. I don't get this."

"Me either. Has to be he's captured more of the Kyger gang."

"Yeah, but why? And how? He robbed that stage ten miles east of town not more than three hours ago!"

"I can't figure it, myself," the deputy said, shaking his head.

"Let's act like everything's all right till we get the outlaws in their cells. Then you keep alert while I put a gun on Stranger. If he tries to resist, shoot him."

John Stranger swung his long leg over the saddle and dropped to earth as the two lawmen drew up.

"Well, Mack, ten down and one to go," he said, grinning. "I found the hideout and gave these boys a little surprise, but Wade wasn't there. Got no cooperation when I asked where he was and when he'd come back. I'll head right back and see if I can catch him there. The hideout's no more than eight or nine miles due north."

"Great! Who've we got here? Some more on the wanted list, I imagine."

People on the street gawked at the scene in front of the sheriff's office as they recognized that it was John Stranger talking to the sheriff and his deputy.

Stranger gave Jensen the outlaws' names. Every one of them was on the wanted list.

When the four men were behind bars, the two lawmen led John Stranger from the cell block back into the office. Bob Harmon's nerves were stretched tight as he watched his boss.

Jensen smiled at Stranger, clapped a hand on his shoulder, and said, "Mighty good work, John."

"I try. Well, I'm going to head back. I hope Wade will be there wondering where his boys are. Maybe I can wrap this thing up before sunrise."

As he spoke, Stranger headed for the door.

Jensen went for his gun.

When Stranger heard the sound of metal brushing against

leather, he stopped. Before he could turn around, the hammer was cocked with a dry, clicking sound.

"Get those hands in the air, Stranger!" Jensen said. "You've got two guns on you. Don't do anything foolish."

The tall man lifted his hands shoulder high and slowly pivoted. A quizzical look was on his face.

"Mack, what is this?"

"You're under arrest for robbery, assault, and murder, mister!"

"This is a joke, right?"

"No joke! Bob, get his gun."

When Stranger had been disarmed, the sheriff said, "Okay, pal, there's a cell back there for you! Let's go."

"How about telling me who I robbed, assaulted, and murdered?"

"Don't have to. You know. I'll have eyewitnesses here soon enough. You're going to hang, Stranger!"

After the tall man was in a cell with the Kyger men looking on in astonishment, Jensen stepped close to the bars and said, "It's a dirty shame what you've done to that sweet little nurse. She really thinks you're innocent. Won't hear to it that you've deceived her."

"I am innocent of whatever I'm supposed to have done, Mack," Stranger said, looking him straight in the eye.

"Well, like they say, tell it to the judge."

Within half an hour, Dale Anderson, Seth Porter, and Lance Garcy stood with sheriff and deputy in front of John Stranger's cell. Stranger did not know Porter, but he knew the other two. When all three had identified him as the man who had committed the crimes, he looked at them and said, "I don't know why you men would want to incriminate me, but you know it isn't so."

"Let's get outta here, fellas," Lance Garcy said. "The man's an actor. He can look his victims straight in the eye, and if I didn't know better, I'd say he was tellin' the truth."

Immediately after holding up Seth Porter's stage, Rick Dane galloped his mount to the west side of Billings, stashed it in a thicket along the Yellowstone River, then sneaked into town. He worked his way between two buildings across the street from the Montana Stagelines office and waited in the shadows.

Dane watched the stage roll into town and cursed to himself when it stopped in front of the sheriff's office a block away. He watched closely, but could not hear the interchange between the driver and the short, fat man.

A crowd began to gather. People were coming out of shops up and down the street, talking excitedly. Soon Dane picked up that the stage was going to head to the hospital. A woman passenger had been shot, but was still alive. He also overheard someone say the name John Stranger.

Dane smiled to himself. After the stagecoach passed him on its way to the hospital, he turned toward the alley. He froze, however, when he saw a cluster of people there talking about the robbery. A man was saying that he just couldn't believe John Stranger would do a thing like that. A woman said he had to believe it. Eyewitnesses who know Stranger had identified him as the robber and killer.

Rick Dane had to duck down low to keep from being seen. Time seemed to drag. Wouldn't those people ever leave? When the crowd in the alley finally broke up, there were still a lot of people moving up and down it. Dane had to stay where he was.

Finally, dusk began to settle on the land, and traffic in the alley diminished to nothing. Dane was about to sneak away when he heard excited voices on the street. People were shouting that John Stranger had just been captured and locked up in jail. There would be a quick trial, and Stranger would hang.

Rick Dane made his way to the alley, ran to the nearest side street, and hurried out of town. When he found his horse, he swung into the saddle and headed for the Kyger hideout. Stranger was in the hands of the law, and Wade Kyger owed him a thousand dollars.

When the news that John Stranger had been captured reached the hospital, Breanna was cleaning-up in the examining room. She left the job unfinished, told another nurse where she was going, and ran toward the jail.

Deputies Herb Doud and Larry Slocum had returned to town for the night and were happy to hear that John Stranger had been captured. Sheriff Jensen and all three deputies stood before the cell door, talking to Stranger through the bars.

"Sheriff, you've got to believe me," John said. "There's something terribly wrong here. I am not the man who pistol-whipped Lance Garcy, and I am not the man who robbed the stages and killed those people."

"Hello?" came a woman's voice from the office. "Sheriff Jensen, are you here?"

"It's Breanna," John said.

Jensen turned to Bob Harmon. "Bring her in."

Harmon headed for the door that led to the office, calling, "We're back here, Miss Baylor!"

When Breanna saw the man she loved standing in his cell, she gasped and ran to him. They embraced through the bars. The seven members of the Kyger gang looked on in silence from their cells.

Breanna turned and said, "Sheriff, you're making a serious mistake!"

"That's what I've been telling him, Breanna," John said. "But three men have identified me as the one who committed the crimes. He really has no choice but to lock me up and send me to trial."

"But there's some kind of conspiracy going on, Sheriff," Breanna said. "You must get to the bottom of it before John goes to trial. If three men stand up in court and point him out as the guilty party, the judge will sentence him to the gallows!"

"Look, I want to believe you, John," Jensen said. "And I will say this…I'm having a hard time figuring out how you managed to capture those four outlaws and rob the stage, all in the space of two or three hours."

"That's just it, Mack. I didn't rob those stages and murder those people. You've got to find the man who did."

"Sure. Find a man who looks exactly like you, even to the scars on his cheek. I'm sorry, John, but everything points to you. Whether I like it or not, I have the guilty man locked up."

"But there is some doubt in your mind, isn't there, Sheriff?" Stranger asked.

Jensen gave him a blank look.

"Since there's doubt," John said, "and you aren't going to look for this man who's impersonating me, let me out of here so *I* can go after him. Let these two deputies who were looking for me go with me."

"John, I can't do that," the sheriff said, shaking his head. "If you wanted to, you could give them the slip. No, that's out. I have no choice but to let you go to trial."

Tears brimmed Breanna's eyes. "Sheriff, if you won't let John go after this impostor, won't you go? Please."

"You'll have to leave now, ma'am. My deputies are going to their homes. It's my turn to bring in food for the prisoners, and I must get to it."

Breanna thumbed away her tears, kissed John through the bars, and told him she would be back tomorrow. The three deputies ushered her through the door. When they were gone, the sheriff moved close to the bars and said, "Chief Duvall's going to be shocked when he hears about this."

"Won't he though," Stranger said.

Suddenly his right hand shot out, grabbed Jensen's shirt, and yanked him face-first against the bars. The blow knocked Jensen out. Stranger eased him to the floor, took the key ring off his belt, and unlocked the door. The outlaws looked on speechless as Stranger dragged Jensen inside the cell.

John took Jensen's revolver and locked the cell door, then hurried to the office. He left the sheriff's gun on the desk, grabbed his bone-handled Colt .45 from the gun case where Jensen had left it, and dashed out the door.

His blaze-faced bay gelding was still at the hitch rail. The street was virtually deserted. Stranger vaulted into the saddle and galloped north out of Billings.

CHAPTER

SEVENTEEN

John Stranger found the hideout unoccupied. He lit a lantern and looked around. On the floor, he found an envelope postmarked August 4...only a few days previous. It had been mailed in Jefferson City, Montana, and was addressed to a Sanford Roberts, general delivery, Billings. Inside was a letter that began, "Dear Wade," and ended, "Your little brother, Wilson."

In the letter, Wilson told Wade that he had recently moved to another hideout. It was still high in the Rockies near Jefferson City, but was well-hidden in a dark box canyon with a narrow entrance. The letter mentioned an enclosed map, but the map was missing.

Stranger rode as fast as he could in the dark back to Billings. He must tell Breanna where he was going and why.

Stranger tied the blaze-faced bay in the alley behind the Big Sky Hotel, mounted the rear stairs, and tapped on Breanna's door. When there was no answer, he went to his own room and wrote Breanna a note. In it, he asked her to tell the sheriff he was sorry he had had to knock him out, but he was determined to prove his innocence. He told her he loved her with all his heart, signed it, and slipped it under her door.

Stranger rode west at a full gallop until the country became too rough to cover safely in the dark. The sky was clear, but there was no moon. Riding the horse at a walk, he soon came upon a small brook lined with cottonwoods and oaks. There he let the bay drink his fill, then ground-reined him so he could graze on the brown grass.

John stretched out on top of his bedroll and stared at the star-studded sky. Suddenly he was aware of bright flashes to the north. He sat up and watched jagged bolts of heat lightning against the velvet darkness. He didn't like to see it. As dry as Montana was, he knew the lightning could start a fire.

After awhile the lightning ceased, and John Stranger fell asleep.

Hours later, the bay nickered. Stranger came awake instantly and sat up. There was a light breeze, and it carried the smell of smoke. As he rose to his feet, he saw that the north sky was lit up in a fan-shaped aura of orange light. Stranger hopped the brook and scurried to the top of a small hill. Prairie grass was burning in a widening swath. He hoped it would burn out before it reached one of the forests that dotted the area. He hated to see a forest destroyed.

The breeze was from the north, driving the fire his direction. He mounted up and pushed westward, and soon the orange sky and smoke were behind him. Since dawn was still several hours away, Stranger found another spot and soon was asleep.

Bill Arkin and Fred Vogel were perched on opposite sides of the narrow entrance to the box canyon where the Wilson Kyger gang was now hiding out. They were only forty feet apart as they sat, rifles-in-hand, atop the sheer granite walls. It was some eighty feet to the canyon floor.

All around were giant rock formations amid thick forests of pine, birch, and aspen. The mouth of the canyon faced southward, and from their lofty position, the outlaws could see a great distance.

It was early afternoon when Vogel spotted movement amongst the trees some five hundred yards to the south. "Somebody comin'," he said to Arkin, who was watching two large hawks circling lazily in the azure sky.

"From which direction?" Arkin asked, running his gaze over the vast sweep of Rocky Mountain ruggedness.

"Due south."

Arkin squinted, lowering the brim of his hat over his eyes to shade them. "Looks like a lone rider."

A quarter-hour passed. As the rider drew nearer, Vogel said, "You know who that is, Bill? That's Wilson's big brother."

"Well, sure enough, it is Wade!"

At the cabin in the heart of the box canyon, Wilson Kyger welcomed his older brother. Wilson introduced Wade to two new gang members, George Dartt and Clem Landon, and told about Jake Ransom being sent to prison.

Wade described what happened at Billings and how John Stranger had methodically taken his gang apart. Wilson well remembered Stranger as the man who had captured his brother and taken him in to be hanged. Wade shared his fear that Stranger would track him down and kill him.

"I don't blame you, Wade," Clete Sarno said. "I've heard he's the best tracker in the West. As one guy put it, Stranger can track a diamondback rattler over a bed of smooth rock."

Wilson laid a hand on his brother's shoulder. "You don't need to lose any sleep about Stranger gettin' at you here, Wade. I always keep two men on top of those walls at the canyon entrance. Nobody can get in here without bein' seen. Me and the boys ride at night, but George and Clem stay right here while we're gone and guard the canyon. If that dude shows up here, he'll get himself filled with hot lead."

"What do you boys do, ridin' at night?" Wade asked.

He was impressed when Wilson told about his deal with Baxter Beaumont and the kind of money Beaumont was going to pay the gang when the last of the squatters pulled out.

Bone tired, Breanna Baylor climbed the hotel stairs just before midnight and moved down the dimly lit hall toward her room. She had stayed with Darla Case until another nurse could relieve her. Darla was doing as well as expected after her surgery, but she had a reaction to the ether and could not be left alone.

Breanna inserted the key in the lock, opened the door, and stepped into the pitch-black room. Her foot brushed something on the floor. By the vague light from the hall, she saw that it was a folded slip of paper. She picked it up, groped her way to the night stand, fumbled for a match, and lighted the lantern. After closing and locking the door, she unfolded the paper and slanted it toward the light.

Her heart pounded as she read John's hastily written words. When she finished, she said, "O Lord Jesus, please let John clear himself."

Breanna left the hotel and walked the dark street to the sheriff's office. Finding the door unlocked, she lit a lantern and carried it into the cell block. The prisoners were all asleep on their cots, but an angry Mack Jensen was standing at the cell door.

"John left me a note, Sheriff," Breanna said in a half-whisper. "I just got to my room. I couldn't leave you here all night."

"I appreciate that, but is that man of yours ever in trouble now! There should be a key— "

"John left this one on the desk," she said, unlocking the door. "Your gun is out there, too."

Jensen was fuming as he shoved the cell door open.

"I want you to read this note, Sheriff," Breanna said.

"In the office," he said. "Not here."

When they reached the office, Jensen read the note, then handed it back to Breanna. "I'm sorry, ma'am, but only a guilty man would do what he did."

"That's where you're wrong, Sheriff. Put yourself in John's place. If you were accused but were innocent, wouldn't you have done the same thing he did? Escape so you could find the guilty party and bring him in?"

The lawman's jaw muscles were working as he clenched his teeth.

When he didn't answer, Breanna said, "You did see that part where he said he's sorry he had to knock you out, didn't you?"

"Yeah. I bet he's sorry."

"Sheriff, John is innocent. He will prove that to you."

"I'm glad you have so much faith in him, ma'am. But in my way of thinking, an innocent man doesn't run."

"You mean he should've just stayed here and let the judge hang him for something he didn't do? That's exactly what would've happened!"

"He'll never come back, ma'am. I'm telling you, he'll never come back."

"I'm a Christian, Sheriff, and I don't gamble. But if I were a betting woman, I'd bet you a year of my pay against a month of yours—John will be back."

Another day passed. On the morning of the next day, Breanna Baylor was giving Darla Case a sponge bath in her room when there was a tap on the door.

"Yes?" Breanna called.

"It's Myron Case, Darla's husband. May I come in?"

"Just a moment," Breanna said, picking up the small pan, washcloth, and towel. "Now, we can let him in."

Breanna carried the bath items to a table in the corner, then opened the door and smiled. "Good morning, Mr. Case. Come in. I'm Nurse Baylor. Your wife is doing fine."

"Thanks to you, Breanna," Darla said.

Myron went to the bed, kissed his wife, then asked about her wound as he held her hand. Breanna gave him a thorough explanation of the damage the bullet had done, then told him Dr. Hackman's prognosis.

Myron smiled warmly at the nurse. "From what Darla said a few minutes ago, it seems you've been a real help to her."

"She's been an angel," Darla said.

"Thank you," Myron said to Breanna, then looked into Darla's eyes with love and concern. "Guess it could have been worse, honey."

Darla nodded, giving him a weak smile.

"Now, I want to know about this lone gunman who shot you. The wire that came from Sheriff Jensen's deputy didn't tell me much."

Breanna moved to the opposite side of the bed and laid a hand on her patient's brow. She was glad Darla's temperature felt normal.

Darla looked up at her husband and said, "Myron, you won't believe who it was."

Myron's eyebrows raised. "You mean you know him?"

"Yes, and so do you. It was Rick Dane."

"Rick Dane! Rick Dane held up the stage and shot you?"

"Yes."

"Are you sure, Darla?"

"Absolutely. It was him. He had some scars on his face I've never seen before, but it was him."

"Maybe he's always covered them with stage make-up for his performances."

"Must have, but there's no mistaking who it was, Myron."

"Well, we know he was a gunfighter," Myron said, "but I never dreamed he was a robber and a killer."

Breanna tried to speak, but the shock of what she had just heard sent her mind spinning around an uncertain center.

Myron noted her strange look and said, "Miss Baylor, are you all right?"

"Did…did I hear you right?" Breanna said. "You people know the man who shot Darla?"

"Yes," Darla said. "Does the name Rick Dane mean something to you?"

"No. It's just that—Well, I'll explain later. Tell me about this man."

Still holding his wife's hand, Myron said, "Rick Dane is an actor at the Miles City Playhouse. We've gone to his plays many times. He was once a gunfighter but quit before it was too late. He's been accused of murder, but no one could ever prove it. You know the law—innocent until proven guilty."

"Yes, or so I've heard. Would…would you describe this Rick Dane for me, Mr. Case?"

"Well, he's tall. Very tall. Somewhere around, oh, six-four, six-five. Slender but wide in the shoulders. Dark complected. Black hair. Well-trimmed mustache. Angular features."

"What color are his eyes?"

Myron looked down at Darla. "What would you say, honey? Pale blue?"

"Yes. Pale blue."

Breanna clapped her hands together and said, "Praise the Lord! The man committing the crimes for which John is being accused is practically his twin. Oh, praise the Lord! Sheriff Jensen needs to hear this!"

Breanna hurried out into the hall and found the hospital's janitor. She asked him to go tell Sheriff Jensen she had some big news for him and to ask if he would come to the hospital as soon as possible. The janitor agreed and rushed out the lobby door.

"Pardon me, ma'am," Myron said when Breanna returned, "but what's this all about?"

Once Breanna told them the story, it was the Cases' turn to be surprised. They told Breanna they hoped John Stranger would soon clear himself.

Dr. Glenn Hackman entered the room for a routine check on Darla, and Breanna excused herself, saying she had other patients to look after. She would return when Sheriff Jensen arrived so Myron and Darla could tell him about Rick Dane.

Mack Jensen entered the hospital lobby just shy of an hour after Breanna had sent the janitor to get him. Betsy McCall had been briefed by Breanna and told Sheriff Jensen to wait at the desk until she returned. Moments later, Betsy appeared with Breanna at her side.

"I understand you have some big news for me," Jensen said.

"I sure do, Sheriff. Come with me."

Breanna ushered the sheriff into Darla's room, introduced him to the Cases, and told him what she had learned about actor Rick Dane. Myron and Darla backed up Breanna's every word, and Darla made sure Jensen understood that there was no mistake about it—Rick Dane was the man who had shot her.

"Do you see it, Sheriff?" Breanna said. "Sure as anything, this Wade Kyger conspired with Rick Dane to commit the crimes and let the blame be laid on John. Being an actor, Dane used stage make-up to paint some fake scars on his face. The whole thing was a set-up to incriminate John so you'd arrest him, and he could no longer be a threat to Kyger."

Jensen rubbed the back of his neck. "Well, it sure looks like John has been framed, all right. I'll wire Marshal Ashley in Miles City and ask him to find out if Rick Dane has been out of town the last few days. Be back to fill you in when I get an answer."

It was nearly noon when Mack Jensen returned to the hospital and approached the reception desk. Betsy McCall smiled at him.

"Miss Baylor told me to keep an eye out for you, Sheriff. You're to go to Mrs. Case's room. I'll find Miss Baylor and let her know you're here."

Jensen thanked her and headed for Darla's room. Minutes later Breanna came in, a questioning look on her face. "What's the word, Sheriff?" she asked.

"Rick Dane has indeed been away from Miles City for several days. He arrived back there just yesterday according to his cousin, Emerson Wheeler. It was Wheeler that Marshal Ashley talked to. Seems Dane is now on his way to Cheyenne City by stagecoach. He left early this morning. Wheeler says Dane is going to take a train from there to San Francisco."

"So I assume you'll wire the authorities in Cheyenne City," Breanna said.

"Already have. The Laramie County sheriff will pick Dane up and jail him. He's to let me know once he's done so. I'll send one of my deputies down there to bring him back."

"Good!" Breanna said.

"I also sent a wire to Sheriff Lloyd Gross in Jefferson City. I didn't wait for a reply from him, but it'll probably be at the Western Union office when I stop by there on my way back to the office. I told him to be on the lookout for John and to tell him he's been cleared of all crimes."

Breanna clapped her hands together, threw her head back, and said, "Oh, praise the Lord for answered prayer!"

"Miss Breanna," the sheriff said, "you are some kind of lady! I have to admire your faith in God...and your faith in John Stranger."

"Both are well-founded, Sheriff," she said, smiling happily. "Didn't I tell you John was innocent?"

"Yes, you did. And I hope you can understand the difficult position I was in. I'm just glad it's turned out the way it has. And I can't wait to see Rick Dane in that courtroom facing the judge!"

Sheriff Lloyd Gross read the lengthy telegram from Sheriff Mack Jensen, which a messenger boy had delivered to his office. Just as he finished reading it, his deputy came in from the street.

"Jerry, I just got a wire from Mack Jensen over at Billings!"

"Must be a good one," Jerry Zeller said.

"It is. You know I've been trying to locate John Stranger through Chief Duvall, but Duvall's on a trip to Kansas City and can't be contacted."

"Yes."

"Well, of all things, Jensen's wire says Stranger is on his way to this area right now."

"Oh?"

"He's trailing Wade Kyger, Wilson Kyger's brother. Wilson's supposed to be around these parts. And you know what I'm thinking?"

"Probably the same thing that just went through my mind. This gang of masked riders might be Wilson Kyger and his bunch."

"Exactly! I'll tell you the details later, but we've got to alert the townspeople and the local ranchers to keep an eye out for Stranger." Gross looked down at the telegram's second page. "He's riding a bay gelding with white blazed face and four white stockings. Everything he's wearing is black except for his shirt, which is white."

"Then let's get the word out," Zeller said. "We don't want to miss him."

"No, and not only because we need his help. From what I understand from Jensen's message, Wade Kyger hired some actor who looks like Stranger to rob and kill people, then let Stranger take the blame. Stranger's after Kyger in order to clear himself with the law. It's already been done, but Stranger doesn't know it. I'm supposed to tell him."

"I'll get some men to help me spread the word."

CHAPTER

EIGHTEEN

———✦———

G entlemen, as you know, five more families have pulled out
in the past week." Zachary Meadows stood before the large
group of small ranchers he had called to a meeting in the
town hall at Deer Lodge City. "I know the lawmen and their posses
have been doing all they can, but the truth is, they need help. The
problem you and I face is that we can't form posses among ourselves because it would take us away from our families at
night…just when the riders strike. All of us keep hearing from the
ranchers with the big spreads that they have nothing to do with the
masked riders."

"That's what they keep tellin' us!" someone called out.

"Well, I suggest that we little guys pay visits to the big guys
and ask them to provide us some men. There are easily enough
ranch hands among them to form three dozen posses of ten men
each. An army like that would send that masked bunch running
out of this valley. If not, we'd soon have them in custody. Either
way, the harassment would stop.

"Let's put these ranchers to the test. They say they're not
behind the raiders. Let's see if they'll help us!"

The crowd was unanimously behind the idea.

Zach pulled out a sheet of paper with the names of all the big ranchers on it. "Okay, gentlemen, I'm going to call off the names, and if you'll make a visit to that rancher, just give a holler."

After ten minutes of reading off names, Zach was down to the one name everyone was waiting to hear. Because the small ranchers outnumbered the big ones, there were many who had not yet volunteered to make a visit.

"Well, gentlemen, just one name left on this sheet. Who will volunteer to visit Baxter Beaumont?"

Dead silence.

Zach looked around, searching faces. "Nobody wants to call on the Big Bull?"

Dead silence.

A smile worked its way across Zach's face. "Well, tell you what. I figured it would be like this, so my name's already written here beside Beaumont's."

One man stood up. "Zach, I'll go along with you."

"Me, too!" came another voice.

This brought an avalanche of volunteers.

Meadows raised his hands to call for silence. When the voices trailed off, he said, "I appreciate so many of you volunteering to go with me, but that wouldn't be wise. I'm afraid we'd raise Mr. Beaumont's hackles if more than one of us showed up on his doorstep. No, I'll go alone."

It was midmorning the next day when Zachary Meadows trotted his horse up to the imposing gate marked with a huge wrought iron square that contained two Bs. A pair of ranch hands stood in front of the gate, bearing rifles.

One of them stepped forward and said, "State your business, mister. Who are you?"

"A neighbor. I own a ranch over that way," Zach said, motioning with his head. "The *Diamond M*. My name's Zachary Meadows."

"And your business?"

"I'd like to see Mr. Beaumont."

"You mean *the* Mr. Beaumont? Not Cory or Mason?"

"Yes. Baxter Beaumont."

Lillian Beaumont was on the front porch of the huge ranch house with Joline. Together they were beating rugs draped over the porch railing. Joline looked up and saw the three riders trotting their direction.

"Mom…"

Lillian looked first at her daughter, then let her line of sight trail to the riders. "I'd say that's Zach Meadows, wouldn't you?"

"That's what I figured. Wantin' to see Daddy, I'd say."

"And your father won't lay out the welcome mat."

Lillian and Joline gave Zach Meadows a warm welcome as he rode up between the two ranch hands.

"This guy wants to see Mr. Beaumont, ma'am," said one.

Lillian smiled. "I believe that can be arranged."

Lillian ushered Zach down a long hallway toward the rear of the house. The door to Baxter Beaumont's den was open. Lillian stepped in ahead of Zach, who paused out in the hall. Beaumont was at his desk with a pile of papers in front of him. When he raised his head, his dark eyes flicked to his wife, then to Meadows. A frown followed.

"Baxter," Lillian said, "Zachary Meadows is here to see you."

"What is it, Zach?" Beaumont said with a scowl.

"Just need a few minutes of your time, sir, if you don't mind."

"Well, I'm busy, but come on in."

Lillian excused herself and left. Beaumont looked up at Meadows without a thought of offering him a chair.

"Well, what do you want?"

Zach brought him up to date on the harassment of the small ranchers. He told him of all the animals that had been killed and the buildings that had been burned, then listed the names of the families that had left the valley.

Beaumont's features remained like stone.

"And then there's poor Ted Sullivan," Zach said, watching Beaumont's eyes. "He'll never walk another step, or ride another horse, or brand another calf. The life he chose here in this valley is all over for him because he dared to stand up against some greedy skunks who did their best to drive him off his own land."

"So get to the point."

Zach leaned over and placed his palms on the desk. "The point is, Baxter, I'm here to ask for your help."

"*My* help?"

Zach told him about the meeting in Deer Lodge City.

Beaumont eased back in his chair and shook his head. "I can't spare any men. There's too much work to do on this ranch."

"The other big ranchers are promising to help us. Does this mean you don't care enough to join them? Could it be you're in favor of this harassment?"

Beaumont leaped to his feet, his face flushed beet-red, and bellowed, "Are you accusin' me of hirin' those masked riders?"

"No, not accusing you," Zach replied evenly. "But you do put a question in my mind when you won't even offer one man to help us put a stop to this."

The veins bulged in Baxter Beaumont's thick neck. "You *are* accusin' me! Get out! Get outta my house! Get off this ranch! Now!"

Lillian and Joline appeared at the door, eyes wide.

"Baxter," Lillian said, "what's going on?"

"This man has just accused me of bein' behind the gang that's been givin' the squatters a hard time, that's what!" He moved toward Zach and gave him a shove toward the door. "Out, I said! Out!"

Beaumont ushered Zach Meadows down the hall, cursing and

swearing at him. Lillian and Joline followed quietly, holding on to each other. When the two men reached the porch, Beaumont shouted at a group of ranch hands who sat their horses nearby to see to it that Meadows rode off the property immediately. Lillian and Joline stopped just inside the door and watched as Zach mounted his horse and rode away with the cowhands escorting him.

"Cal!" Beaumont called to one of his men who was passing the house. "Go find Cory and tell him I want to see him immediately!"

As the man scurried away, Lillian stepped onto the porch. "Baxter, what's Cory got to do with this?"

"Plenty! He's thinkin' of marryin' that Meadows girl. Well, he ain't gonna do it, not after the way her old man accused me just now!"

"Dear," said Lillian, laying a hand on his arm, "are you sure Zach accused you? Did he actually say that?"

"I don't care what he said, I know what he meant! He's one of your lowdown, hypocrite *Christians*. No son of mine is gonna marry his daughter!"

Lillian kept her voice level. "Baxter, you can't penalize Cory for what you think Zach was intimating."

"Just watch me!"

"But...none of this is Cory's fault. He and Sage are very much in love. They — "

"Bah!" Baxter marched into the house and down the hall. "Send Cory to my den when he gets here!" he called over his shoulder. Then the door slammed hard.

Mother and daughter were quickly in each other's arms. They stole away to the sewing room and prayed.

It was nearly an hour before Cory Beaumont stepped into the house. Lillian and Joline were there to meet him.

"What's up with Pa?" Cory asked. "Cal said Zach Meadows was here and Pa wanted to see me right away. Said Pa seemed to be upset."

Lillian was fighting tears. She could hardly speak. "Zach— Zach upset him. He— Your father will tell you, Cory. Go on and talk to him. Joline and I have been praying."

Cory hurried on down the hall and tapped on the den's door. "Pa, you wanted to see me?"

"Yes, come in!"

Stepping in, Cory saw his father seated at his desk, looking at him with burning eyes. He closed the door and quietly approached the desk.

"You are to break off your relationship with Sage as of now, Cory!" Baxter said. "I don't want to hear any more talk about marriage between the two of you. Do you understand me?"

"I understand what you're saying but…I want to know what happened to bring this on."

Baxter told Cory of his conversation with Zach Meadows.

"But Pa," Cory reasoned, "from what you're telling me, I think you've jumped to a conclusion. Maybe you need to rethink the whole—"

"I don't need to rethink nothin'. Meadows made his accusation, and no son of mine is going to marry that man's daughter."

"But you can't order me to break it off with Sage! I'm very much in love with her and—"

"This discussion is over!"

Voice low, Cory said calmly, "Pa, isn't this really about my being a Christian and planning to marry a Christian girl?"

Baxter was breathing hard, but he did not reply.

There was genuine love in Cory's voice as he said, "Pa, there's a war going on between you and the Lord Jesus Christ…and you're the one making the war. If you would just open your heart to Him, He would take all this turmoil away. You don't know the kind of peace and joy Jesus brings to a person's life until you let Him save you and wash away your sins in His blood. That's why He died on the cross, Pa...so He could keep you from going to hell and take you to heaven when you die. But you have to let Him. You have to—"

"Cory, that's enough! I've told you before, I don't want to hear that Jesus stuff! Now, you break it off with Sage like I told you. End of conversation."

"Pa, I'm not a child. You can't run my life anymore. I have a right to choose whom I marry. Sage is a wonderful girl. She's—"

"She's out of your life as of right now, and that's final! If you don't tell her, I will!"

"And what happens if I don't put her out of my life?"

"Then you are disinherited, fired as foreman of this ranch, and no longer welcome in this house."

Cory took a deep breath. "All right then...that's the way it is. I love Sage with everything that's in me. I will not give her up!"

Baxter was so angry, he couldn't speak.

"Pa, I have no desire to cause a rift between you and me," Cory said. "I love you, and I want only to honor you. But I am an adult, and you can no longer control my life."

"Get out!" Baxter screamed. "Get out of my sight and out of my house!"

The door swung open, and Lillian rushed in. Joline was on her mother's heels.

"Baxter!" Lillian gasped. "What on earth is all this shouting about?"

Footsteps were heard in the hall, and Mason appeared at the door, eyes wide.

"This...this son of yours has just been disinherited!" Baxter said. "He's fired as foreman of the ranch, and he's been told to get out of this house! He's a traitor to his own father, and he's no longer welcome here!"

Lillian stepped between Cory and Baxter and faced her husband. "Are you telling me that because Cory has refused your command to break it off with Sage, that makes him a traitor?"

Baxter swore. "It sure does!"

"But even if Zach Meadows was accusing you, that's no fault of Sage's...nor Cory's."

"There will be no more discussion on this matter, Lillian. The traitor, here, is to pack up his belongings and remove himself from this ranch immediately!"

"What did Meadows accuse you of, Pa?" Mason asked, moving in closer.

"Of hirin' those masked riders."

Mason sent a hot look at his brother. "And you'll still marry his daughter?"

"Sage can't help what her father does," Cory said.

"But she's still his daughter. Pa's right—you are a traitor."

A smile broke out on Baxter Beaumont's hard face. "You ought to listen to your little brother, Cory. He's got more good sense than you'll ever have. Now pack up your stuff and get out."

An hour later, Lillian and Joline stood on the porch and watched as Cory tied his horse behind one of the ranch wagons. Dave Nix would drive the wagon that bore Cory's belongings. Cory was sure the Meadows family would give him a place to stay until he could find a job. Dave would return with the wagon once he had delivered Cory to the *Diamond M*.

Tears were shed as Cory embraced and kissed his mother and sister. They agreed they would continue to pray hard for the salvation of Baxter and Mason. Cory said he would at least get to see his mother and sister at church, then he kissed them again and climbed into the wagon.

Mother and daughter held on to one another and wept as the wagon moved away.

The Meadows family welcomed Cory Beaumont when he told them what had happened between his father and himself. Zach immediately hired Cory as his ranch hand, saying he could live in the small bunkhouse that had recently been built. Zach told Cory he would become foreman of the *Diamond M* when the ranch grew to the place where more help was needed.

When Sage learned that Cory had refused to break off their relationship at his father's command, it made her love him more than ever, and she told him so in the presence of her parents.

Fred Vogel and A. J. Titus were perched high on the rim of the box canyon. The sun scorched the dry mountain land, and both men drank frequently from their canteens. They watched the shimmering heat waves on the southern horizon and the jagged bolts of heat lightning.

"I'd give a month's pay to see it rain," Vogel said.

"Yeah, me too," Titus said. "I know August is usually a dry month in Montana, but not this dry. What worries me is all that heat lightnin'. Dry as everything is, it sure could cause a bad fire."

"I don't even wanna think about it," Vogel said, taking another sip from his canteen. Suddenly his attention was drawn to a patchy shaded area in the distance to the southeast. "A. J.," he said, pointing, "see if you can tell what that is down there. I saw movement, I'm sure."

Titus brought up the binoculars he was wearing around his neck and turned the focus wheel until the area came clear. "Don't see anything."

"Well, somethin' moved. Might've been a cougar…maybe a deer."

"Or a mountain goat."

"Yeah. Or the law."

"Well, if it's the law, we have enough fire power to— "

"See it?"

"Yeah. It's a lone rider."

"Watch for some more behind him."

"I am, but there ain't no more. He's alone."

Vogel lowered the brim of his hat and strained to see the rider. "Well, for sure it ain't one of us. All of our boys are in the canyon… and we ain't expectin' no visitors."

"Since we ain't expectin' visitors, maybe we'd better get Wilson up here so's he can check the dude before he gets too close."

Ten minutes later, both Wilson and Wade Kyger were on Titus's side of the canyon's mouth, hunkering down. Wilson peered at the oncoming horse and rider through the glasses.

"I've got a funny feelin' runnin' up and down my spine," Wade said.

"You think it's Stranger?" Wilson asked.

"Wouldn't surprise me none."

"Well, if it's him," Fred Vogel said, "he's a dead man. He'll never get near you, Wade."

"I'd like to be the one to *make* him a dead man," Wade said.

Wilson continued to watch the rider through the glasses. After a few more minutes, he said, "It's a man dressed in black. White shirt. He's on a bay with white blaze and four white stockings."

"Lemme have those glasses!" Wade said.

Wilson relinquished them to his brother. Wade put them to his eyes, worked the focus wheel for a second, then sucked in a sharp breath. He lowered the binoculars and looked at Wilson. "It's him! It's Stranger!"

"You're sure?"

"Positive. That's the horse he's been ridin', and them's the clothes he wears. Black gunbelt, too. I can even make out the bone-colored handle on his gun."

Wilson took the glasses back and looked again at John Stranger. "We gotta get the rest of the boys up here. We'll give that dude a reception like he ain't never seen! Rate he's comin', he'll be right below us in ten minutes. A. J., get the rest of the boys up here. I want half of 'em on that side, and the other half on this side. We'll just catch Mr. John Stranger in a circle of fire!"

Wade Kyger laughed with glee as A. J. Titus scurried down into the canyon. He grabbed the binoculars from his brother and focused on the lone man astride the bay. "C'mon Stranger, you slimy snake! We've got a little surprise for you!"

In barely more than five minutes, ten men hunkered down amid the rocks atop the jutting walls that formed the canyon's mouth. Their repeating rifles were cocked.

"Okay, guys, when the nose of his horse crosses that patch of shade beneath those bushes down there, we'll let him have it."

"Wilson," said Wade, who was bent low beside him, "I want to fire the first shot."

"I think you deserve that honor," agreed the younger brother. "You boys hear that? Wade'll fire the first shot. Then we'll all have us a little fun."

Wade's whole body tingled as John Stranger drew near. He wiped his sweaty palms on his Levis as horse and rider approached the jaws of the canyon. Almost there. Just a few more yards. Then Wade's victim was in his sights.

"Good-bye, John Stranger." Wade held his breath…and squeezed the trigger. The rifle bucked in his hands.

"Yahoo-o!" Wade yelled when he saw the bullet punch a black hole in the white shirt.

Before the man-in-black could even fall from the saddle, a staccato of gunfire tore into him. The blaze-faced bay started to bolt, but went down in a heap as hot lead plowed into it.

As if they were in a shooting contest, the ten outlaws kept jacking cartridges into the chambers of their rifles and firing into the lifeless forms of horse and rider eighty feet below.

When every rifle had been emptied, Wade Kyger jumped to his feet and danced with glee atop the canyon's rim. Shaking his rifle in defiance, he shouted, "John Stranger is dead, and *I* killed him!"

CHAPTER

NINETEEN

O n Monday, August 15, Sheriff Mack Jensen entered Billings General Hospital just before noon. Betsy McCall greeted him with a smile.

"Good morning, Sheriff."

"Morning, Becky."

"You look like you're carrying the weight of the world on your shoulders."

"Close to it," he said. "I must talk to Nurse Baylor, but I need Dr. Hackman or Dr. Farner with me when I do it."

"Sounds serious."

"It is."

"Wait here and let me see what I can do."

In just a few minutes, Betsy returned. "I told Nurse Baylor you were here, Sheriff. She'll be able to see you in about five minutes. Dr. Farner is in surgery, but Dr. Hackman is free. He said to come on back to his office. Miss Baylor knows to meet you there."

Jensen thanked her and made his way to Dr. Glenn Hackman's office and tapped on the door. Hackman opened it and said, "Hello, Sheriff."

"Hello, Doc."

The doctor looked at him with some concern. "You look tired, Mack. You making sure you're getting enough rest?"

"Tired isn't the word, Doc. *Burdened* might be more appropriate."

Hackman pointed to a chair in front of his desk. "Please, sit down."

The sheriff lowered himself onto the chair as the doctor sat down behind his desk.

"Burdened," Hackman said, looking across the desk. "This has something to do with Breanna, I assume."

"Yes, sir, I—"

"Good morning, gentlemen," Breanna said as she passed through the open door. "Betsy said you wanted to talk to Dr. Hackman and me, Sheriff."

Both men rose to their feet. Hackman left his desk to close the door.

"Sit down, Breanna," he said.

"Well, I really need to talk to *you,* ma'am," Jensen said, "but it's of a nature that I requested it be in the presence of either Dr. Farner or Dr. Hackman."

Breanna's smile faded. She sat down and held a steady gaze on Jensen.

"What is it, Sheriff?"

Both men took their seats. Jensen's hands trembled slightly.

"Miss Breanna, I received a wire earlier this morning from Sheriff Lloyd Gross in Jefferson City." He cleared his throat nervously. "It seems that ranchers in the canyon country west of there heard gunfire in the afternoon on Friday. A whole lot of gunfire. They investigated and, after some time, found the body of a man at the bottom of a ravine, along with the man's dead horse."

Dr. Hackman watched Breanna closely.

"Well, ma'am," the sheriff continued, "the horse was a bay gelding with white blazed face and four white stockings. Sheriff Gross has the man's body at the local undertaker's. The dead man…ah…has a pair of twin scars on his right cheek. He's tall and dark and was wearing—"

Breanna closed her eyes and clenched her hands into fists. "No! No, Sheriff, it can't be! Not John!"

Dr. Hackman rounded the desk and laid a hand on Breanna's shoulder. "May I get you some water?"

She shook her head. "No, Doctor. Thank you."

Jensen spoke softly. "I'm sorry, ma'am. Sheriff Gross said the bodies had been dragged into the ravine from somewhere else. He doesn't know where. He asked if he should send John's body here. I wired him back and told him to do so. It'll be on the afternoon stage from Jeff City tomorrow."

Breanna's eyes had a faraway look as she said, "This can't be. It just can't be."

"Sheriff Gross believes John was ambushed by the Wilson Kyger gang," Jensen said. "Since John was trailing Wade Kyger toward Jeff City, Gross figures Wilson is hiding out in the area and may be responsible for some horrible crimes that've been committed there in the past few months. He thinks the gang set up the ambush for John, knowing he was after Wade."

"No. John can't be dead," Breanna said, still staring vacantly. "He can't be!"

The tears finally surfaced, and she lowered her head and began to sob.

Both men stood beside her, gripping her shoulders and occasionally offering words of sympathy and solace. Breanna wept for several minutes, then began to bring her emotions under control. Dr. Hackman handed her a cloth to use as a hanky.

All my dreams of a future with that wonderful man are gone, she thought as she wiped her tears. Lord, why? Why would You allow John and me to fall so deeply in love, then take him from me?

Dr. Hackman knelt in front of her. "I want you to take the rest of the day off—tomorrow, too. I'll send one of the nurses to your hotel to stay with you."

"That won't be necessary, Doctor," she said, sniffling. "I'll be all right."

"But you shouldn't be alone at a time like this."

"I'll be fine, Doctor. I have the Lord. He'll be there to comfort me."

"Not to belittle His help and presence, ma'am," Jensen said, "but sometimes we need help and comfort from mortal beings. My wife would be glad to come and spend the night with you. Or better yet…you could come to our house and stay."

"Thank you, Sheriff," Breanna said through a faint smile. "I appreciate your offer, but really, I'd like to just be alone."

"Okay. But I'll walk you to the hotel."

In her hotel room, Breanna wept and prayed. She was not angry toward God, nor bitter, but she told Him she did not understand. She opened her Bible and read in both the Old and New Testaments, then prayed some more. Eventually a warm, sweet peace flooded her soul. She told the Lord that even though she did not understand His ways, she would trust Him. She thanked Him for the peace that only He could give, and told Him she knew He never made mistakes. She would follow Him by faith and let Him work it out.

The next day, Sheriff Jensen knocked on Breanna's door at a quarter till three in the afternoon. The stage from Jefferson City was due in fifteen minutes. As they walked toward the Montana Stagelines office, Jensen asked how she was doing.

"Grieving, of course," she said, trying to smile, "and will be for a long time to come. But the Lord has given me the peace He speaks about in His Word…the kind that passes all understanding. Only God can give that kind. I can't explain it, Sheriff, but I can almost feel His strong arms around me."

"I'm glad," Jensen said.

Breanna and the sheriff were almost to the stagelines office when they saw the stagecoach coming toward them from the west end of the street. Breanna's heart leaped in her breast when she saw the coffin in the rack on top.

Chet O'Dell was waiting in front of the stage office with his hearse to take the coffin to the funeral parlor. The agent emerged from the office and met the passengers as Jensen enlisted some men on the boardwalk to help the driver and shotgunner take the coffin from the rack and place it in the hearse.

Jensen turned to Breanna, who stood looking at the hearse with tears in her eyes, and asked, "Would you like to view the body? I've made arrangements with Chet for you to do so at the funeral parlor if you want to."

She sniffed and nodded.

"All right. I'll walk you."

A short time later, Jensen led Breanna into the funeral parlor. O'Dell had told the sheriff he would place the coffin on a viewing table in the back room where Breanna could view the body in private, if she wished.

As the sheriff and Breanna headed for the rear of the building, the undertaker emerged from a small room and said, "The coffin is in there, ma'am. I have the lid off so you can see the body. I should warn you that it is a very unpleasant sight. The bullet holes, you understand."

"Yes," she said softly.

"Do you want me to go in with you?" Jensen asked.

"No. Please, I'd like to be alone with...with him. But thank you."

Jensen nodded, walked her to the door, then leaned against the wall as Breanna entered the room.

Three lanterns burned in the room to make plenty of light. Breanna closed the door and turned her gaze to the coffin. She could not see John's head from where she stood, but she could see his arms folded over his chest. And the bullet holes fringed with dried blood.

Her knees felt watery, and her mouth went dry. She took a deep breath, braced herself, and stepped up to the coffin.

When her gaze fell on his face, her hand went to her mouth and a tiny mew came from her throat. She brushed tears from her eyes to get a clearer look.

"Sheriff!" she cried. "Sheriff, come here!"

Jensen burst into the room. "What is it?"

"It's not John! *It's not John!*"

"What?" he gasped, moving up beside her.

"This isn't John," Breanna said. "It has to be Rick Dane!"

"You're just tired and upset, Miss Breanna. This has to be John. Rick Dane's being picked up by the sheriff in Cheyenne City right now."

Breanna reached out and brushed her thumb across the scarred cheek of the dead man. The scars smeared.

Breanna looked toward heaven, tears flooding her eyes. "Thank You, Lord! My John is still alive! Oh, thank You!"

"I don't understand this at all," said the sheriff, shaking his head. "I'm going to wire Marshal Ashley in Miles City and tell him Rick Dane has turned up dead. Something was wrong with the information he wired me on Friday."

Breanna wiped the tears from her cheeks with the back of her hand. "Let me know what you find out, will you?"

"I will."

It was late afternoon when Sheriff Jensen sat down with Breanna in a small room at the hospital.

"This is really something, Miss Breanna," he said, shaking his head. "I wired Marshal Ashley, and he wired me back almost immediately saying that he sent me no wire on Friday."

"He didn't?"

"Turns out that Rick Dane's cousin, Emerson Wheeler, who

owns the Miles City Playhouse, had received a wire from Dane telling him that a man owed him money—which, of course, had to be Wade Kyger. Dane told Wheeler the man was on his way across Montana, and he was going after him to collect the money." Jensen pulled a lengthy telegram from his shirt pocket and unfolded it. "So here's what happened. Dane knew that his cousin was a close friend of Miles City's Western Union agent, Clyde Patton. Dane asked Wheeler to ask Patton to intercept any wires that came in concerning him, and to let Wheeler see them. Wheeler knew what to do."

"So we have some skullduggery going on here."

Jensen held up the telegram. "Says here that when my wire arrived on Friday, Wheeler intercepted it. Knowing Dane wouldn't want to be followed, he made up the 'stagecoach to Cheyenne City and train to San Francisco' story. Both Wheeler and Patton have been arrested."

"Good."

"And then I had to solve the other mystery."

"What's that?"

"The fact that Dane was riding a horse identical to the one John bought from Fred Ryal. Well, I rode out to the *Flying R Ranch* and talked to Fred. Just as I thought, Dane had come in and bought a bay gelding with the same markings. Fred thought the man was John Stranger and asked him why he wanted a second one. Dane gave him some cock-and-bull story about the first one breaking a leg and having to shoot it."

"Sheriff…"

"Yes'm?"

"It just struck me…John's still on his way toward Jefferson City. Shouldn't we wire Sheriff Gross and let him know that the dead man he sent us was Rick Dane…and to be on the lookout for John? He needs to know he's been cleared with the law here in Billings."

Mack Jensen grinned. "I've already done that, Miss Breanna. I got a wire right back, and Sheriff Gross assured me he'd be watching for him. He was glad to hear that the body he sent us belonged to Rick Dane, not John Stranger."

As John Stranger approached Jefferson City, he decided to move about town and see if he could pick up any hints from the locals about the hideout's location. He wished the letter had given more information than that the hideout was somewhere in the mountains around Jefferson City.

Stranger rode slowly down the town's main thoroughfare. His eye caught the sign above the sheriff's office, but he told himself if the local law knew anything about the outlaw hideout, the gang would already be in custody. The best places to learn the kind of information he needed were the saloons.

Just as he was riding past the sheriff's office, Stranger saw a man wearing a badge come out the door. The man was suddenly staring at him.

"Hey, John Stranger!" the lawman yelled.

John's skin prickled and his heart thudded against his rib cage. Mack Jensen must've wired lawmen all over Montana to be on the lookout for me! he thought. There was nothing he could do. To spur the horse would get him a bullet in the back. There was no way he would draw his gun on the lawman. He must find a way to escape this sheriff as he had Mack Jensen.

Stranger pulled the horse's head around, expecting to find himself looking down the muzzle of the sheriff's gun. Instead, the man was smiling, and his gun was still in its holster.

"Mr. Stranger!" called the lawman, hurrying toward him. "I'm Sheriff Lloyd Gross, and I have a message for you!"

"A message for me? How—?"

"Come to my office. I'll explain it there."

Stranger dismounted and led the bay to the hitch rail in front of the sheriff's office. As they stepped inside together, Gross said, "Sit down, sir."

Stranger eased onto a straight-backed wooden chair in front of the cluttered desk, and Gross sat down behind it. "I'm sure I've got you completely puzzled, haven't I?"

"You might say that."

"Well, Mr. Stranger, I've been in contact with Sheriff Mack Jensen down in Billings the past few days, and I've got some good news for you."

"Good news, I can use. Been having quite a bit of the other kind lately."

Lloyd Gross carefully laid out the whole story, including Rick Dane's masquerade as John Stranger and his death by ambush in the mountains west of Jefferson City. Gross said that he now knew why Dane was killed. The Kyger gang was somewhere up in that canyon country, and they mistook Dane for Stranger. John was relieved to know that he had been cleared in the eyes of the law and of the people in Billings.

"You truly are the bearer of good news, Sheriff," John said.

"Now, let me tell you something ironic," Gross said, leaning forward with his elbows on the desk. "I've been trying to locate you through Chief Duvall, but he's headed to Kansas City and I couldn't get ahold of him. And now here you are, right out of the blue!"

"Why were you trying to find me?"

Gross told him about the masked riders and their harassment of the small ranchers. He told him of Ted Sullivan being paralyzed, of animals being killed, of ranch houses and outbuildings being burned, and of the many families who had already pulled up stakes and fled.

The sheriff shared his conviction that wealthy rancher Baxter Beaumont, the Big Bull of Deer Lodge Valley, was paying the gang to drive off the small ranchers. He hastened to add, however, that he had no proof. It was just gut instinct.

Gross also told about the posses he and Sheriff Hank Hawkins had formed and of their fruitless efforts to catch the gang red-handed. They needed John Stranger's help.

"You will help me track down that bunch, won't you?" Gross said, looking the tall man straight in the eye.

"Be more than glad to. Now, where was Dane ambushed? The hideout must be somewhere nearby."

"Not necessarily. We found the bodies of Dane and his horse in a ravine, but they were taken there from wherever the ambush took place. The horse had been dragged quite a ways, from the looks of it. And for that matter, the ambush could have happened a long way from the hideout."

A wire was sent back to Sheriff Jensen and Breanna Baylor, telling them that John Stranger was going to help Sheriff Gross track down the Kyger brothers and Wilson's gang. Deputy Jerry Zeller was at the office when Stranger and the sheriff returned from sending the telegram, and Gross filled him in on the situation.

"Sheriff," Stranger said, "I'm going to start by asking questions on the street and in the saloons. It's amazing what people don't realize they've seen or heard until they're asked something that triggers their memory. One way or another, I'll find that hideout."

"Too bad we couldn't squeeze the location of the hideout out of Jake Ransom, Sheriff," Zeller said. "Sure would've made things a lot easier."

"Who's Jake Ransom?" Stranger asked.

"Part of Wilson Kyger's gang," Gross said. "I arrested him on good hard evidence, and he's now serving a long sentence in the Territorial Prison at Deer Lodge City."

"But he refused to tell you how to find the hideout, eh?"

"Even when he was told he would get a reduced sentence, he flat refused to tell us anything. We tried everything we could short of torture to squeeze it out of him."

"Yeah," said Zeller, chuckling. "I wanted to beat it out of him, but ol' softy here wouldn't let me."

Stranger smiled at Zeller, then said, "Sheriff, I think I can get the information you want out of this Ransom fellow."

Jake Ransom lay dozing on his cot in midafternoon at the Montana Territorial Prison. He heard footsteps and voices in the corridor, followed by the rattle of a key in his cell door.

He was lying on his back with an arm resting over his eyes. He moved the arm and saw a man being shoved through the open cell door by two guards. The man stumbled slightly, then wheeled around as the key rattled in the door again.

"You think you're pretty tough, don't you?" one of the guards snapped at him. "Well, we'll see how tough you are after you've been in here for twenty years! New cellmate for you, Jake. Wake up and give him a warm welcome!"

Jake sat up, eyeing the man he would now share his cell with. For some unexplained reason, his other cellmate had been taken to another cellblock earlier that morning.

The new prisoner watched the guards walk away and mumbled in a low voice, "Twenty years. Hah! I won't be in here twenty days, dog face."

Jake stood up. "Dog face, eh? Good name for that stinkin' guard." He extended his right hand. "I'm Jake Ransom."

The dark-complected man nodded and shook Jake's hand. He eyed the cot Ransom was not using and sat down.

Jake eased down on his cot, peered at his new cellmate for a moment, then asked, "How'd you get those scars on your face? They're shaped exactly alike, like maybe somebody had you tied down and carved 'em in your skin."

The man did not reply.

Jake studied him a moment longer, then said, "I told you my name, but I still don't know yours."

"John."

"First name or last?"

"First."

"What's your last name?"

"Claxton."

"What you in for?"

"You been in prison long, Jake?"

"No."

"Man needs to learn that in a place like this, you can ask too many questions."

"Sorry. You said a few minutes ago that you wouldn't be in here twenty days. You plannin' to make a break?"

"Yep. No prison I've ever been in has been able to hold me."

"Really?" said Ransom, his eyes lighting up.

"Really. And this one won't hold me, either."

"How soon you gonna make your break?"

"Not long. Just gotta look the place over a little."

"How about takin' me with you?"

"I don't need any excess baggage when I go," he said, shaking his head. "I just want to get out and lay my hands on plenty of money."

Jake laughed. "My sentiments exactly. Listen, John…if you take me with you, I can cross your palms with plenty of money. I belong to a gang. We've made lots of it. I mean lots. If you let me break out with you, I'll take you to my boss, Wilson Kyger. On my recommendation, he'll take you into the gang."

Stranger raised his eyebrows. "Wilson Kyger. Is he any kin to Wade Kyger?"

"Brothers."

"Well, what do you know? I've admired Wade from a distance for a long time. Is Wilson as tough and shrewd as Wade?"

"Every bit."

"So where's this gang located?"

"Right here in Montana. In fact, not more'n three hours' ride from Deer Lodge City. Take us about nine or ten hours to walk it."

"In the mountains?"

"Yeah. They changed locations a couple weeks ago. Reason I know is, my best friend in the gang is a fella named Clete Sarno. He put on a disguise and came to visit me just yesterday. The hideout's now in a box canyon with a real narrow entrance. From what Clete said, it's a virtual fort. Any lawmen come around there, they'll die."

"You know how to find this canyon?"

"Sure. Clete told me exactly where it is."

"And you really think Wilson will take me in?"

"If I tell him it was you who broke me outta here, he'll welcome you with open arms. And by the way. Clete told me Wade is with 'em now. You'll get to meet him."

"How come he's with Wilson's gang?"

"Clete didn't tell me a lot about it, but it seems some mysterious dude who moves like an Indian and works like a devil took Wade's gang apart."

"One man?"

"Yeah. I told you, he works like a devil. Or should I say worked like a devil. Clete told me he's dead."

"What happened?"

"Remember I said if any lawmen ever try to get into the canyon, they'll die? Well, this dude was after Wade. Tracked him to the canyon and got himself blown to pieces. I mean, they cut him to shreds after Wade put the first bullet right in his heart."

"You know this guy's name?"

"Well, he had the same first name you do. But his last name's really weird. It's *Stranger.*"

"Stranger, huh? I've heard of him before. Glad to hear he's dead. From what I've heard, he could make life pretty miserable for men like you and me."

"I ain't never heard of him before. Anyway, you gonna take me with you?"

"You bet I will. It'll take me a day or two to get the layout of this place, but once I do, you and I will be long gone."

"Great!"

John Stranger and Jake Ransom talked for some time about the Wilson Kyger gang. Ransom told him they had been hired by Baxter Beaumont to drive the small ranchers out of the valley. He spiced up his invitation for John to join the gang by telling him the kind of money Beaumont was going to pay them when the job was finished.

At 5:00 o'clock the supper bell clanged. Tough-looking guards let the prisoners out of their cells and ushered them to the mess hall. Stranger stood in line behind Jake Ransom, who was introducing him to the men close by.

Stranger's gaze strayed to the men who stood in the long line behind him when suddenly he recognized Jason Vennard, whom he had captured in Denver when the outlaw put a gun to Benny Cumberland's head. Stranger recalled that Vennard was wanted in Montana. The man was less than twenty feet from him.

Jason Vennard recognized Stranger at the same time. There was a thin glitter of hatred in Vennard's eyes as he said, "Hey! I know you!"

TWENTY

---◆◆◆---

J ohn Stranger dropped his tin plate and cup and bolted for Jason Vennard. Vennard braced himself, dropping his own plate and cup with a clatter, and swung at his attacker. Stranger dodged the punch and landed a hard blow to Vennard's jaw. Men scattered as Stranger's punch sent Vennard backpedaling into a nearby table. The table went over with a crash, and Vennard dropped to the floor.

Guards came running.

Stranger grabbed Vennard by the shirt and jerked him to a standing position. Just before the first guard reached him, he unleashed a blow that sounded like a flat rock dropping into mud when it connected with Vennard's jaw. The outlaw went down hard, unconscious.

John Stranger had met all the guards, a few at a time, in the prison superintendent's office that morning. The one who reached him first was Herb Berry.

"Don't move, Claxton," Berry snarled, raising his club, "or I'll split your skull!"

The clamor of voices gave enough cover for Stranger to say to Berry, "Get him out of here before he comes to. You'll have to put him in isolation. He knows me."

Berry shouted to his fellow guards, "Pick Vennard up and take him to isolation, men! I'll deal with Claxton myself!" He looked around at the convicts. "Okay, excitement's over! Pick that table up and go on with your supper!"

Jake Ransom watched as Herb Berry escorted John Claxton out of the mess hall. Jake's countenance fell. No doubt John would be thrown in solitary, too. No telling how long he would be in there. The escape would have to wait.

Jake Ransom stirred on his cot when he heard the outer door to the cell block clatter and swing open. It was nearly midnight, and the prisoners had been asleep for two hours. Footsteps echoed in the corridor, and by the light that flowed from a lantern that hung on the wall outside the cell, Jake recognized Herb Berry and Lester Fordham as they stopped in front of his barred door.

"Hey, you guards!" came a voice from a cell adjacent to Ransom's. "What's the idea of makin' all this noise in the middle of the night?"

"Shut up, Jenkins!" Fordham said. "Seems Ransom here told a bunch of stuff to that new clown Claxton today. We just want to find out what he told him."

"I didn't tell him nothin'! What's he talkin' about?"

"Come along, Jake!" Berry said. "You can do your talking in the office."

Berry and Fordham ushered Ransom down the corridors toward the offices. Jake was cursing himself for having told Claxton about his link to the Wilson Kyger gang…and that he knew where the hideout was.

When the guards ushered Ransom into the office, John Claxton was there. Ransom glared at him.

"Do you want to tell him, John, or should I?" Berry said, closing the door.

"Go ahead."

"Tell me *what?*"

"Look, Jake," Berry said, "Les and I are old friends of John's from the Civil War. He saved our hides at the second Bull Run battle."

"So what."

"So, John was telling us about you offering to get him into the Kyger gang, and he's telling us the kind of money he's gonna get his hands on. This true, what you told him?"

"Why should I tell you?"

"Well, John has agreed to share some of it with us. How about you? If we let you escape, will you give us your word to put ten thousand dollars in our hands? Between you, I mean."

Jake smiled at John.

"I told you I'd get us out of here," John said.

Jake looked at Berry. "Whatever John says is fair to give you, I'll go along with it. But exactly how is this escape gonna work?"

"I won't bore you with the details. We'll handle our end in here. You two just ride hard and fast once you're out of here!"

Jake's eyes lit up. "You mean now?"

"Yes, now."

With the help of the two guards, Jake and John stole two horses from the prison corral, and just after one in the morning, the two of them were riding hard toward the mountains.

John Stranger wanted to arrive at the hideout before dawn. Since Wade Kyger was there, he didn't want to be recognized until he could get the drop on the gang. He would have to play it all by ear. He prayed for God's help.

They neared the small town of Garrison, and Stranger asked if Jake knew if it had a gun shop. When Jake said it did, Stranger told him they should break into the shop and arm themselves. Jake agreed, and they broke in through a window in the alley.

They took rifles, revolvers, gunbelts, and ammunition. When Jake wasn't looking, Stranger dropped enough money to more than pay for what they were taking and for the broken window.

Riding on, they soon veered east among the towering peaks dappled with moonlight. Scattered clouds floated in the sky overhead.

John Stranger knew that Wade Kyger thought he was dead. He could hardly wait for the moment when Wade would see his face.

The vague light of dawn was in the eastern sky as the two riders approached the narrow mouth of the box canyon. Stranger was glad it was no lighter when he saw the two figures standing atop the towering walls. Jake had told him that Clete Sarno said there would be two guards at the mouth of the canyon.

They reined in as one of the guards shouted down, "Hold it right there! Who are you, and what's your business?"

"Hey, Fred, it's me! Jake!"

"Jake!" Fred Vogel exclaimed in disbelief. "How'd you get out?"

"Long story. I'll tell you about it over breakfast!"

"Who's that with you?" Vogel asked.

"He's part of the story—the *main* part! Name's John Claxton."

"Well, let me be the first to welcome you, John," Vogel said.

"And I'll be the second!" said Bill Arkin, the other guard. "Come on in. We'll meet you about two hundred feet inside. We're supposed to be relieved of guard duty in about an hour. Won't hurt to leave our posts for that long."

The faint light of dawn was not enough to reveal John Stranger's face as they met up with Arkin and Vogel inside the canyon and dismounted. He kept his hat tilted low. His nerves were strung tight, and he was praying hard.

As they walked deeper into the canyon, Arkin said, "You

won't get to see Wilson and Wade, or A. J., Clete, and Leo for a couple of days, Jake."

"Where'd they go?"

"Up north to a town called Red Mountain."

"Oh, yeah, I know where that is. About sixty miles or so from here, if I remember right."

"Yep. Wilson found out an old friend is up there. Wanted to see if he'd like to join the gang. Wade and the others went along for the ride. Should be back in two-three days. So the squatters are gettin' a little reprieve right now."

"Clete was tellin' me a bunch more have pulled out."

"Yeah. Baxter's real happy about it."

"Clete was also tellin' me about the two new guys Wilson took on."

"George Dartt and Clem Landon. Good guys."

"So that leaves how many here at present?" Stranger asked.

"Five, before you and Jake showed up."

Lantern light was showing in the cabin as it came into view. Tendrils of smoke trailed skyward from the chimney.

"Looks like the boys are up and at 'em," Vogel said.

George Dartt and Clem Landon were sitting on the front porch of the cabin, smoking cigarettes. The sky was growing brighter by the minute.

As they drew up, Arkin said, "George...Clem...you've heard us talk a lot about Jake Ransom. Well, this is him—he busted outta prison! And this is his friend, John Claxton."

Roy Coulter appeared at the door. "Breakfast is ready!" he said.

"Hey, Roy!" Fred Vogel said. "Come out and see who's here!"

Coulter stepped out on the porch. When he saw the familiar form of Jake Ransom, he laughed and said, "Hey, Jake! What a surprise! How'd you get out of prison?"

"I'll tell you all about it over breakfast," Jake said.

The brightening dawn put enough light on John Stranger's

face for Coulter to see the scars on his right cheek. His jaw slacked and he gasped.

"Who's this? Jake, what're you doin' travelin' with a dead man!"

As Coulter spoke, his hand went for his gun. Stranger's weapon was out and cocked before Coulter could clear leather.

"Hold it right there!" he said.

Stranger quickly took a step back so he could cover all of them. He commanded them to drop their gunbelts and put their hands over their heads.

"It is him!" Bill Arkin said, unbuckling his gunbelt.

"Who?" Jake demanded.

"John Stranger!" Vogel said. "We killed him! How can this be?"

Jake Ransom was so stunned, it had not yet dawned on him that his friend, John Claxton, meant for him to drop his gunbelt too.

"Jake! Drop it!" Stranger said.

"What's goin' on here?" Jake said.

"You're all going with me to Sheriff Gross's office, that's what's going on!"

Jake unbuckled his gunbelt with shaky hands. "Who *are* you? You can't be John Stranger—he's dead! And there ain't no such thing as a ghost."

"Lets' just say I'm Justice, and I'm going to see that you get your due."

"You rat! You tricked me!" Jake Ransom felt a savage compulsion to lunge for the man holding the gun and tear him to pieces.

"Let's get the saddle and bridles on, boys," Stranger said. "We're all going for a ride."

"Without breakfast?" Coulter spat.

"Without breakfast."

By nine o'clock that morning, the gang members were in jail.
Sheriff Lloyd Gross was smiling as he returned to the office and
tossed the cell door keys on his desk. Deputy Jerry Zeller was on his
heels. John Stranger was exchanging the revolver and gunbelt he
had acquired in Garrison for his regular ones that he had left at
Gross's office.

"I'd like to go with you and see the face of that Big Bull when
you arrest him, Sheriff," Stranger said as he tightened the buckle on
the gunbelt, "but it's important that I head for Red Mountain right
away."

"I understand, John. You've provided me enough evidence to
lock Baxter Beaumont up for a long time. I'm sure the judge and
jury will see it that way, too."

John Stranger rode northward in the tinder-dry forests of the Rocky
Mountains. He was astride the same horse the prison had provided
for his escape. He loved this part of Montana...its big sky and lonely
stretches of meadows and forests, its rugged rock formations and
deep canyons that scarred the land. All of this surrounded by jagged
peaks that seemed almost to touch heaven.

Miles fell behind him as he worked his way across brown-
grassed open stretches, over ridges and saddles, and through the
dense woods. He was awed by a pair of bald eagles racing each other
high overhead. Soon they swooped down and disappeared over a
rocky ridge. He saw a pack of wolves, like gray ghosts, slink through
the trees off to his right.

Part of the time his thoughts were on the remainder of the
Kyger gang, whom he was determined to see behind bars. At other
times he thought of Breanna and of how very much he loved her.

And at times his mind went to his faithful and gallant horse, Ebony. He missed his big friend and companion. He hoped Ebony would soon be fully recovered.

The streams in the mountains were running low. Every so often, Stranger stopped to water the horse, take a good drink for himself, and fill his canteen.

It was midafternoon when horse and rider were rounding a massive rock formation, and the gelding nickered nervously and began to tremble. Just as Stranger was about to pull rein, wondering what kind of danger the horse sensed, they came upon a black she-bear licking a bleeding leg of her cub.

The bear reared up on her hind legs and roared. Before Stranger could wheel the horse to retreat, the bear charged. The gelding whinnied, shied, and bolted away in terror. As Stranger was trying to bring him under control, the horse stumbled and fell. Stranger went sailing out of the saddle and landed in a patch of bushes. He scrambled to his feet and looked back at the bear, but she had returned to her cub.

The horse was trying to get up, but his right foreleg was bent beneath him. Stranger bent down, patted his neck, and said, "Here, boy. Let me get a look at that leg."

It took only a second to see that the leg was broken. The horse nickered as Stranger stood up and said, "I'm sorry, boy, but this is the end of the road for you."

He pulled the rifle from its saddleboot, jacked a cartridge into the chamber, and put the horse out of its misery. He removed the saddlebags and draped them over his shoulder, then hung the canteen around his neck and started walking, rifle-in-hand. Stranger could not remember where the nearest ranch might be, but he figured to run onto one as he continued north toward Red Mountain.

The afternoon passed, and the sun went down. No sign of a ranch so far. It was almost dark when Stranger came upon a small creek that had been reduced to little more than a trickle. He filled his canteen and drank from it as he ate hardtack and beef jerky.

Soon a full moon came over the peaks to the east, spraying its silver hue everywhere. A soft breeze came up, rustling the limbs of the giant pines that surrounded him. For a while, Stranger stood on the bank of the creek, smelling the night smells and listening to the night sounds.

He took his Bible from the saddlebags, angled its pages toward the moon, and read for about an hour. Then using the saddlebags as a pillow, he stretched out his weary body and closed his eyes. He was about to fall asleep when he heard the distant, mournful howl of a wolf. Seconds later, the wolf's mate answered from the opposite direction. Twice he heard the scream of a cougar, then all was quiet.

Again, he was about to fall asleep when he heard the shrill whinny of a horse. The sound was close. He sat up and looked around. He heard the whinny again. Then he saw him—a magnificent black stallion, wild and beautiful.

He was skylined on top of a craggy bluff with the full moon behind him. He stood with his regal head held high and ears forward, looking at Stranger. The breeze fluffed his mane and tail. He bobbed his head, snorted, and pawed the earth.

Stranger rose to his feet. He thought of the time when God said to Job, "Hast thou given the horse strength? hast thou clothed his neck with thunder? Canst thou make him afraid as a grasshopper? the glory of his nostrils is terrible. He paweth in the valley, and rejoiceth in his strength."

The stallion snorted again, snuffed up the breeze in his nostrils, then reared up, pawing the air with his forelegs. When all four hooves were on solid ground again, he whinnied, darted off the bluff, and vanished from sight.

"Marvelous, Lord," John said to his God. "What an animal!"

John Stranger sat on the creek bank and ate a cold breakfast at dawn. There was a rustle in the air behind him, and he turned to see a magnificent bald eagle silhouetted above him against the brightening sky. The eagle ejected a cry, then shot downward on the sweep of the morning wind, swooped close to the earth, then flapping its great wings, headed for massive cliffs to the west.

John picked up his saddlebags and canteen and proceeded north. The sun had been up about an hour when he saw a few horses moving through the pines on a rise above him. They moved too swiftly for him to get a good look, and he instantly thought of the Kyger gang.

He hurried and hid himself behind a giant pine, then peered around it. The horses were dropping down from the heights and coming his way. He was about to work the lever of his rifle when the horses broke through a heavy stand of trees some sixty yards from him. They were led by a large black stallion and bore no riders.

It was the same stallion he had seen the night before.

The stallion hauled up some thirty yards away, and the dozen-and-a-half wild horses that followed him skidded to a halt. The black looked straight at Stranger, laid his ears back, and reared up, whinnying and pawing the air.

"I sure would like to borrow your back for a while, big boy," Stranger said. "I need a ride out of here."

The stallion shook his head, flopping his mane, and whinnied shrilly once more. He reared, stomped down hard, then wheeled and galloped toward the forest with his herd behind him. Within seconds, they were swallowed by the tall timber.

Stranger draped the saddlebags over his shoulder once again and plodded on. The parched grass crackled beneath his feet. He stopped and filled his canteen at a trickling stream, then pushed on.

Later in the afternoon, Stranger still had not caught sight of a ranch. He stopped to mop his brow with a bandanna and once again caught a glimpse of the stallion moving amongst the timber on higher ground. The stallion paused for a moment, looked down at the lone traveler, then snorted, tossed his head, and disappeared.

A few seconds later, Stranger saw a large male cougar slinking through the trees where he had last seen the stallion. The cat hissed and passed from view.

Stranger pressed on. The sun was about to disappear behind the peaks to the west when Stranger found himself moving through dense timber. Soon he broke out from the trees into a slender meadow divided by a small meandering brook. Down a gradual slope to the north was a narrow gap between trees that led to more open country. He estimated the gap to be some six or seven miles from where he stood.

Bone-tired, he decided to spend the night there in the meadow. He halted at the brook bank, eased the saddlebags and canteen to the ground, and laid down the rifle. At the same moment he saw the black stallion break out of the woods and come prancing toward him with marvelous ease and swiftness, head and tail erect. He came within some twenty yards, then swerved and climbed to a rock ledge above where Stranger stood and looked down at him.

This time he was close enough for Stranger to get a good look at him, and John marveled at what he saw. He was a giant of a horse, all muscle, grace, and power. Everything about him spoke of unbroken spirit...from the keen intelligence of his expressive eyes and the flare of his nostrils to the way he held his head and swished his tail. He stood like a monarch and looked down at John Stranger.

John was wondering where the rest of the wild herd was when without warning, the male cougar he had seen earlier sprang over the rocks above the stallion and landed on his back. The horse screamed, reared, and bucked, but the cougar's claws were buried deep. The horse bolted and charged down from the lofty spot, kicking and bucking violently.

Stranger grabbed his rifle and jacked a cartridge into firing position. The stallion was on his level now, bucking in a tight circle. Stranger shouldered the rifle, took careful aim, and squeezed the trigger. The .44 caliber slug struck the cougar like a sledgehammer, knocking him off the horse's back. The cat hit the rocky ground with a painful screech, rolled over, and struggled to get up.

Stranger quickly positioned himself for the best angle, took aim between the cat's eyes, and fired. The cougar fell dead.

Surprisingly, the stallion had not run away. Stranger laid the rifle down, displayed open hands, and moved toward the stallion slowly, saying in a low voice, "Hold it, big boy. Your back is bleeding. I'd like to take a look at it."

The big black nickered but did not move.

When John was within ten feet of him, he was glad to see that the cougar's claws had not ripped the flesh. He moved closer.

"Hey, boy, those scratches have got to hurt. If you'll let me, I'll bathe them with some cool water."

The stallion gave a soft nicker, bobbed his head, and nickered again. Stranger felt if he could just lay one hand on the animal, he could show him he meant no harm, then he would go after his canteen.

"That's a good boy," he said, stretching out one hand. "Let me just—"

Suddenly the big black shied, wheeled, and galloped away, vanishing into the forest.

Stranger paused at the dead cougar, then walked to the stream bank. Removing his hat, he knelt down and began washing his face and head in the cool water. He scooped water into his cupped hands and was drinking his fill when he heard hoofbeats behind him. He turned on his knees, smiled, and stood up.

The stallion came within ten feet of him, bobbed his head, and nickered.

Stranger smiled again. "I think you and I might just become friends, big guy."

TWENTY-ONE

J ohn Stranger picked up his canteen and slowly rose to his feet. The stallion did a soft nicker, flicking his ears.

John held out an empty hand, palm-up, and said in a soothing tone, "I know those scratches hurt, boy. If you'll just trust me, I can make them feel better."

Still the big black did not move.

Stranger continued to talk to the horse as he stepped closer. When he could reach the muzzle with his extended hand, he carefully stroked it. "See, big guy? I wouldn't hurt you. I'm your friend."

The horse remained as Stranger patted his head, then his neck. "Okay, boy," he said, lifting the canteen over his back, "let's see how this feels."

Carefully, John poured the cool water on the scratches at both the withers and the loins. The blood had already begun to dry, for which Stranger was thankful. He washed it off with his free hand as he poured the water. When he had emptied the canteen, he took a step back and laid the canteen on the ground.

He moved up close again, patted the horse's neck, and said softly, "I'm sure you've never had a man on your back, but you sort of owe me. How about it, pal? I'd like a ride at least to a ranch where I can buy a horse. I've got a gang of outlaws to bring in."

Still the stallion did not move.

"Okay," Stranger said, "let's see just what kind of friends we really are."

When Stranger gripped the long mane and bent his knees to swing aboard, the big black shied and bolted away into the timber.

"Well, I guess we're not so close, are we? I should've known better but…oh well, it was worth a try."

Stranger settled down on the bank of the small stream and ate a cold supper. As dusk settled over the Montana Rockies, he stood up and scanned the area. His line of sight took in the dark line of trees that fringed the slender meadow on both sides, then he looked northward to the narrow break in the forest that led to more open country. He hoped that out there in those wider spaces he would find a ranch.

When darkness fell, he spent time in prayer, especially asking God to watch over Breanna and keep her from harm. Then he wearily laid down, put his head on the saddlebags, and soon was asleep.

He had been asleep about an hour when he was jerked awake by the vicious crack of lightning that split the sky directly above him. It was so close he felt the heat of its flash. Sitting up, he saw another bolt a hundred yards to the east, then another struck just beyond that. The whole sky seemed alive with daggers.

After an hour or so, the fiery display began to subside, and soon all was quiet and dark again. Drowsiness overtook him, and once again he fell asleep.

Sometime during the night, John was awakened when the wind began to pick up. He stirred briefly, then rolled from one side to the other and was asleep again.

It was just before dawn when he was awakened by the smell of smoke on the wind. His eyes fluttered and suddenly popped open with a start. The sky was filled with orange-colored smoke. He sat up and looked around. The forest behind him to the south was ablaze, as was the timber on both sides of the meadow.

On his feet quickly, John saw that the only place the fire was not burning was in the gap between the timber to the north. The wind, however, was forcing the flames further that direction, narrowing the gap and driving the fire closer to him on the other three sides. A circle of fire was fast closing in on him!

John Stranger's only hope of escape was the gap six or seven miles to the north. He hated to leave the saddlebags with his Bible and food in them, but he dare not try to take them. Hitching at his gunbelt, he ran toward the gap as fast as he could. In his heart, he knew if the wind continued to close the gap at the same rate it was at the moment, he would never make it.

John Stranger was in a race with wind and flame. There were miles of meadow and forest, dry as powder, ahead of him. He thought of Breanna as he ran. He must live! They must have their lives together as they had planned. For the love of Breanna, he ran.

The heat was oppressive. Billows of smoke swirled across the open meadow. The air seemed too thick to breathe and it burned his lungs.

"Too far!" he said hoarsely. "I'll never make it! Dear Lord in heaven...it looks like...I'm coming home! Take care...of my precious Breanna!"

Suddenly, off to his right, Stranger saw the black stallion come charging down an area of solid rock. His herd of wild horses came behind him, whinnying in terror. The horses must have thought they were in a safe place, then as the heat pressed down on them, realized they would have to get out.

The stallion saw John running toward him and skidded to a halt. The herd galloped past their leader, heading for the gap at the end of the meadow. The stallion watched John for a moment, then reared, pawed the air, and galloped after his frightened herd.

"No! Come back! Come back! You're my only chance!"

John Stranger ran on. The smoke swirled in the wind like a fog around him, stealing the stallion and his galloping herd from sight. He knew he would not make it now. But he would die trying.

Suddenly, through the roar of wind and fire, Stranger heard a thrilling sound...the rapid, rhythmic beat of hooves.

Through the thick smoke ahead of him, Stranger saw a phantom-like form. The black stallion came thundering through the smoke, eyes bulging. He stopped in front of Stranger, whinnying shrilly.

Without hesitation, Stranger stepped up to the horse's left side, grabbed a fistful of mane, and swung aboard. "Okay, big boy, you're my only chance! Let's ride!"

The horse whinnied, then plunged straight north into a heavy cloud of smoke. John's eyes smarted and stung, but a moment later, he could see the gap at the end of the meadow. He judged it to be less than five miles away. Though it was narrower than when he last saw it, it was still open.

Off to his left, he saw flames run up a nearby pine tree, which exploded as if its trunk were loaded with gunpowder.

Stranger bent low, gripping the long mane. The fierce wind seemed determined to close off their escape. The great stallion sensed it, too, and found the strength to add more speed. Horse and rider flew faster than the wind.

The tips of the blazing pines at the sides of the gap were bent before the wind. Flames were building across the small opening just as horse and rider thundered through and into the open area beyond the burning forest.

"Thank You, Lord!" John shouted as the stallion slowed but continued to move away from the fire.

John looked back. Behind him the fire flared and the smoke rolled ever upward. It was an unearthly spectacle.

When they were about a mile from the fire, John was suddenly struck with a different scent than smoke. Looking skyward, he realized that it was not smoke above him but rain clouds! And cool drops were striking his face.

He patted the horse's neck and tugged on the mane. "Whoa, boy!"

The stallion came to a halt. At the same moment, his wild herd appeared, galloping over a rocky rise. All eighteen horses bunched up and came to a stop a few feet away. The stallion greeted them with a shrill whinny.

The rain was falling harder every minute. Stranger slid off the horse's back, patted him, and said, "Thank you, big fella. I saved your hide, now you've saved mine. I'll never forget you. And I've thought of a good name to remember you by—Chance. Seems fitting since you were my last-chance escape from death."

Chance nickered and bobbed his head as if he understood. He turned his head toward the herd, then looked back at Stranger, whose hatbrim was now dripping with rain.

John stroked Chance's neck and patted his shoulder. "I know it's time for you to lead your herd, ol' boy. Go on. I'll be fine now."

The stallion nickered, wheeled, and galloped toward a rocky ridge eastward with his herd trailing behind. Through the driving rain, Stranger watched the big black horse lead his herd over the ridge and disappear.

The rain came hard and heavy as Stranger plodded northward, but he didn't mind. It felt good to be wet and cool.

At a small ranch a few miles due north of where John Stranger last saw Chance, the Kyger brothers, along with A. J. Titus, Leo Davey, and Clete Sarno, had taken refuge to wait for the distant forest fire to burn itself out.

The outlaws had been at the ranch since the middle of the night when they had kicked open the parlor door, bowled their way inside, and dragged Harvey Smith and his wife, Elsa, out of bed. Elsa had been forced to cook them breakfast, and Harvey bore purple welts on his face from refusing to obey their commands.

It was three hours past breakfast, and the outlaws continued to lounge around in the parlor. Harvey and Elsa sat together on the couch. Elsa was pale and frightened, and Harvey held her hands in his own, telling her that the men would soon be gone.

Rain spattered the windows as A. J. Titus grinned at the woman and said, "You just listen to your husband, lady. He had to learn the hard way that we don't take no guff offa nobody. We're men of our word, though. Like Wilson told you, if you'll just be good and do what we tell you, as soon as the rain stops, we'll be on our way. Rain as hard as this is bound to put out that forest fire."

As he spoke, Titus left his chair and walked to the front door, which stood open. There were several places where the rain was dripping through the porch roof onto the porch floor.

A. J. leaned against the door frame, folded his arms, and watched the rain. After a while, he said over his shoulder, "Looks like it's easin' up. Maybe we'll be leavin' real soon, folks."

Elsa looked at her husband and mouthed, *I hope so.*

The rain had become a drizzle as John Stranger neared the barn, corral, and ranch house. There were several horses in the corral. John would offer the rancher a fair price for whatever one he would sell and be on his way toward Red Mountain. No doubt the Kygers and their henchmen would be on their way south by now.

Inside the ranch house, the aroma of hot food floated from the kitchen to the parlor. The outlaws had Elsa cooking another meal for them before they pulled out. Leo Davey was in the kitchen to watch her, while the rest of them kept Harvey in the parlor.

Titus left his chair again, strolled to the open door, and leaned against the door frame. Outside, the clouds were thinning and the sun was peeping through, its warmth causing mists to rise from the wet earth.

The outlaws talked about the man they had gone to see in Red Mountain. Wilson had been very upset when they arrived there and learned that his old friend had been shot and killed the day before in a saloon fight.

Harvey Smith sat alone on the couch, wishing he could get to his double-barreled twelve-gauge shotgun, which stood in a corner of the closet next to the front door. If he could just get the drop on them…

Wade Kyger looked across the room at his brother and said, "I figure as soon as the ol' girl's got lunch fixed, we oughtta just go ahead and do it, don't you, Wilson?"

"Do what?" Harvey asked.

"Take care of you and the ol' lady," Wade said, a sneer on his face.

"What do you mean?"

"Do I have to draw you a picture, pal? Look, we don't need you puttin' the law on our tails. If you and your ol' lady are dead, you can't do that, now can you?"

Smith's mouth went dry. "But…your brother said if Elsa and I did what you told us, as soon as the rain stopped, you'd be on your way." He gestured toward the door. "And this man said you were men of your word."

Wilson laughed, but his eyes were without a trace of mirth. "Oh, we are. Soon as we've had lunch, we'll be on our way. I didn't say what condition you and the missus would be in when we go."

Smith's features lost color. "Now, look. Elsa and I have done nothing to you. How can you be so— "

"Shut up!" A. J. Titus hissed.

Every eye turned to Titus, who was staring into the mists toward the south.

"What's the matter?" Wilson asked.

Still peering hard, Titus said, "I…I thought I saw somethin' out th— Yeah, I did! We got company!"

There was a rumble of boots on the wooden floor as the

Kyger brothers and Clete Sarno hurried to the door. Looking past A. J.'s shoulder, they saw a tall, dark figure coming their way through the gray mists. He wore a white shirt and flat-crowned black hat.

Titus blinked and swallowed hard. "Wade…"

"It *can't* be him!" Wade said. "I killed him! It's his ghost! He's come back to get me!"

Wade Kyger turned and ran in blind panic through the kitchen and out the back door.

Leo Davey came on the run, shouting, "What's the matter with Wade?"

No answer came, for Wilson had whipped out his gun and blared, "Dead men don't come back, boys! It's Stranger, all right! Let's get him!"

John Stranger was within forty yards of the ranch house when he heard the shouting and saw men moving about at the front door. Just before the first man came charging out, gun blazing, Stranger heard the man say his name.

Stranger leaped out of the line of fire and dived behind a buckboard as the rest of the gang blazed away at him. Bullets struck the bed and wheels of the buckboard, chewing wood and ricocheting off the metal rims of the wheels.

Stranger fired back, dropping Clete Sarno. A second shot missed, but a third shot from Stranger's Peacemaker put a slug through Leo Davey's heart. Both outlaws lay sprawled in the yard.

Wilson Kyger and A. J. Titus both dashed for the protection of a massive oak tree that stood in the yard, firing toward the buckboard as they ran. Stranger's bullets chewed bark as the two men ducked behind the oak. Hunkering behind the old vehicle, Stranger fired his sixth shot. While he was reloading, Wilson shouted, "Let's rush him, A. J.!"

Suddenly a voice cut the air behind them. "You ain't rushin' nobody! Drop those guns!"

The heads of both outlaws came around. Harvey Smith was on the edge of the porch with a double-barreled twelve gauge trained on them.

Titus swore and brought his gun to bear. The shotgun roared, and the outlaw took the full charge in the chest. The impact of it lifted him off his feet and flopped him on his back.

Stranger was coming on the run as Wilson Kyger threw his gun down and lifted his hands. Smith stepped off the porch with blue-white smoke trailing from the right barrel of the shotgun.

"I guess you've got better sense than your pal had," he said to Wilson. Elsa Smith was at the door looking on.

As Stranger drew up, Smith said, "Are you really John Stranger, mister?"

"The one and only," Stranger said.

"I've heard of you."

"Well, I'm much obliged to you, sir." Stranger looked around at the three dead men, then pinned Wilson with icy gray eyes. "There's one missing here. Where's your brother?"

Wilson licked his lips. "How do you know I'm Wade's brother?"

"Same distasteful family resemblance. Where is he?"

"He ran out the back door when he saw you comin', Mr. Stranger," Smith said. "Said you were Stranger's ghost come back to get him. Funny thing. Wade was talkin' about your dead body not more'n a couple hours before you showed up. By the way, my name's Harvey Smith. That's my wife Elsa on the porch."

Stranger smiled at Elsa and touched his hatbrim. "Nice to meet you, ma'am. And nice to meet you, Mr. Smith. Keep this no-good covered while I find his brother."

"You can count on it," Smith said. "He had just told me they were gonna kill Elsa and me when that dead guy over there saw you comin'."

"Well, their killing days are over, Mr. Smith. Don't let him move a whisker."

"If he does, I'll give him a shave with some hot buckshot."

Stranger hurried toward the back of the house, carefully scrutinizing his surroundings. When he reached the backyard, he could hear someone sobbing and whimpering. The sound was coming from the woodshed, which stood near the toolshed a few steps from the back porch.

Stranger eased up to the door of the woodshed and found it standing open two or three inches. He pulled it all the way open and saw Wade Kyger lying on the floor in a fetal position. There was stark terror in his tear-filled eyes as he looked up and saw the tall, dark man. His entire body trembled.

"No-o!" Wade screamed. "No, please! I'm sorry I killed you! I'm sorry! Don't take me with you! I don't wanna go to wherever you've been!"

"I haven't been where you think I've been, Wade," said Stranger, bending down to relieve the outlaw of his revolver. "I'm not a ghost, and I haven't been to the regions of the dead. I'm taking you to Sheriff Gross's jail. The judge will take it from there."

Harvey Smith still had Wilson Kyger standing like a statue with his hands over his head when Stranger ushered Wade Kyger around the corner of the house.

While Stranger and Harvey Smith tied the outlaws' hands behind their backs, Stranger explained why he was trailing them and said he was eager to get them to Jefferson City so they could stand trial. Smith volunteered to bury the three dead ones. Stranger thanked him and said he would take one of the dead outlaws' horses, and the Kyger brothers could ride their own.

"Wilson, how'd he live through it?" Wade said, still trembling. "I know I shot him through the heart. And the rest of you shot him over and over. How'd he live through it?"

Wilson looked at Stranger. "Yeah, how did you?"

Stranger grinned furtively. "One of life's little mysteries."

With the outlaws bound and in their saddles, John Stranger rode Clete Sarno's horse as they headed due south. When they neared the blackened area where the fire had raged, Stranger's attention was drawn to the sound of thundering hooves off to the east. Moments later, he saw Chance come over a rocky ridge, followed by his herd.

The herd stopped on the crest of the ridge, but Chance galloped toward Stranger with a high-pitched whinny. Stranger pulled rein and swung from the saddle as Chance drew up.

"Sit tight," he said to the outlaws.

The stallion bobbed his head and nickered as the tall man reached up and patted his neck.

"Howdy, boy," he said softly. "To what do I owe this special favor?" Stranger rubbed the horse's long face. "Thank you, Chance, for saving my life. I'm glad the Lord sent you when I needed you. And even if there'd been no fire, I'm glad we met and became friends. I'll never forget you."

With that, Stranger turned and mounted again, a lump in his throat. As they moved out, Stranger expected to see Chance return to his herd and gallop away. Instead, the great stallion nickered and began to follow. The herd remained on the crest of the ridge.

When Chance had followed for half a mile, Stranger drew rein and dismounted again. He saw the herd looking on from the now distant ridge as he approached the big black. Chance nickered affectionately, shaking his head.

Stranger patted the long, muscular neck, ruffled the mane, and said, "Chance, you belong in the wild. It's in your blood. I don't think a horse with your make-up would be satisfied in captivity. Besides...those stallions and mares need you." Stranger hugged Chance's neck. "Go back, big guy. They're waiting."

Chance nickered, stomped his forelegs, wheeled, and galloped away. Stranger stood and watched as the gallant horse raced back to the crest of the ridge and joined his herd. He reared, pawed the air, and whinnied a final farewell. Then he disappeared over the ridge with the wild bunch following.

John Stranger walked to his mount, still fighting the lump in his throat and blinking against the tears that flooded his eyes.

CHAPTER

TWENTY-TWO

Deputy Sheriff Jerry Zeller carried meal trays into the cellblock at noon and distributed them to the prisoners. Jake Ransom and Bill Arkin shared a cell, as did Fred Vogel and Roy Coulter, and George Dartt and Clem Landon. Baxter Beaumont was alone in his. As usual, the Kyger bunch complained about the food.

"Listen, there's nothing wrong with this food," Zeller told them. "It comes from the café across the street, and that's one of the best in town. The problem's not the food, it's where you're eating it. And whose fault is it that you're behind bars?"

"John Stranger's," Roy Coulter said, and the other Kyger men agreed. Baxter Beaumont remained silent, only staring at his food.

"What do you mean it's John Stranger's fault?" Zeller said. "You wouldn't be in here if you hadn't broken the law! You want to see whose fault it is that you're in here, Roy? Go take a look in that mirror!" Zeller said, pointing to the mirror above the wash basin in Coulter's cell.

The prisoners mumbled curses and groaned, then began gobbling the food they said they didn't like.

Zeller turned to leave and noticed Beaumont wasn't eating. "I know it might not be as good as your wife's cooking, Baxter, but you'd better enjoy it. The cooking at the Montana Territorial Prison's a lot worse than this. Ask Jake."

Beaumont gave him a bland look and went on staring at his food. Zeller shrugged and left the cellblock. As he entered the office, his boss was just coming in from the street.

"Get the prisoners fed?" Sheriff Lloyd Gross asked.

"They're wolfing it down right now…after telling me how bad it is. That is, except for Baxter."

"Baxter's been in his turtle shell ever since we arrested him," Gross said. "It's got to be hard to go from being a rich hotshot rancher one minute to a jailbird the next."

"Should've thought of that when he hired the gang," Zeller said.

"Yeah. Tell you who I feel sorry for—his family. Poor Lillian. She tried so hard to believe he was telling her the truth."

"Cory and Joline, too."

"You think Mason knew it all along?" Gross asked.

"He'll never admit it, but he and his daddy are awfully close. I can't believe Mason didn't know."

"Well, I hope the kid'll learn from seeing his father go to prison. I'd hate to see him turn out bad."

Lloyd Gross's attention was drawn to three riders pulling up at the hitchrail in front of the office. He chuckled and said, "Well, Jerry, look what we've got out there!"

Both lawmen hurried out the door to greet John Stranger, who had the Kyger brothers bound and in tow. Stranger helped Wade off his horse, and Zeller helped Wilson.

"So what about the rest of them?" Gross asked.

"Dead."

Gross nodded. "Well, I'd say justice has been served."

Wade and Wilson gave the sheriff malevolent looks as they were ushered through the office and down the corridor to the cellblock. Shock showed in the eyes of the other prisoners when they looked up and saw the two brothers being led into the cellblock.

"Look who we have here, boys!" Gross said. "I believe you all know each other."

No one spoke. The Kyger brothers were given a cell together, and Stranger and Zeller untied their wrists.

"Well, what a relief to have this mess cleared up," Gross said. "The circuit judge will be here day after tomorrow, John. Baxter'll have his trial. Can't say how it might turn out for him. Probably at least ten years at Deer Lodge. Ransom will go back there with more years added on for escapin'. And as for the rest of these no-goods, they all have murder raps hangin' over their heads. I'm sure Judge Larkin will sentence them to hang."

A dead silence prevailed in the cellblock.

Gross turned to Zeller as the Kygers' door clanked shut. "Jerry, I guess you'd better get some lunch for these two. John, how about I buy you lunch at the café across the street? You hungry?"

Stranger grinned. "I'll take you up on that."

Gross stepped to Beaumont's cell and noticed he had not touched his food. "Myrna said they'll be here about two o'clock, Baxter."

Beaumont looked up, nodded, and said, "Thanks."

"Okay, John," Gross said, "let's go."

The Mountain View Café was full, but a man and woman were just leaving their table as Stranger and Gross walked in. One of the café's two waitresses welcomed the sheriff, saying she would clean off the table. Two minutes later, Gross and Stranger were seated and enjoying cups of coffee. They talked about the forest fire and the welcome rain before giving the waitress their order.

"John, there's no way I can thank you properly for cleanin' up that gang," Gross said.

"Don't have to, Sheriff. Just glad I could help. It's gratifying to know the world's better off with that bunch out of business."

"I wish we could put all the outlaws out of business," Gross said with conviction.

Stranger grinned. "But, Sheriff, if there weren't any bad guys, you'd be out of a job."

Gross laughed. "Can't argue with that, John. But if I could guarantee the world no more criminals, I'd gladly do somethin' else for a livin'."

"I'm sure you would."

Soon their meal was on the table. While some people gawked, Stranger bowed his head and thanked the Lord for the food.

As they began to eat, Gross looked at his friend with a glint in his eye and said, "I…ah…I've got a little somethin' to tell you, John."

"By the look in your eye, I'd say you've been holding out on me."

"Well, sorta. I just wanted to get all this other business taken care of before I give you some real good news."

"Real good news?"

Gross grinned impishly. "Well, three days ago I met this real pretty lady, and—"

"Sheriff! What did your wife say about that?"

"Hear me out, will you? I've got a story to tell, and it's good news for your ears, not mine."

"Sorry. Proceed."

"Well, you see, this pretty little nurse came in on the stage from Billings on Saturday and—"

"Are you telling me that Breanna's here?"

Gross shrugged, cocked his head, and grinned. "Yes."

"Well, where is she?"

"First let me tell you why she's here. She came in on the stage and marched herself right here to my office. Told me who she was and of her relationship to you. Explained about her job at the hospital in Billings."

"Mm-hmm."

"Told me it was time to return to Denver, but she came here instead. Said she wired her sponsoring doctor in Denver and told him she was coming to Jeff City to wait for you. She didn't want to go home till she'd seen you and knew you were all right."

"Bless her," John said. "She's some kind of lady. So which hotel is she staying in?"

"Neither. You see, I was walkin' her to the Claymore Hotel, carryin' her baggage for her, and while we were walkin', I was tellin' her about what Wade Kyger and his gang had been doin' to the small ranchers in these two counties. I told her about so many pullin' up stakes and all...and I told her about Ted Sullivan bein' paralyzed. When she heard that, she said she wanted to meet Ted and Myrna."

"Sounds like my gal."

"Well, we checked her into the hotel, then I took her out to meet the Sullivans. Guess what."

"What?"

"Your Breanna offered to teach Myrna how to care for Ted, and right away the Sullivans asked her to stay with them. So yours truly had to come back to town, check Miss Baylor out of the Claymore, and take her baggage out to the Sullivan place."

Stranger laughed. "Maybe that's the kind of thing you'd do if there weren't any bad guys. You'd make a good delivery boy."

"Thanks a lot. Anyway, she's stayin' with the Sullivans till you show up."

"Well, if you'll tell me how to find the place, I'll ride on out there soon as we finish here."

"You won't have to."

"Hmm?"

"You heard me tell Beaumont that Myrna said they'd be in town about two o'clock."

"Yes."

"Well, Baxter Beaumont is a broken man, John. He's showing real remorse for his crimes. He knows it's his fault that Ted Sullivan is paralyzed. He wants to see Ted, so Myrna and Breanna are bringing him to the jail."

Stranger swung his gaze to the clock on the café wall. "Ten after one. Well, let's get this food down, Sheriff. I want to be there to meet Breanna when she gets here."

Both lawmen and John Stranger were sitting in the sheriff's office talking when the Sullivan wagon hauled to a stop outside. Breanna was at the reins, and Myrna was seated beside her. Ted lay on a cot in the wagon bed.

John dashed out the door with Gross and Zeller right behind him. Breanna saw him immediately.

"John!" she cried, smiling. "O John, you're here!" He hurried up to the wagon and helped her down. "I'm so glad you're all right," she said as they embraced.

Breanna took John by the hand and introduced him to Myrna, then to Ted. Jerry Zeller took Ted's wheelchair out of the wagon, and John picked Ted up and carried him into the office. Jerry sat the wheelchair down, and John placed Ted in it. Myrna and Breanna were there to brace Ted up and make him as comfortable as possible. He smiled and thanked them for their help.

"Jerry and I will bring Baxter in here," the sheriff said. "We'll be right back."

Breanna's eyes were shining as she took John's hand and said, "I assume Sheriff Gross told you why I'm here, and why I'm staying with Ted and Myrna."

"He did. And I'm very happy about it."

Ted sat with his back flat against the back of the wheelchair and his arms resting on the arm supports. He wore a brace to hold his head erect. "Myrna and I have both heard of you, Mr. Stranger," he said. "And—"

"*John,*" corrected the tall man. "Friends of Breanna's are friends of mine…and friends aren't formal with each other."

"All right, John. Anyway, we've heard of you for several years, and we knew before we met Breanna that you're not only good at ending the careers of outlaws, but you're a born-again preacher of the gospel. We're both very honored to meet you."

Myrna nodded her assent. "And we love our little nurse very much!"

John smiled at Breanna. "I can understand that, Myrna. I love her a little bit myself."

"Only a little bit?" Breanna asked.

"Well, maybe a little bit more than a little bit."

Ted and Myrna both laughed.

Footsteps were heard in the corridor, and the lawmen came through the door with a handcuffed Baxter Beaumont preceding them. Beaumont's face was gray and his eyes downcast. The ladies took off their bonnets as Baxter was seated on a chair, facing Ted. Breanna moved to where John stood, and Myrna took her place beside her husband.

Baxter Beaumont was somber. He adjusted himself nervously on the chair and cleared his throat.

"Ah...Ted, I...I want to tell you how sorry I am for what happened to you. I ain't gonna throw the blame on anybody but myself. I wanted to run you people out of the valley. I wanted more for Baxter Beaumont."

There was a silent moment, then he said, "Ted, I want you to know that those men I hired never meant to kill you. They had strict orders from me never to take a life. They were only trying to frighten you. The man who—well, no sense coverin' for anybody now—Jake Ransom just flat didn't cut that rope thin enough."

There was another silent moment. Baxter leaned forward on his chair. His eyes moistened.

"Ted, I...I'm asking you to forgive me. I don't deserve it. By all rights, you oughtta have somebody take me out and break *my* neck. But then, you're not the kind who'd do that."

"As a Christian," Ted said, "I could never do a thing like that."

The mention of the word *Christian* unsettled Baxter

Beaumont momentarily. He took a deep breath, then said, "No matter what the law does to me, Ted, I'll never have a day's peace or a decent night's rest unless I have your forgiveness."

"You have it, Baxter. I forgive you."

The moisture in Beaumont's eyes threatened to spill down his cheeks. He raised his shackled hands and wiped the tears away. His voice quavered as he said, "Thank you, Ted. I don't know how you can find it in your heart to forgive me, but thank you."

"There's only one way I can forgive you, Baxter," Ted said. "It's because I've been forgiven for mountains of sins I've committed against God. I obtained that forgiveness through His only Son, the Lord Jesus Christ. Baxter, Jesus died for you as much as He did for me. I've forgiven you for what you did to me, but you need God's forgiveness even more."

Baxter Beaumont was staring at the floor. He let a few silent seconds pass, then rose to his feet, looked at Ted Sullivan through a film of tears, and said, "Thank you for meeting with me, Ted. And more than anything, thank you for forgiving me."

"Better think on what I just told you," Ted said.

Beaumont gave a nod, then turned and headed for the corridor door. Jerry Zeller followed him.

"Well!" Myrna said. "I've got some shopping to do. Breanna, I know you'd like to spend some time with Mr. Stra—with John. Why don't I do my shopping and come back here in an hour or so?"

"That's fine."

"And then John can come home with us for supper," Myrna said.

"Sounds good," Stranger said. "I'll take you up on it."

Myrna bent over her husband. "Honey, would you like to wait here or ride along in the wagon?"

"I'll go with you if somebody'll put me back in the wagon."

Stranger carried Ted to the wagon, and Sheriff Gross followed with the wheelchair. When Ted was settled on the cot, Myrna thanked them, then said to Breanna, "See you in about an hour."

"Well, I've gotta get over to the telegraph office and wire Sheriff Hawkins," Gross said. "Gotta let him know that John has put an end to the Kyger threat."

John helped Myrna into the wagon seat as the sheriff hurried down the boardwalk. Just as Myrna was picking up the reins, a rider drew up in front of the sheriff's office and dismounted.

"Mason Beaumont," Myrna said in a low voice. "Baxter's youngest son."

Jerry Zeller was coming out the door. Mason hurried by him and vanished inside.

"I've never known anyone more hardened to the gospel than those two," Myrna said. She then told John and Breanna how harsh Baxter had been to the rest of the family when they became Christians and how Baxter had disinherited his son Cory and run him off the ranch when he refused to break off his romance with Sage Meadows, a Christian girl from a strong Christian ranch family.

"Well, you two enjoy some time together," said Myrna, firming up on the reins. "Ted and I will see you later."

"Breanna," John said. "Do you have your Bible with you?"

"I have my small one here in my purse," she said. "Do you need it?"

"Yes. The Holy Spirit wants me to go talk to Baxter right now. His boy can run away if he doesn't want to hear it, but Baxter can't go anywhere."

Breanna handed the Bible to John and said, "I'll be praying."

"*We'll* be praying," Myrna said. "Shopping can wait. Ted, Breanna, and I will have a prayer meeting right here at the wagon."

Sage Meadows had just spent a few minutes with her father and Cory Beaumont at the *Diamond M* barn. She was heading toward the house when she saw a wagon barreling up the road. It took only a few seconds for her to recognize Lillian Beaumont at the reins and Joline beside her. Sage saw her mother come out onto the porch and study the oncoming vehicle.

Wanda called to her daughter. "It's Lillian and Joline, Sage. I wonder what's happened. They seem in a hurry to get here."

Sage broke into a run, stepped up on the porch, and looked toward the bounding wagon. "We're about to find out."

Lillian slowed the team before reaching the house, then drew them to a halt at the porch. Concern was evident on the faces of both mother and daughter. Steve Meadows emerged from inside the house.

Lillian looked at Wanda and said, "Could we have a prayer meeting?"

"Well, of course."

"Let me help you down," Steve said. He helped Lillian down first, and she stepped up on the porch while he helped Joline.

"Mason and I just had a real fight...an argument, I mean," Lillian said. "He left the house, cursing me, riding for town." She burst into tears.

Joline hurried to her mother and put an arm around her shoulder. Wanda sent Steve to bring Zach and Cory, then took Lillian and Joline inside.

Moments later, Lillian told everyone that at lunch, Mason had blown up because she had prayed for his salvation while thanking God for the food. He angrily told her he was happy believing what his father had taught him, and he hated "this Jesus stuff." He stormed out of the house, swearing, saying he was going to go see his father.

Cory said he could see the Lord answering prayer. The conviction of the Holy Spirit does upset lost sinners. Zach suggested that they ask the Lord to make both Mason and Baxter so miserable that they would turn to the Lord.

They discussed for a moment the shame that had come to the Beaumont family since Baxter's arrest. Sage said she knew it had been hard for Lillian, Joline, and Cory to deal with Baxter's crime, but she felt the Lord would use it for His glory in the end.

All agreed, then went to prayer.

At the Jefferson County Jail, Baxter Beaumont sat on a chair close to the bars, looking at his youngest son. Tears filled his eyes. Neither was aware that John Stranger was standing in the corridor listening to their conversation. John had halted before entering the cellblock because he had heard Baxter weeping.

"I've got to think this whole thing over, son," Baxter said. "Lately I've been thinkin' that your mother, Cory, and Joline may have the right thing after all."

Mason shook his head and ran shaky fingers through his hair. "Pa, I don't get it. All these years you've taught me that this Jesus stuff is a bunch of bunk! Now you're tellin' me you may have been wrong?"

"Yeah. That's what I'm tellin' you."

"But you always said the Bible was just a book of myths and fairy tales…that it wasn't true. Why all of a sudden do you think it might be true?"

"Somethin' your mother asked me when she visited me here the second day I was in. She wanted to know if I'd ever found one thing in the Bible that'd been proven to be untrue. When I said I hadn't, she started listin' off a bunch of things it says that nobody can argue with. *I* couldn't argue with it."

"Like what?"

"Well, she showed me where it said that whatever kind of seed a man puts in the ground, that same thing will come up. I can't quote it exactly, but it's somethin' like that."

"You mean, 'Be not deceived; God is not mocked: for whatsoever a man soweth, that shall he also reap'?"

Both Beaumonts looked up at the tall, dark man as he entered

259

the cellblock carrying Breanna's Bible.

"Yeah, that's it," Baxter said.

"Hard to argue with that one, isn't it?" Stranger said.

"Can't. It's a fact."

"Who're you?" Mason asked.

"His name's John Stranger, son. He's the one who broke up Wilson's gang."

"Oh, so it's his fault you're in here."

"No, Mason, it's not his fault. The fault's all mine."

"The Scripture I just quoted is Galatians 6:7, Baxter," said John, thumbing through Breanna's Bible. "Let me show you one akin to it that's just as true. I believe you'll agree." When he found Numbers 32:23, John pushed the open Bible through the bars. "See where my finger is?"

"Yeah."

"Read it to me."

Baxter squinted at the page. "'Ye have sinned against the LORD: and be sure your sin will find you out.'"

"Is that true or not, Baxter?"

Baxter bit his lower lip. "It's true. Of course it's true."

Stranger looked at the youth. "Is it true, Mason?"

"I guess so," he said.

"How about it, boys?" Stranger asked, looking around at the other prisoners. "Did your sin find you out?"

Nobody answered.

John turned back to Baxter and Mason and, using passages from the Bible, gave them both a clear explanation of the good news that Jesus Christ had shed His blood to take away their sins and to redeem their souls. He could see the Holy Spirit using the Word of God to break down Baxter's resistance.

"If you'll call on Him, believing what I just showed you is true, He'll forgive you and save you, Baxter," Stranger said.

Baxter Beaumont smiled. "See, son? Your mother's been right all along."

Mason Beaumont's heart seemed to flutter in his chest. Tears surfaced. "Yes, Pa."

The many months of witness, and John Stranger's apt use of the Scripture coupled with the power of the Spirit of God, were enough to break both father and son down. They opened their hearts to Jesus and called on Him to save them.

TWENTY-THREE

B reanna Baylor was sitting in the seat of the Sullivan wagon beside Myrna. They had finished praying, and the Sullivans were asking questions about John Stranger, whom Ted had labeled the "Mysterious Man of the West," when Stranger and Mason Beaumont emerged from the sheriff's office.

The beam on young Mason's face told the story.

Breanna smiled and said, "Look at that face!"

"Mason, you know the Sullivans," Stranger said as they drew up to the wagon. "I'd like to introduce you to my fiancée, Miss Breanna Baylor."

"It's a pleasure to meet you, Miss Baylor," Mason said, smiling. "Nice to see you, Mr. and Mrs. Sullivan." His eyes still showed a trace of the tears he had shed inside the jail.

"These people are Christians, Mason, and while I was in there talking to you and your father, they were out here praying. You want to tell them?"

Mason's eyes shone with fresh tears. "Pa and I both opened our hearts to Jesus," he said with a quaver in his voice.

Breanna and the Sullivans rejoiced together, praising the Lord for answered prayer.

Ted asked John if he would mind taking him to Baxter, and

Myrna, Breanna, and Mason went along. There were happy moments in the cellblock as Baxter's Christian friends shared in the jubilation while the prisoners looked on dumbfounded.

Before they left, Baxter looked through the bars at Mason and said, "Son, go tell your mother, Cory, and Joline, will you? And tell them I want to see them as soon as possible."

"I will, Pa. I'll go right now."

John and Mason rode their horses while Breanna drove the Sullivan wagon. Myrna rode in the wagon bed with Ted. When they arrived at the *Box Double B,* one of the ranch hands told them that Lillian and Joline had gone to the Meadows ranch.

A half hour later, they rode onto the *Diamond M.* Mason's heart drummed his rib cage as they drew up beside his mother's wagon. John left the saddle and stood beside the wagon next to Breanna. Mason dismounted and had just stepped onto the porch when Zach Meadows appeared at the open door.

"Mr. Meadows," Mason said, "I'd like...to talk to my mother and sister if I may. And Cory, if he's here."

"They're all here, son," Zach said. He turned and called into the house, "Lillian, Mason's here!"

It took only seconds for everyone in the house to appear at the door. Zach stepped aside, allowing Lillian to step onto the porch.

Tears filled Mason's eyes as he moved closer and said, "Mom, I'm sorry for the way I treated you today...and for the way I've treated you and Joline and Cory ever since you became Christians. I...I came to tell you that, but even more, I came to tell you that Pa and I just became Christians, too."

It took a brief moment for Mason's words to filter into the minds of all who stood listening at the door. When they finally struck home, Lillian choked up and wrapped her arms around her son. They clung to each other and wept. Cory left Sage's side, took his sister by the hand, and they embraced both Lillian and Mason. Everyone was crying.

Finally, Mason turned and introduced his family and the Meadows to John Stranger and Breanna Baylor, then told them how John had come into the jail and led his father and him to the Lord. There was much rejoicing.

When things had settled down, Mason said, "Mom, Pa asked that you, Cory, and Joline come and see him as soon as you can."

"We'll go right now!" she said.

For the ride to the Sullivan ranch, John Stranger tied his horse behind the wagon and held the reins. Breanna sat beside him.

"How about I fill you in on how the Kyger gang had its fall?" John said, holding the team to a leisurely pace.

"Oh, good!" said Myrna from the wagon bed. "May Ted and I listen too?"

"Be my guests," John said, smiling over his shoulder. He took Breanna's hand. "You heard about the big forest fire north of here, I assume?"

"Yes. I knew you were somewhere up there, so I rattled heaven's gates with prayer."

"Well, the Lord was listening. Let me tell you about a big black horse He sent to save me from that fire..."

Circuit Judge Caleb Larkin arrived on schedule. The first trial held was for the Kyger brothers and their gang. Since Jake Ransom was the only one who had not previously been convicted of murder, he was ordered back to the Montana Territorial Prison, with an additional five years to serve because of his escape. The rest were sentenced to hang the next day at sunrise.

Baxter's trial was scheduled for nine o'clock the next day, three hours after the hanging. Townspeople and ranchers from both counties attended the hanging, glad to know that the awful harassment was over.

At 8:45 that morning, the courtroom was packed, with hundreds of people standing outside. Sheriff Lloyd Gross stationed himself next to Baxter Beaumont at the front, near the judge's bench. The Beaumont family sat on the front row with the Meadows beside them. Sage and Cory were seated together, holding hands. Ted had stayed home with a neighboring rancher looking after him.

As soon as Judge Larkin opened the trial and asked the defendant how he pled, Baxter Beaumont stood and told him he was guilty of hiring the gang to harass the small ranchers. He admitted it was because of his greed, and he showed sincere regret for having done it. He told the judge he deserved whatever sentence he was given, and did not plead for mercy.

Sheriff Lloyd Gross, who had arrested Beaumont, testified about the information he had received from the gang members themselves.

When Judge Larkin had heard from both men, he asked Baxter Beaumont to stand. Everyone in the courtroom had been touched by Baxter's confession and his willingness to take whatever punishment the judge felt he deserved. Lillian Beaumont and her children looked on, praying that the judge would show leniency.

"Mr. Beaumont," Larkin said, "I do not need to tell you that this trial would have been totally different if someone had been killed during the harassment you financed. Had this been the case, you would have died at the end of a rope as did the murderers at sunrise this morning."

"Yes, sir," Baxter said, his features solemn.

"I am told that seventeen families left this valley because of the harassment. They are gone, and there is nothing I can do to see that they are reimbursed for property and animals destroyed. However, I am assigning both Sheriff Gross and Sheriff Hawkins to go to those ranchers who have stayed. They will total up their losses of property and animals caused by the gang you hired, and you will reimburse every last dollar."

"Yes, sir."

Judge Larkin cleared his throat. "Now, Mr. Beaumont, this restitution would not be possible with you behind bars. For this reason, and because I see genuine remorse in you for your part in these crimes, I sentence you to five years' probation. You will be on weekly report to the sheriff's office in this county."

The gavel banged on the judge's desk, and the trial was over.

The Beaumont family and their Christian friends shed tears of joy. Many ranchers who had despised Baxter Beaumont took the time to come by and tell him they were happy to see the change in his demeanor. He was quick to tell them it was because he had become a Christian, and Jesus Christ had made him a new man.

Lillian clung to her husband while people talked to him. When the courtroom was almost empty, she hugged him hard, weeping and thanking the Lord for answered prayer.

Baxter, who had shown no affection to his children before, opened his arms to them and told them he loved them.

"Bring Sage to me," he said finally to Cory.

Sage tried to smile as she stepped up to Baxter with Cory beside her. Baxter embraced her, asking her to forgive him for the way he had treated her. Sage told him she loved him.

Baxter blinked against his tears. "Son," he said, holding onto Sage's hand, "as of this moment you are restored to your original place in the inheritance. And whether you choose to come back and work at the *Box Double B* or stay on with Zach, I want you to marry this girl!"

Sheriff Lloyd Gross came to Baxter and discussed arrangements for his reports. He said he and Hawkins would present Baxter with the amount owed the small ranchers within a couple of weeks.

When Gross walked away, Baxter asked Myrna Sullivan if it would be all right if he went to see Ted. She assured him it would be fine. John and Breanna were invited to go along to the Sullivan ranch since Breanna still had her things there.

Ted Sullivan lay on his special couch in the parlor and rejoiced that Baxter had been given probation. He was also relieved to know that his fellow ranchers would be reimbursed for damages.

Myrna stood next to Ted. Lillian, her children, and Sage, and John and Breanna made a half circle around them. All were wondering what Baxter had on his mind.

Baxter dropped to one knee beside the couch and said, "Ted, you have forgiven me already for the sorrow and untold harm I've caused you."

"Yes, I have."

"You know that I've been ordered by the judge to reimburse the small ranchers for their losses."

"Yes."

"Well, I have some more reimbursing to do. There's been no time to talk to Lillian about this, but I have no doubt she'll go along with it one hundred percent. We're going to pay off the mortgage on your ranch. It'll be yours free and clear."

Ted's eyes were swimming. "But Baxter, you—"

"Not only that, but we'll meet the payroll of whatever men it takes to run the ranch...and we'll be depositing a sizable amount in your bank account every month to meet your needs. This will go into our will, so if Lillian and I should go to glory ahead of you, the money'll still be there."

Overwhelmed, the Sullivans shed tears of joy, thanking Baxter and Lillian for their generosity. Everyone in the room rejoiced in the goodness of the Lord.

The next day, after all the good-byes were said, John and Breanna deposited their luggage at the stage office an hour before departure and took a walk outside the town limits.

"How I thank the Lord for sending that wonderful wild horse to you," Breanna said as they strolled across an open field.

She noticed tears in John's eyes as he stopped, looked northward, and sighed. He was silent for a moment, then in a steady but soft voice said, "Out there somewhere is a wild, gallant, and brave black stallion. I owe Chance my life, Breanna. Without him, I would've died in that circle of fire."

Journey of the Stranger Series

One dark, mysterious man rides for truth and justice. On his hip is a Colt .45…and in his pack is a large, black Bible. He is the legend known only as the stranger.

An Exciting New Series
by Bestselling Fiction Authors

Let Freedom Ring
#1 in the Shadow of Liberty Series

It is January 1886 in Russia. Vladimir Petrovna, a Christian husband and father of three, faces bankruptcy persecution for his beliefs, and despair. The solutions lie across a perilous sea.

ISBN 1-57673-756-X

The Secret Place
#2 in the Shadow of Liberty Series

Popular authors Al and JoAnna Lacy offer a compelling question: As two young people cope with love's longing on opposite shores, can they find the serenity of God's covering in *The Secret Place?*

ISBN 1-57673-800-0

A Prince Among Them
#3 in the Shadow of Liberty Series

A bitter enemy of Queen Victoria kidnaps her favorite great-grandson. Emigrants Jeremy and Cecelia Barlow book passage on the same ship to America, facing a complex dilemma that only all-knowing God can set right.

ISBN 1-57673-880-9

Undying Love
#4 in the Shadow of Liberty Series

19-year-old Stephan Varda flees his own guilt and his father's rage in Hungary, finding undying love from his heavenly Father—and a beautiful girl—across the ocean in America.

ISBN 1-57673-930-9

Angel of Mercy Series

Post-Civil War nurse Breanna Baylor uses her professional skill to bring healing to the body, and her faith in the Redeemer to bring comfort to thirsty souls, valiantly serving God on the dangerous frontier.

Mail Order Bride Series

Desperate men who settled the West resorted to unconventional measures in their quest for companionship, advertising for and marrying women they'd never even met! Read about a unique and adventurous period in the history of romance.

#1	Secrets of the Heart	ISBN 1-57673-278-9
#2	A Time to Love	ISBN 1-57673-284-3
#3	The Tender Flame	ISBN 1-57673-399-8
#4	Blessed are the Merciful	ISBN 1-57673-417-X
#5	Ransom of Love	ISBN 1-57673-609-1
#6	Until the Daybreak	ISBN 1-57673-624-5
#7	Sincerely Yours	ISBN 1-57673-572-9
#8	A Measure of Grace	ISBN 1-57673-808-6
#9	So Little Time	ISBN 1-57673-898-1

Hannah of Fort Bridger Series

Hannah Cooper's husband dies on the dusty Oregon Trail, leaving her in charge of five children and a general store in Fort Bridger. Dependence on God fortifies her against grueling challenges and bitter tragedies.

#1	Under the Distant Sky	ISBN 1-57673-033-6
#2	Consider the Lilies	ISBN 1-57673-049-2
#3	No Place for Fear	ISBN 1-57673-083-2
#4	Pillow of Stone	ISBN 1-57673-234-7
#5	The Perfect Gift	ISBN 1-57673-407-2
#6	Touch of Compassion	ISBN 1-57673-422-6
#7	Beyond the Valley	ISBN 1-57673-618-0
#8	Damascus Journey	ISBN 1-57673-630-X

Battles of Destiny Series

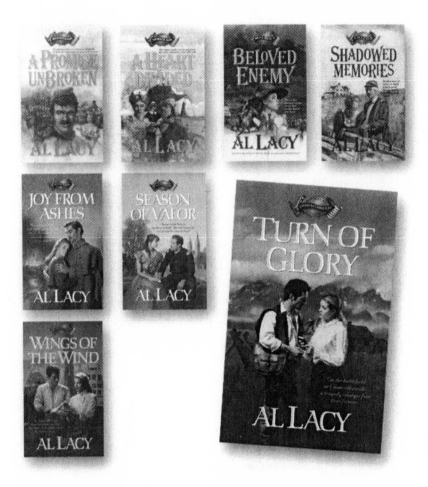

It was the war that divided our country and shaped the destiny of generations to come. Yet out of the bloodshed, men, women, and families faced adversity with bravery and sacrifice…and sometimes even love.

#1	A Promise Unbroken	ISBN 0-88070-581-7
#2	A Heart Divided	ISBN 0-88070-591-4
#3	Beloved Enemy	ISBN 0-88070-809-3
#4	Shadowed Memories	ISBN 0-88070-657-0
#5	Joy From Ashes	ISBN 0-88070-720-8
#6	Season of Valor	ISBN 0-88070-865-4
#7	Wings of the Wind	ISBN 1-57673-032-8
#8	Turn of Glory	ISBN 1-57673-217-7

Printed in the United States
74475LV00002B/89